Signs of Courage

by Christopher Karam

© 2014

Cover Photography by Derek Lewis

Text copyright © 2014

All rights reserved. No part of this book may be reproduced in any manner whatsoever without written permission from the author, except in the case of brief quotations in reviews and articles.

This is a work of fiction. Names, characters, places and incidents either are the product of the author's imagination or are used fictitiously. Any resemblance to actual events, locales, organizations, or persons, living or dead, is entirely coincidental and beyond the intent of either the author or the publisher.

Also by Christopher Karam:

- Signs of Life

To Alison, my sunshine.

Chapter I

It was more than three-quarters of the way up the giant eastern white pine when John Thompson decided to make his first cut. He had already removed the lower branches necessary to use the tree as a spar, and had rescaled the trunk to now remove the top. Once he topped the tree, he would attach a pulley and rigging needed to haul other trees onto the landing. Yesterday was one of the longest days he had remembered working. It had rained hard in the afternoon. Hard enough to knock dried needles off the tall Adirondack pines. Hard enough to penetrate his waxed cotton jacket. Hard enough that he still seemed to feel the cold dampness, even after a night's sleep and two cups of the morning's hot coffee.

The new day's sky had started with a pinkish-red hue, but had now changed to a melancholy shade of gray. The wind blew lightly from the north, and John knew this afternoon would once again offer a more challenging environment to work in.

He had been a tree topper, or high climber as they called him in camp, for over two years, and had worked in all kinds of weather. Of all the jobs offered in camp, the high climber paid the best due to its dangerous nature, but the job wasn't without its unique pleasures either. It offered him a feeling of independence and solitude. He looked across to a nearby pine, as the repetitive song of a Carolina wren caught his attention. He smiled and whistled back to the wren before she flew off, flittering through the dense green branches.

John tightened the leather belt, which wrapped around his waist and the tree itself. He had made it from an old harness with brass hardware, which he had just recently retired to hang in his barn. While most men used a rope to scale trees, John preferred his custom belt. He had fashioned it so as he climbed higher, where tree trunks grew thinner in diameter, he could stop and adjust its length through the brass hardware.

He dug his bootjacks into the soft bark and pulp of the pine to gain leverage as he pulled the head of the axe out of the wood. When he swung his axe a second time, a large chip flew out from the tree. He always enjoyed following the flight of the first chip as it made its way to the ground below. One..two..three..four, he counted, as he estimated the one hundred and ten-foot height from where he worked to the forest floor below.

His axe's edge was keen, and his subsequent chops dug deep. Within a few minutes, he was more than halfway through the two-foot diameter trunk. He knew that as soon as the top leaned and snapped loose from the remaining trunk, he would feel that terrible vibration, which had shook many a high climber loose from their perch.

The wind changed and now blew across his face as he worked. He had always tried to position himself with the wind at his back, so any breeze would aid in blowing the top off and away from him. But it was too late to change position now, as he had completed his front cut and only needed to start his back cut, which would allow the top to fall forward. He swung his axe at the trunk and it bit deep into the soft pine. His following cut exposed the back hinge he had so carefully carved. He knew his next chop might be the one to start the chain of events that could not be stopped.

But before he could pull his axe head from the hinge, a gust of wind blew hard through the forest and pushed the mighty crown of the tree like the sail of a ship. He could feel the tree sway in the wind, and his axe head was locked in place by the weight of the wood above it. He pulled and jerked the ash handle hard to remove the axe, but it was frozen stiff. As he looked up at the top of the tree, he could see it start to spin slowly, as if being twisted by some invisible hand. A cold chill went down John's back, as he tried not to panic. His instincts took over as he quickly attempted to shift his body to the other side of the trunk, but it was too late. With a loud crack, the tremendous top of the tree broke free from the trunk and slid down diagonally off its pillar. What happened next only took a second, but to John, the moment slowed in his mind. Time stood still, as every movement and detail became crystal clear. The bottom of the crown slammed into John's chest with the force of a giant sledge hammer, and he felt the bones in his chest give way. An equally excruciating pain shot up from the small of his back, just before the straining leather lifeline snapped from the tremendous force.

For a few seconds, John felt weightless. He could smell the scent of the pine needles and the waxed cotton of his jacket. He thought of the bandage-wrapped cut on his hand he had recently acquired from the buck saw, and how he had worried about it getting infected. He thought of his wife and son, and the fishing trip he had promised Andrew they would all go on when he returned home next week. The panic he had just experienced was immediately replaced by a sad calm, knowing he would never see his family again.

None of the other men at the site saw his body fall, or heard any cry carried on the wind. As he accompanied the mighty crown to the needle-laden forest floor, John's world went dark.

Feeling no pain, he felt himself effortlessly rise up. He could see the dull, gray day turn bright, as the sun came out from behind the clouds. Bright rays of light streaked diagonally through the trees as it illuminated their branches in a peaceful glow. There was an eerie silence to his surroundings, as if he had gone deaf. He continued to feel weightless as he rose higher and higher, until he could look down on the illuminated green canopy below him.

The startling silence was suddenly replaced by the beautiful song of the Carolina wren in the distance.

Chapter II

At the top of a hill, deep in the Adirondack woods, Andrew Thompson woke from his sleep, his back against the trunk of a tall red cedar. He looked up at the full December moon, as he yawned. The hill, which overlooked a great span of oak and cedar trees, was comprised of ledge, long since deposited by an ancient glacier.

He thought about the dream and how foggy bits and pieces were clearer than others. He thought it strange to dream about something he knew little about. His mother had always kept the details of his father's death from him. Perhaps his subconscious mind was trying to fill in the blanks. His cold hands suddenly turned his thoughts back to the dark green forest world, which surrounded him. He slowly rubbed his hands together to get some warmth back in them. Deer hunting was a quiet chore. One where a man could experience the world waking up around him. But in exchange for this drama, it often required sitting perfectly still against the early morning cold and the urge to move around to get warm.

Each warm breath that passed from his mouth formed a silky mist, which rose upward in front of his view of the moon and then vanished. He wondered if James, a mile away, was looking at the same luminous scene unfolding before him.

Across the valley, James Riley turned the collar of his wool jacket up against the back of his neck. He slowly shifted his weight from one side of his backside to the other, trying to keep his legs from cramping.

He liked the cold weather when he hunted. It gave him a feeling of peace. In this stillness, a man could reflect on his life, his family, his accomplishments and sorrows. At the age of fifty-eight, he had plenty to look back on. In his middle age, James had married a widowed woman, Wendy Thompson. In doing so, he had become stepfather to young Andrew Thompson. Ever since Andrew was eleven years old, James had felt as if Andrew were his real son. He and Wendy had watched Andrew grow into a fine young man, who was now twenty-one years of age and held a job at the livery as a blacksmith. Following in his stepfather's footsteps, he also worked as a guide in the Adirondack mountains.

James remembered when he was that age. Strong and ambitious, it was as if he would live forever. Life was one adventure after another. Each year contained another little victory. Now, he felt the years of hard work tugging at his shirt tail. Every year seemed to be a little harder than the previous to accomplish the same daily chores. Even getting up early to hunt was not as easy as it used to be. His muscles seemed to need more time to get warmed up and going. His neck would sometimes stiffen, the result of years of harvesting firewood and sleeping on the cold ground while on a hunt. But he took great joy in watching Andrew in the life they had built together. It was as if he were reliving parts of his youth.

It was the rustling of a mouse under a few layers of oak leaves that brought his attention back to the hunt. He had wished for some snow, which would quiet his footsteps should he decide to still-hunt. But the winter had been a dry one so far, which was unusual for late December. So instead, he kept himself perched on his ledge, scanning the woods for any sign of movement. He double-checked the cap on his black powder rifle. At least the crisp weather would keep his powder dry.

To the east of the oak trees, he could see a far away hill across the valley with a single, large white birch, which was adorned by moonlight.
To the west was a wetland with a stream that ran through tangles of briars, bushes and reeds. From the ledge, he could overlook any deer that would pass through the wetland area and work its way up the draw toward the hill of oaks.

Every so often, he would turn his head very slowly, from the wetland to the oaks and back to the birch tree on the far hill. He had yet to see any deer on this hunt, but was content with the landscape before him. He knew the full moon would often cause deer to feed at night and sleep through the early hours of the morning.
Estimating it was just before six a.m., he could see the top of the sun start to peek above the far hills to the east. As the sun rose, the part of the sky just above the horizon changed to a purple-red hue. The birch trees across the valley seemed to soak up the colors, which were now filling the sky.

James had seen quite a bit of deer sign while scouting the area a few days prior. They had split up, with Andrew hunting the lower portion of the ridge to the northeast.
Should one of them harvest a deer, the other would hear the shot and come to the other's aid by bringing up their horses to help carry out the carcass.

As the sun continued to rise, his thoughts turned to Wendy. "Right about now she'll be stoking the stove in the kitchen to warm the house, and then head out to the henhouse to gather the eggs. Eggs, bacon and coffee sure would taste good right about now." His hand slowly reached into his coat pocket and produced a small strip of jerky. His hand moved even slower as it made its way to his mouth. He let the piece sit between his lower cheek and gums and become soft as he enjoyed the smokey flavor.

With the sun now fully up, sitting on the horizon like an orange ball, Andrew Thompson heard what sounded like a footfall in the leaves. "Too quiet to be a squirrel," he thought to himself. His head slowly turned from the rising sun toward the direction of the noise. Forty yards in front of him was a small doe, and ten yards behind her was a rather large buck, which he estimated to be 220 pounds.
It made no difference to Andrew the gender of the animal he hunted, as James had taught him to hunt for the experience and the food, and not the trophy. A rewarding experience was trophy enough.
The buck would provide enough meat for many meals during the winter.
Andrew slowly cocked the hammer of his muzzleloader, using his other hand to cup over the top of the hammer, hoping it would block some of the noise.
A soft "click" caused the buck to stop and lift its head. The doe kept walking as the buck lifted its nose into the soft breeze. Its ears rotated in Andrew's direction as it stood motionless and waited. Andrew dared not lift his gun to his shoulder with the buck in such an alert stage. Excited from seeing the large male appear in front of him, he just concentrated on slowing his breathing. Within a minute, the buck

lowered its head again and continued on the path of the doe. When its head went behind an oak tree, Andrew slowly raised his muzzleloader to his shoulder and placed his cheek on the stock.

When the buck cleared the tree, Andrew placed the front brass bead on the small area of its chest, directly behind the front leg. With his finger now on the trigger, he slowly let out his breath while gently squeezing. The sound of the muzzleloader going off was like a small crack followed by the boom of thunder, which echoed across the valley.

The buck shot forward with a bound, and seemed to cover fifty yards in a matter of a few seconds before Andrew saw it collapse and roll on its side.

Andrew put down his rifle, slowly stood up and placed his hands on his lower back, stretching his frame as he kept his eyes on the downed buck. He took his time gathering his gun and possibles bag before approaching the deer. Walking up to the buck, he could see his shot was a well placed one. Straight through the heart and lungs. Confirming its death with the nudge of his rifle barrel, he took out his knife and cut a small bough off a nearby sapling, just as James, his stepfather, had taught him, and placed the branch in the large buck's mouth as he knelt over it. A traditional ritual, the "last meal" was a prayer of respect for the animal who gave its life so others could benefit. He then started cleaning the animal, knowing James would arrive soon after hearing the shot.

It was half an hour later that James came up the hill, leading the horses. "Nice buck," he said as he dismounted his horse. "Anything I can do to help?"

"Well, if we can get this big guy across the back of Ruth here, I'll walk beside her down the ridge."

"Wow, feels like he's close to two hundred pounds dressed out," said James, puffing through his cheeks as he and Andrew hoisted the large buck over the saddle of the tan mare.

"Gettin' too old to be lifting heavy loads."

"You're still plenty strong, Pa," said Andrew as he patted James on the back. "Ma is going be proud when she sees what I brought home."

"She is. ...We both are."

The sun continued to rise in the sky as they slowly worked their way down the ridge.

They shared memories from past hunts together as they headed toward home. Stories of snow storms and driving rain, long hikes and peaceful moments, like the one they shared this morning.

It seemed like a good time to segue into what he had long wanted to ask James... "Pa, how old were you when you headed out west?"

"Oh, I was about eighteen I think. Old enough to be on my own, but it wasn't an easy decision. I had close ties to my family, but I needed to find a place where I could search out my own fortune. I learned a lot, but eventually left to come back home. I knew it was back here where I truly belonged. But I guess I wouldn't have found that out, if I hadn't spread my wings."

A good amount of silence passed with just the sound of the squeaking of saddle leather and hoof falls from the horses.

"I was thinking... maybe I'd want to see the west. Before it changes too much. I've only read about it in the papers and dime novels. I mean, I like my job at the livery, but I've always felt there's something bigger out there waiting for me. Something I haven't experienced yet."

"It's a place of constant change, Andrew. A place filled with adventurous men, each trying to get a share of something they can't get back here."

"Like what... land?"

"Yes, land for some, wealth for others, and for others still, a way of life filled with motion. Some men just aren't meant to settle in one spot. It's like they always have to keep movin' on.

If there does come a day when you find yourself on your own, you'll need to know when to keep to yourself, and when you might need to share your company with others. I guess what I'm trying to say is, use your best judgement when it comes to dealing with strangers. It's different here, where pretty much everyone knows everyone else, but just like the woods we hunt in, there are predators out there."

"When you were younger, did you need to fight any of those 'predators', Pa?"

"A ruttin' buck doesn't use up his energy tryin' to fight bears. There's a right time to stand up for yourself, and a right time to walk away. Just make sure that if there is a time you need to stand up for yourself, you're in the right. A man who is in the right, will most always come out on top.

The man who fights when he knows he's wrong has to fight two battles, the man he's up against and his own conscience. For me, I had my fill of adventure with the army, and when I had seen enough, I decided it wasn't for me anymore and I headed for home. One day, I just got on my horse and rode. I'm glad I came back."

Andrew said nothing, as he let his father's words sink in.

"Do you think Ma would understand if I decided to head out west?"
"I think Ma would understand, but don't expect her to get excited about the notion. If you had a good job waiting for you and promised to write every so often, it might take some of the sting out of the proposition."
"Would you back me up after I speak with her about it?"
"Yes sir, I will."

Chapter III

The spring crocuses had started to push their way up through the soil of the flower beds to catch the warm rays of the sun, as Wendy Riley hung her laundry on the clothesline in back of the house.

It had often made her smile in the past, when Andrew's clothes seemed to magically grow in size from one spring to the following. No longer a child, Andrew's clothes didn't change in size any more, but had remained the same for the past few years. She missed those days, and although she loved the man he had grown into, it was a bittersweet feeling that he was less dependent on her.

"Can I speak with you, Ma?" a voice came from behind her.
"Certainly," she answered without turning around so as not to show him the wetness of her eyes.
"I've been thinking about traveling out west for a while. I'd like to see what it has to offer. Mr. Hollings at the livery has talked several times about his cousin who has a ranch out in southern Colorado. He's always going on about how he could set me up with a job, a room and three squares if I was interested."
"This is something... something you really want to do?"
"Yes, Ma. I've been thinking about it for quite a while, since last fall. It's like I've got this urge to travel where I haven't been and see what the west might have to offer. I've put enough money aside to buy myself a ticket on the railway. I figure, if I don't like it, I can always find a way to head back. But I wouldn't want to go without your blessing."

"I knew there would be a day when you might want to see other parts of the country and make your own way in the world. I just didn't think it would come so fast. It seems like yesterday, you were coming home from school and asking me to help you with your homework." Wendy stopped to wipe her tears and then placed her hands squarely on her son's shoulders. "I want you to follow your dreams Andrew, and if that means going out west, then that's where you need to go. Just remember how much your pa and I love you, and that we're always here for you."

"I will, Ma. Please know that I'll write when I can."

"I'd expect that, son."

"I love you, Ma." Andrew wrapped his arms around his mother and hugged her. He hugged her so hard he almost lifted her off the ground. He hugged her for the lonely times after his father had died, when she was all he had before James had come along. He hugged her for the two jobs she worked every day, and all the meals she cooked to feed him. He hugged her for the happy childhood she had given him. But most of all, he held her tight for the bond between a mother and her son that has no comparison.

The following week, when the plans with Mr. Hollings had been finalized, James, Wendy and Andrew rode into town to see Andrew on the train bound for the west.

James drove the buckboard up to the train station in Altamont. The station had been built several years ago by John Hurd, who owned Hurd's Lumber Mill, to meet the demands of sending the lumber to market. Originally named the Adirondack Railroad, it later became the

Northern New York Railroad after it was sold to a private syndicate due to Hurd overextending his business.

James jumped to the ground, and then walked to the other side to help Wendy down. They continued to the boardwalk, where several others awaited the train.

After Andrew purchased his ticket, he walked over to the steel rails, which made up the long, thick track. He stared in awe of how the rails, bracketed by the trees, extended for miles and grew thinner as they converged, until they disappeared into the horizon. He studied the spikes, which were driven into the cross beams that held the rails firmly in place. How could such a thing this massive be built across an entire territory, much less a country? Where was the end and what would its path have in store for him?

Then he heard the train whistle in the distance, as a small black dot appeared to grow in size as it came closer. He could see the smoke billowing from its stack and could feel the vibrations in his foot, which still rested on top of one of the rails.
He stepped a few paces back as he continued to watch the train approach. But there was a dangerous curiosity, which kept him from moving too far back. The whistle blew again, sounding much louder as the train was now only a half-mile away. As it pulled up to the station, the engine slowed and the loud screeching of the wheels against the rails could be heard as the engineer applied the brakes. Andrew was mesmerized by the size of the engine and its many passenger cars. He had never seen anything like this up close. He walked down the length of the engine and felt the heat from its boiler.

The engineer told Andrew he must step further back, and he did, just as the engineer purged some of the steam from the boiler. Few people got off the train. The ones that did looked like business men. Probably associated with the logging companies, he thought. Some stayed aboard, and Andrew could see the blank stares of their faces close to the glass windows of the cars.

As the conductor called for passengers to climb aboard, Andrew turned and walked back to his parents to say good bye.

"Please write when you can," Wendy reminded him, as she hugged him one last time and kissed him on the cheek.

"I will," he replied. "And don't worry, Ma. I'll be just fine."

James reached out and shook Andrew's hand, then pulled him in close and hugged him. He took a pocket watch from his front pants pocket, unclipped the fob from his belt and placed it in Andrew's hand. It was a beautiful silver Waltham watch, with a deer head for a fob at the end of the chain, where it clipped to a belt. The patterned lines of the engraved design on the outside were partially worn from years of use.

"This was my pa's. I have always had every intention of passing it on to you someday. Now just feels like the right time. Besides, it just might keep you from missing a train."

Andrew opened the watch and looked at the inscription. It read: "There is nothing so precious as family." He smiled as he closed the clasp and tucked it in his pocket.

"Thanks, Pa. I'll keep it safe."

"Just enjoy it. It's yours now; and don't forget what we spoke about, son."

"I'll remember, Pa."

James tucked three folded dollars into Andrew's shirt pocket. "Just in case you should need something along the way."

"Thanks, Pa. I'll make you both proud."
"We know you will. We love you. Remember that, too. Safe travels son." As he clasped the hand rail and climbed aboard the train, Andrew smiled and looked back at them.
He then walked down the narrow isle and stopped about halfway down the coach, stowing his bag and choosing a seat on the same side as the boardwalk. Smelling the cigarette smoke in the air mixed with the leather scent from the seats, he opened the window wide to invite in some fresh air.

As he heard the last call to board, Andrew watched his parents through the large open window. It framed them as if they were both in a picture. They waved to him as the iron horse jerked forward, spewing large amounts of smoke and steam, and slowly moved its way down the track under the power of the great engine.
He waved back, and continued to watch as they slowly moved out of the frame. Other passengers opened windows and leaned with their arms out, waving to loved ones, as if either savoring or prolonging their good-byes.

Andrew just sat back in his seat with his hat resting on one knee, and placed his folded hands in his lap as the train picked up speed.
He felt the nervousness of leaving his family behind, after living all of his life in the small town, which continued to grow. But he also felt a sense of adventure, the eager excitement of discovering what lay ahead.

When the porter came through to ask for tickets, Andrew held his out. The porter punched the ticket with a small metal tool, and Andrew then placed it in the inside rim of his hat, and tilted the brim forward as he put it back on his head. The motion of the train soon helped him nod off.

It wasn't until the train pulled into Allentown, Pennsylvania, late that afternoon, that Andrew woke and stood to stretch his legs. He thought of the states he would be passing through on his way to Colorado. "One down, only six more to go," he said to himself, as he walked down the street looking for a local tavern, hungry for something to eat. He had thirty-five minutes before the six p.m. train would depart, which seemed to be enough time for a quick meal.

Around the corner and down the street, he found what he was looking for. Iron Mill Tavern was on the sign above the double doors. He could hear the voices from those within carrying on conversations about various goings-on in the town. He wasn't used to this much noise in one place, especially when sitting down to a meal, and it appeared to be more of a saloon atmosphere inside. Many of the men looked as though they came directly from working in the iron mills. Andrew couldn't help but stare at one large fellow who spoke with a very loud voice. He carried on his conversation with his fellow workers by yelling above the hum of the room, as if he dared for anyone to be louder than himself. His face still smudged with dirt and sweat, he hoisted the beer mug to his face and then after drinking half of its contents in a few gulps, wiped the corner of his mouth with the back of his hand. He went on about being underpaid at the iron mill and how if any of his higher-ups should be in his shoes, they would instantly understand the direness of his situation. He banged his empty glass down on the bar with such force, that Andrew was surprised it did not burst. Upon receiving a full measure, he then dared any man to an arm wrestling match on the bar. The first man to match him slammed two coins down and took the loud man's hand in his own grip. The struggle was short, as the loud man

quickly swung the other man's hand down with such force that a loud boom was heard from the bar top. Then he took the two coins and placed them in his shirt pocket as the crowd yelled and raised their glasses. As the man scanned the room, looking in his direction for another taker, Andrew broke his gaze and headed to a table in the far corner, avoiding eye contact from the men at the foot-rail of the bar.
A woman came by to take his order, and Andrew asked for a ham sandwich, a bowl of soup and a tall glass of milk. Ten minutes later, the meal was at his table. "That'll be twenty-five cents please," said the woman.
Andrew placed three dimes in her hand and told her to keep the change. "That's very generous of you, sir," she replied.
The soup was beef with barley and it filled the hollow spot in Andrew's stomach just fine. He mopped up the broth with the last of the ham sandwich and washed it all down with the milk.
As he rose to head out the door, he heard the large man with the loud voice call out.
"How about you, sir? Feel like trying your luck at arm wrestling?"
Andrew wasn't sure if the man was addressing him and felt it might be best to keep walking, instead of stopping to look.
"What's the matter lad? It's only a twenty-cent bet."
Andrew wasn't sure what inside him made him stop to look over at the man, but when he did, it was obvious that he was indeed speaking to him.
"I just paid for my meal and I need to catch a train."
The crowd laughed from his response and someone heckled from the bar. "Leave him alone Sam, he's probably got his mom waiting for him at the station." The comment was followed by several laughs and Andrew smiled himself, more out of embarrassment than humor.

As he looked at the man in detail, he noticed he was big in stature, but not much bigger than himself. He reminded himself he was a blacksmith by trade and was strong in his own right, from his time behind the anvil and hammer.

He also knew the man had at least three beers in his belly, and had already arm wrestled twice for what it was worth.

Andrew stepped forward and reached into his pocket. He placed two dimes on the bar and asked to see the same. "He doesn't trust you Sam," a voice yelled out.

"The lad's not from here, so that's expected," answered Sam, as he also placed twenty cents on the bar. Placing his beer down, he pushed his sleeves back past his elbows as he glared straight into Andrew's face, trying to intimidate him. Andrew placed his right elbow on the bar and reached over with his open hand, inviting Sam's grip.

"Are you ready lad?" asked Sam as he squeezed Andrew's hand tight.

"Yessir," answered Andrew, as he stared back at him with a grin.

"GO!" yelled the bartender.

Andrew leaned into Sam as he pulled against the large man's weight. Sam leaned in as well and glared at Andrew as he pulled, puffing air out of his enlarged cheeks. Andrew focused on his grip, which he knew was key to him winning. For the past few years he had gripped the large forging hammer every day, and the muscles in his hand were powerful and accustomed to extended use. He could feel his wrist bending slightly forward as Sam's began to bend back. Sam looked surprised as he broke his gaze from Andrew's face and instead stared at their two hands in disbelief. Sam made an all-out move and forced the rest of his breath out of his cheeks, like the sound of a train engine purging steam. But the assault was stopped as Andrew pulled hard, forcing Sam's arm back past the halfway point. Andrew now made his own move and squeezed tight, while pulling as hard as he could. The veins in his forearms were now accentuated against his skin. His eyes focused on Sam's face. The expression of defeat was upon him. As Sam's arm gave way to the strength of Andrew, his hand slammed down on the bar with a bang.

A shout went up around the room as Sam slapped his hand down on the bar in frustration. An older man next to Andrew grabbed his hand and raised it high in victory.

"You beat me fair n' square lad," said Sam, with a voice that was less than loud. "What would be your name?"

"My name's Andrew, and if I'm ever back in town, I'll offer you a rematch," he said with a humorous grin as he placed the forty cents in his pocket.

It then dawned on him that in all the excitement, he wasn't paying attention to the time. He pulled his pocket watch out and checked the time. Three minutes to six, the dial read.

"Thank you. It's been fun, but I have to go," he said, as he made his way through the people at the bar and ran out the door and down the street toward the station.

As he ran down the street, he could just see the setting sun behind the silhouettes of the buildings. He heard the conductor calling out the "all aboard" in the distance, accompanying the sound of the ringing bell. As he rounded the corner he could see the steel wheels already turning, with large puffs of smoke coming from the stack. Without time to spare, he ran alongside, reached out for the iron bar on the side of the passenger car and pulled himself up onto the steps of the train as it picked up speed. Slightly winded, he sat himself down in an empty seat, spread out his legs and subconsciously rubbed his sore arm. As he slid his hat forward over his eyes, he could still hear the cheers from the tavern in his head.

Chapter IV

The next time Andrew woke, the sun was already up above the trees. He stretched as he yawned and then got up to stretch his legs. Not able to afford a bed in the sleeper car, he made due with his second class ticket seating for the night. He walked through the passenger car to the next car down, which was the dining car, to get a cup of coffee and perhaps a biscuit. A man walked over to take his order. He was tall, thin and looked to be a little older than Andrew.

"What can I get for you, sir?" he asked, as he wet the tip of his pencil with his tongue.

"How much is a cup of coffee and a biscuit?"

"Ten cents, sir," he replied.

"Does that biscuit come with butter?"

"Yes, sir."

"How much for a cup of coffee and two biscuits?"

"Fifteen cents, sir."

"OK, then make it two biscuits. Oh, by the way, where are we anyhow? I slept clean through the night."

"We're currently in Indiana, sir. We should be in Illinois by early afternoon and be arriving in Springfield by evening."

"Thanks a heap. I've always wanted to see a big city."

"Well, Springfield certainly does qualify. I'll be right back with your breakfast, sir."

Several minutes later, the man came by with Andrew's coffee and biscuits. They smelled and tasted just as good as his ma's and the coffee wasn't bad either. He watched the scenery pass by as he ate his biscuits. He'd never imagined how much there really was outside of his own town. It was so much different than just looking at a map in the school house. Farm after farm went by his window, along with large lakes, rivers with bridges, and fields of corn as far as he could see. It was truly amazing.

After breakfast, Andrew retrieved his bag and walked back to the seat he now occupied in the passenger car. By two o'clock, the train had crossed over into Illinois.

At six p.m. they pulled into Springfield Union Station, where Andrew was to change trains.

The large brick building dwarfed the other stations Andrew had been to. One of the more prominent features of the station was a three-story clock tower, which was centered on the front of the building.

Upon entering, he was drawn to the beautiful woodwork throughout the station's hall and the ceiling, which appeared to be twenty feet high. Posters framed in glass illustrated rail lines between the big cities of Chicago, Clinton, Springfield and St. Louis.

He walked over to the information desk and asked the gentleman when the train to St. Louis was due.

"Should be arriving at seven-thirty p.m.," the man said in a monotone voice. With over an hour before his train was due, Andrew decided to walk outside, and perhaps get a quick meal.

Two and three-story buildings lined the streets and seemed to peer down on Andrew as he walked down the sidewalk. It was near to impossible not to look up at their imposing size, as they blocked out some of the emerging evening stars from view.

He wished he could spend more time here and see the city in the day time, but that was not an option. He had only walked a half-mile or so, when he came across a small restaurant. The sign read Maldener's, which hung above the entryway. Walking inside, he could smell the wonderful aromas, which reminded him of his mother's cooking back home. A man at the entryway offered to take his coat and hat, which Andrew handed over to the him. They seated him at a table near the window, and he watched the people walk up and down the sidewalk for a few minutes before a young woman came over to take his order. Andrew ordered a steak with potatoes and then sat back in his chair, watching the world outside go by. A wagon stopped nearby and two men dressed in overalls unloaded several large kegs and rolled them down the sidewalk past the window.

Once in a while, a small horseless carriage would roll by, making a low humming sound with smoke coming from its back end as it went past the window. He had heard of these new machines, but had never seen one until now.

The United States was growing, and new inventions and new businesses were appearing every day. He wondered where he would eventually fit in, with what he often felt was an overwhelming country of constant change. His mind went back to the ranch out in Colorado. He hoped that it would bring him the experience and opportunity to learn what it takes to run a ranch and profit from the hard work.

He pulled a pencil and some folded paper from his shirt pocket and began to write his parents about what he had seen so far, and assure them all was well as he made his way west. He would post the letter at the station before leaving for Kansas. When finished, he folded the letter, placing it back into his pocket, just as his steak and potatoes arrived at his table. He thanked the gal as she placed the plate in front of him. The medium rare piece of meat was the largest he had ever seen on a plate. It had to weigh a good pound and a half. The aroma was wonderful and caused him to salivate. The juice from the steak soaked into the large pile of mashed potatoes, which looked equally as good. If not for his mother's voice in the back of his mind, he would have forgotten to say grace. After a short, silent blessing, he carved off a large piece and swiped it across the edge of the potatoes, constructing himself the perfect bite. Fifteen minutes later, the plate was clean and he sat back, sticking two thumbs under his belt to relieve the slight tightness from his full stomach. He was about to ask for the check when the smiling woman twisted his arm for a large slice of apple pie and a cup of coffee.

The whole meal came to fifty cents. Andrew straightened one leg and reached deep into his pants pocket, pulling out one of the dollars his father had given him. He left a five-cent tip and whistled a lively tune as he left the restaurant with a full stomach. Checking his pocket watch, he confirmed the train's arrival in ten minutes. Walking back to the station, he stopped at a newsstand and paid the vendor a penny for the daily news. He folded the paper and tucked it under his arm as he walked, eager to read the stories once back on board.

When he reached the station, he posted the letter to his parents, then climbed aboard the train.

Once in his seat, he could see three burly lawmen with badges displayed and rifles in hand, escorting four other men toward the train. The four other men worked in two pairs to carry two large, padlocked metal boxes toward the train. As the men walked down the length of the train and disappeared from sight, Andrew stuck his head out of the window to see how far down the train they would go. They appeared to stop three cars down from his passenger car.

Each team of men swung their box up into the open car and then walked away. Two of the three lawmen climbed up into the car, where the large metal boxes had been stored. The third lawman produced a padlock from his pocket and, after sliding the car door shut, fastened the lock through the handle on the outside. He then stood with his back to the car, rifle folded across his arms, as he watched the passengers approach the train.

The conductor rang the bell and gave his last call for boarding. Then the engine chugged its way forward, picking up speed as it headed off into the night.

Andrew wondered what was in those boxes that they needed to be guarded so well. Gold, silver, cash money? He sat back, opened his paper and began to read the sports articles inside. He settled in on an article about the new game of baseball and how they had just created the American league to compete against the National league. In boxing, a man named James Jeffries set a record for the fastest knockout in a heavyweight fight against his opponent, Jack Finnegan. His eyes began to feel heavy as the lights from the town faded in the distance.

The next morning, the sun had just broken the horizon when a loud noise woke Andrew from his sleep. Half awake, he batted at the open newspaper that was across his face and shoulders, from where he had left it the night before. Several passengers stood up inside the moving train, trying to gain a better view of what was going on a few cars in front of theirs. Then, suddenly, the train screeched to a halt. Several of the passengers who were standing, were flung into the aisle. Baggage and hats flew down from the overhead shelves. Some of the women screamed. Startled, everyone tried to make sense of what was happening.

As the train let out a large gasp of steam, Andrew and some of the other men helped the passengers who had fallen, back into their seats. The porter, who was in the same car at the time, tried to make his way to the front of the train, only to be pushed back into the car by a burly man wearing a large, tan Montana Pinch hat with a leather band and a handkerchief over his face. His chaps were well-worn and blue shirt was faded. "Sit down!" he yelled with a voice that had clearly seen its share of cigarettes and chaw. His thumb cocked the Colt revolver in his right hand. "I said sit the hell down, now!"

The porter, as well as the other men who were still standing, quickly found a seat.

"Welcome to Kansas. I'm only going to say this once. As I walk down this aisle, you will place any money and personal valuables into this here sack. Anyone failing to do so, will be shot."

The man made his way, row by row down the car. People fumbled with wallets, jewelry and other items as the sack was thrust in front of them, hesitant to part with their belongings.

Andrew pulled his remaining money from his pocket and held it ready as the man approached and shoved the bag in front of him. "It's all I got," Andrew said as he tossed the items into the sack.

"I don't think so," said the man, as he used the barrel of his Colt to raise the chain of his pocket watch.

"That was my pa's."

The man pushed the barrel of the revolver firmly against Andrew's stomach, and glared hard into his eyes. "Put it with the rest."

Andrew reluctantly lifted the watch from his pocket with the chain, and did as he was told. At just inches away from the man, he could smell the stale tobacco on his breath and saw a scar, which started high on his left cheek and ran down underneath the handkerchief that covered his face.

Just then, an explosion rang out from the front of the train. The car shook and dust billowed in through the open windows. Several exchanges of gunshots followed. Andrew could tell the sound of rifles as well as a few shotgun blasts. Then the firing stopped. Another man appeared in the car and shouted to his partner. "Let's go! We got what we came for."

The man with the sack ran down the aisle and went out the rear door. Several men in the car got up and looked out the windows on the far side of the train, only to see a group of four riders heading south, as their trail dust floated off in the wind.

Chapter V

The crow that was flying overhead for several minutes finally landed in a large apple tree, which overhung a man who was fast asleep.

It cawed several times, as if to see if the man were alive; or perhaps the crow was lost and trying to call its way back to its kind. The man softly snored as the sunlight gradually moved onto his legs, which had been in the shade just an hour earlier.

Upon his head was an old, faded green hat, which bore no particular shape other than it had a tall, tapered crown with a dent in the front and a brim, which had long since been warped by sun, snow and driving rain. Around the crown of the hat was a long piece of braided hemp, which served as a hat band. A red-tailed hawk feather jutted out of the band on the left side and rested on the rear of the brim. His face was wrinkled and bearded. His hair, mostly gray from the hardships of life, gave him the appearance of being much older than his age.

His pants were dark brown and stained from working in the hills, and were patched at the knees and on the seat. They bore suspenders, which were criss-crossed over his shoulders. His shirt wasn't really a shirt at all, but rather the top of his faded red long johns, which also had experienced needle and thread many times.

Next to him was a half-full knapsack, which rested against the trunk of the tree. Tied to the outside of the knapsack was a small lantern, a metal drinking cup and a leather-sheathed skinning knife with an antler handle. Beside the knapsack rested an old cap-lock Kentucky rifle that had fended off Indians, provided meat for the soup pot, and had served as a crutch when needed. His boots were well-worn, bearing the scuffs and broken laces from years of hard use. There was a hole in the right sole, below the ball of his big toe, that had appeared just last year after his mule, Jacob, had died during one of the coldest winters on record. His wide chest and fairly big belly, rose and fell as he breathed in the fragrance from the wild flowers, which painted the hillside around the large apple tree.

But his midday nap was about to end. The cawing of the crow finally woke the man, and he stretched his arms wide and then propped himself up, craning his neck back and upwards to locate the noisy bird. "That's no way to make an entrance - waking a man up from his much needed sleep," he said, as he placed his hat back on his head just the way he liked it.

"Cawww," went the crow.

"No sir, I don't have no food neither, so you may as well just be goin'," he answered, as he again lay back and closed his eyes.

"Caaaaaaw, caw, caw," answered the crow.

"Very well then, I'll just be leavin' you to this here tree, since you obviously own it, and do not intend to let me fall back to sleep."

The man stood, reached for his knapsack and swung it over his left shoulder before retrieving his rifle, which he held across his arms as he walked down the hill and back to the main road.

He had walked several miles, when he heard the sound of a gurgling brook nearby. He followed the noise as he walked through a large stand of pines. When he came out the other side, he saw a perfectly wooded spot down a hill, with a stream flowing through some pines and oaks, which shaded the entire area. Large flat boulders that looked as if they were placed here and there by giants with the utmost care, offered him a place to sit, roll up his pants and soak his tired feet. He sighed and slowly leaned his head back, as the cold stream water cooled his aching muscles. He had camped at many a place throughout the years of his travels, but this was truly a secluded Eden. It didn't look to have any of the signs of a spot that was used as a common campsite.

After enjoying the solitude of the shaded spot for a while, he walked back to the bank and cut himself a switch, which he made into a fishing pole with some twine he pulled from his knapsack, and a small hook he had stashed on the inside of his hatband.

"There's just got to be fish in a beautiful spot like this," he said, as he looked under stones for a worm to bait his hook.

Two hours later, the sun was going down and the man sat on the bank of the stream, enjoying a single brook trout he had pan-cooked over a small fire. The fire's glow lit up the underside of the oak trees that overhung the stream and created a warmth, which gave the man a feeling of contentment.

The next morning, the distant whistle of a train woke the man from his sleep. He rolled from his side, onto his back and reached out from underneath the wool Indian blanket that covered him, and grabbed his old pocket watch that he had placed in one of his boots.

Opening it, he saw it was five minutes to nine, which meant there must be a town nearby that the train would be pulling into. Trains were always arriving pretty much on the hour as they pulled into towns.

He never could figure why they were so prompt, and what all the hubbub was about. People had been living their lives for generations in this country, doing what must get done each day, living from sunrise to sunset. Since the trains came west, it just seemed that all of a sudden, people had to be on time for one thing or another. He had decided a long time ago he wasn't going to live that kind of life.

He dressed himself, rekindled his fire from the previous night's remaining coals and decided on some morning coffee. While the pot heated, he made up a small batch of biscuits in his dutch oven and set it beside the coffee pot in the coals. He then walked through the stand of oaks and pines in the direction of the train whistle he had heard, until he reached a hill of wildflowers. Climbing the hill, he could see a ridge only a mile away and could make out what he thought were railroad tracks. He decided that he'd simply follow those tracks into town after his coffee and biscuits.

As he walked back to his campsite, he noticed something he hadn't spotted from the other direction. There seemed to be an odd figure underneath one of the large flat boulders that jutted skyward at an angle, creating an overhang, which shrouded the figure in shadow. He approached the figure slowly, crouching slightly as he drew within a few yards, still not sure what he was looking at. He shaded the sun from his eyes with his hand, and was now sure what he was looking at were the skeletal remains of a man, partially covered with dried oak leaves, from what must have been over a decade of blustery autumns and winters. He bent over to fit under the overhanging rock and slowly reached toward the skeleton, still dressed in what looked to be a Union Army uniform of sorts. The man had served in the army himself, but could not tell the rank of the soldier from looking at his Union coat. Two partially rotted shafts of wood jutted out from the soldier's back. Grabbing the shoulder of the coat, he pulled at the sleeve and the soldier's skeleton rolled onto its back. When the man unbuttoned the tattered wool coat and looked underneath, he confirmed the two Indian arrowheads on the ends of the shafts, still inside the man's chest cavity. The legs of the soldier no longer remained below the knees, and the man figured they were probably carried off by coyotes after the body started to decay. The skeleton was also missing its jawbone and right hand. The soldier's canteen, bullet pouch and belt were clearly army issue. The man searched the inside pockets of the soldier's coat, pulling out a silver flask and also a folded piece of paper, which looked to have been stained by blood. Another pocket held an old leather draw-string pouch. It jingled as the man pulled it free from the pocket. Slowly pulling open the dried leather strings, he turned the pouch upside down over his hat. Several coins jingled into the hat, along with a roll of paper money. He counted exactly forty-eight dollars in paper and coins as he placed them from the hat, back into the pouch. A good amount of money for a soldier to have on him.

Next, he carefully opened the folded piece of paper, which was yellowed and brittle from age. He read the letter aloud to himself, carefully sounding out the words, as he was not a well-educated man.

"To whoever finds this note:
I lie here wounded by two arrows, as I write. A party of Cheyenne ambushed me a few miles south of this pass while I was advance scouting for our company.
I believe I killed two of the enemy. They have tried twice to rush me, but I have shot one dead each time.
I do not think I will live. It is getting increasingly hard to breathe and I cannot remove the arrows from my back. Last night, the enemy retrieved its dead and left the immediate area. I don't know why they didn't finish me. Maybe they figured I wasn't worth losing another

warrior over, or maybe they were just content with taking my horse, since they know I am wounded badly. I am nearly out of water and I dare not venture out into the open, even though there is a stream just yards away, in case their apparent retreat is just a trap to have me expose myself. Please keep my Colt revolver, I hope it serves you as well as it has me. Please send word of my death to D Company at Fort Bayard.

My thanks in passing,
Charles Collins"

The man folded the letter and placed it in his shirt pocket. Looking more closely below the overhanging rock, he felt around for the Colt revolver that the soldier referenced in his letter. His hand met a large piece of metal underneath the dirt and leaves. He pulled out the Colt, which was an 1860 model, only this one had gone through a cartridge conversion and took the self contained .44 Colt cartridge ammunition, instead of the older ball and powder method. Surprisingly, the revolver was in pretty good condition, with what looked to be only some surface rust on the barrel and cylinder. The man opened the loading gate of the revolver and thumbed the hammer back to its halfway position, which was very stiff. The cylinder turned stiffly, and was in need of a good cleaning and oiling. As he looked into each chamber of the cylinder, he noticed that the soldier died with three cartridges still in the revolver. He then thought of the ammo belt pouch the soldier's body still had on his belt. He reached over and opened it, only to find it no longer contained cartridges, but rather a folded piece of tanned leather. The man unfolded the leather, revealing a roughly cut six-inch square that appeared to be drawn upon with ink. Not having enough light to closely study the drawing under the large rock, he took it out into the sunlight and was amazed at what he saw. The drawings and words illustrated a type of map, which contained references to a town named Phillipsburg, and sketches of a few mountains and rivers. He rubbed his whiskered chin as he studied the names of the other towns. Dillon, Anaconda and Southern Cross... none of them sounded familiar. There was no reference to any state, so this could be on the other side of the country for all he knew. What he did recognize was the words "ROCK CREEK MINE". He scoured both sides of the piece of leather with his eyes to see if there were any other clues as to whether it was gold, silver, or some type of coal mine, but there was no other information written on the map.

He placed the leather map inside the collar of his boot, tucked the Colt inside the front of his pants and walked back to his camp.

Sitting in front of the running stream, drinking his coffee, the man studied the map again, but still had no recollection of any of the towns. His thoughts wandered on what to do next. He had no horse or mule. He was alone, and had no friends he could trust.

After reading the letter, he had every intention of traveling to Fort Bayard and finding the soldier's Company so he could deliver the letter and news of his death. But after finding the map, he mind became wary of the thought of someone in the company knowing of the map's existence, and how they might naturally connect the map with him. He decided it would be best not to tell anyone of the body. He comforted his conscience with the thought that the army must clearly have pronounced the soldier dead by now and would have sent word to his kin. Then he came upon a better idea. He could wire the Fort at the next town, and leave the message anonymously. He rubbed his whiskers and nodded to himself.

The next morning, after a biscuit and bacon grease breakfast, he threw the remainder of his coffee in the fire and broke camp. He walked through the oaks, back to the hill of wildflowers. As he reached the top of the hill and started down the opposite side toward the ridge, he heard a faint train whistle in the distance. His walk now turned into a hasty shuffle, moving as quickly as he could without going into a full run.

The metal cup attached to his knapsack clanked against the small lantern just often enough to become annoying, and the Colt would slip further down into his pants every so often and need to be pulled up against his belly. The train whistle grew louder as he reached the bottom of the ridge. Stopping for a moment to catch his breath and readjust his Colt once again, he looked up at the grade in front of him. The train would have to slow as it made its way around the corner and up the ridge. This would be a great place to get on board, he thought to himself. He tied his long rifle to his pack and started up.

Hand over hand, he climbed the steep ridge, looking up every so often to check his progress. He could now feel the vibration as the iron horse approached. When he reached the top, the iron horse came around the corner and the whistle blew a deafening squeal. The man had no time to rest, but needed to now run full-out in order to catch up to the speed of the climbing train. He reached out as he ran alongside one of the boxcars, in a desperate attempt to grab onto an iron side rail. Not used to a prolonged run, he was becoming winded. As he felt himself giving in to his exhaustion, he made one last attempt to grab the rail. But just as his fingers wrapped around it in full stretch, his feet gave out, and he tumbled forward, just missing the steel wheels and landing on his chest beside the tracks. He could feel the hard metal of the Colt revolver jam into his groin as he let out a yell that sounded like a prizefighter who'd been hit in the gut. The front of his legs came off the ground for a split second as the momentum of the fall transferred his weight from his chest, to his face and shoulders. His knapsack flipped over his head, knocking off his hat. The clang of his metal cup and shattering sound as the glass in his lantern broke added a sorrowful accompaniment to the pain and embarrassment of his tumble. As he looked up with a bloody lip and scraped chin, he saw the caboose pass him by, with the whistle blowing loudly once more, as a lasting reminder not to try such a foolish thing again. In seconds, the train had disappeared around the next bend.

The man rolled onto his back and then slowly sat up. He collected his belongings and threw the knapsack over his back in disgust. It would be a seven-mile walk to Durango, and he was not looking forward to it.

It was late afternoon when the man reached the outskirts of Durango. There was a light breeze, which slightly cooled his sweat as he walked under the hot sun. On the wind, he could smell the familiar scents of the local restaurant starting to serve dinner, the raking out of the livery stable, and the burning coals and scorched metal of the blacksmith shop.

Ahead of him was the train station. He strode with purpose down the wooden walkway, passing the familiar cars, which were now empty. It would have been embarrassing to walk by cars full of passengers who might have caught a glimpse of his acrobatic boarding attempt. He stopped at the telegraph window, removed his pack and wiped the sweat from his brow.

"How much to send a short message to Phillipsburg?" he asked the operator, who sat behind the window looking over the top of his glasses at the man.

"That depends," answered the operator. "If you're talking about Phillipsburg, Kansas, it'll cost you about twenty-five cents, if you haven't too much to say."

"What other Phillipsburg would I be talkin' about?"

"Well, there is a Phillipsburg in Montana, but I've never had anyone ask to send a message there. If you did, the wire only goes as far as Fort Ellis, and you'd need to arrange for a rider the remainder of the way. About four days ride from Fort Ellis, I should think. I can help arrange that for you, if you meant Montana."

"No, thank you. I'll uh, wait on that. Instead, I'd like to send a message to Fort Bayard, in New Mexico territory."

"So, you don't want to send a message to Phillipsburg?"

"Nope. Not any more. I want to send a different message to Fort Bayard. It's important. I found this here letter on a dead soldier's remains under a ledge several miles west of here."

The man unfolded the letter he had in his hand and gave it to the telegrapher.

The telegrapher read the letter and then looked at Jeb, adjusting his glasses on his nose to take a good look at him.

"How do I know you didn't kill some poor soldier and write this yourself?"

"Because I can't write so good. I can barely read as it is. I never went to no school. Look, this here's the pistol I found on the remains, mentioned in the letter. He said whoever found him could keep it. You think it would be in this shape, if it just came off a live soldier? Now, can I just tell you what I want to say? I don't write so good."

"Yessir, you can start whenever you'd like. I'll take down your words and read it back to you. But you'll need to answer a few more questions from the sheriff before you can leave."

"Sheriff!" Jeb shouted. "Why the heck should I talk to the sheriff for doin' a good deed?"

"Sheriff Belmont is a good man, and he'll probably only ask you a few questions. You know, to make sure everything is as you say it is."

The man thought for a second before answering. He wouldn't make it a mile out of town if he turned and ran. Besides, the letter didn't mention anything about the map or the mine.

"Alright, I'll come inside and sit a spell while you send for the sheriff."

"Thank you, sir," said the telegrapher. "I assure you, you're doing the right thing."

A few minutes and twenty-five cents later, the anonymous message of the soldier's passing was on its way to the fort. After another twenty minutes and two cups of coffee with Sheriff Belmont, the telegrapher received confirmation about the soldier, who had gone missing in the area years ago. Sheriff Belmont was satisfied and the man walked out the door with a smile on his face.

He stopped to sit down on one of the nearby benches, removed his boots and rubbed his feet. He recounted the money in the leather pouch, still not quite believing his good fortune in finding such a sum.

Chapter VI

As the train pulled into Durango around ten a.m., Andrew looked out the window at the empty platform. It was nothing like the stations he had seen in Harrisburg or Chicago. He had expected at least a few people who might be waiting for family members or maybe a business man or two. But no one stood on the platform. Only a few older men, who lay sleeping with their large sombreros pulled down upon their eyes, accompanied the tumbleweeds that blew past the train as it had come to a stop.

The conductor made his call, and Andrew swung his bag over his shoulder and stepped off the train and onto the platform.

He took his ticket stub and tucked it under the flap of leather on the inside crown of his hat, as a keepsake of his trip.

Andrew looked both up and down the platform, but saw no one to welcome him. He made a stop at the nearby telegraph office to see if any incoming message might be waiting for him, but there was no news. Twenty minutes later, he was beginning to get thirsty as he paced back and forth on the sun-beaten train platform, but resisted the temptation of walking over to a saloon or restaurant for a drink, in fear of missing the person who was late to give him a ride to the ranch. He thought that the owner surely would have sent someone to get him. Even if he knew where the ranch was, he had no transportation to get there. Sitting down on a nearby bench, he tipped his hat forward, only peeking out from under the brim occasionally to make sure his contact didn't mistake him for one of the sleeping old men.

It had been over an hour from when he had gotten off the train, when a tall lean man approached him at a slow gate. His tattered shirt and well-worn pants were in need of a washing, and his boots had leather straps on the side that dangled as he walked. His hat looked worn as well, and had a small tear in the front of the brim. He removed his hat and wiped his brow with a handkerchief he pulled from his shirt pocket, then placed the hat back on his head. "Damn hot today... Might you be Andrew Thompson?"

"Yessir, from Altamont, NewYork. Mr Hollings had..."

"I'm Red Saunders, owner of the Triple Fork Ranch," he interrupted. "Hollings said you be comin' in on the train today. I forgot the exact time. People around here don't pay too much attention to clocks. Mostly get up with the sun and go to bed when it gets dark. Well, we best get movin'. It takes the better part of an afternoon to get to my ranch."

Andrew slung his bag on the back of Mr. Saunders' buckboard and climbed aboard.

"Where do you think you're sittin'?" Mr. Saunders asked, as he wiped his brow again.

"I thought we were heading to your ranch."

"We are, but you'll be driving this wagon. I already rode a spell, and I'm tired. Just head southwest and you'll be fine for a while. You do know which way is southwest, don't ya'?"

"Yessir," said Andrew, as he took the reins of the horse between his first and second fingers of each hand. With a sharp slap of the leather reins, the horse started off down the dusty trail. They were riding for a few hours when Andrew glanced behind the seat, hoping to spot a canteen or a jug of sorts. Mr. Saunders was right. It was hot. Much hotter than back home. Despite the beautiful mountains in the distance and the wild flowers that painted the landscape, there seemed to be no shade around this part of the country. When the wind changed, the dust from the wagon wheels blew back and swirled in front of them.

"What's wrong with ya'?" Saunders bellowed, as he stirred from his half-sleep.

"Nothing sir, just looking for a canteen. My throat is pretty dry."

"Didn't think to bring one. We'll stop a ways ahead. There's a small stream we have to cross. You can drink your fill there."

It was another hour before they reached the stream. The sun was well past its zenith, and Andrew figured it to be mid-afternoon.

The sun's heat could be felt in the iron handrail on the buckboard that Andrew had grabbed hold of to steady himself before he jumped down from the wagon. He looked at the slight red mark on his palm left by the hot metal. Running over to the stream, he let the cool water soothe the burning sensation in his hand. He then dunked his whole head in the stream, letting the cool water run down onto his chest and shoulders as he squatted beside it. Touching his lips to the surface, he sucked in several mouthfuls of the delicious water and then soaked his neckerchief in it, before tying it back around his neck. He remembered some of James' stories from his time out in the desert and could see the reality of his words - out here, water is truly more precious than gold.

Mr. Saunders walked over and sat a few yards away from Andrew. He dipped a small metal cup he had pulled from the back of the wagon and drank his fill as well.

After they had watered the horse, the two men continued on to the ranch. They arrived just a few hours before sunset.

Andrew looked at the small run-down shack of a house, which had just two small windows in front and a modest front porch with one rocking chair. The barn, which was about thirty yards away from the house, also looked in need of repair. There were two corrals next to the barn. A larger one with several horses in it, and a smaller one a few yards from that with a center post in the middle that stood about six feet tall. A few buckets hung on rail posts. In the smaller corral stood a handsome light-gray mare. She seemed to be looking at Andrew as they rode past. Her long, white mane flowed straight down her neck with another long tuft in the front, which hung over her left eye. The rails of the corral looked to be made of cedar trees, and nothing like the fences made from lumber mill board-stock back east. It certainly didn't seem like the ranch he had envisioned in his head after listening to Mr. Hollings' stories.

"You'll sleep in the barn with Walter," said Mr. Saunders as the wagon pulled up in front of it. "There are a few horse blankets you can place over the hay to sleep on. There's a small creek in back of the barn a ways, where you can wash up. We'll have dinner just about sunset, and I'll expect you up just before sunrise to start work."

"Yessir," said Andrew as he jumped down and grabbed his bag from the back of the buckboard. "Who's Walter and what work will we be doing?" he asked, more interested in just carrying on a conversation with the quiet Mr. Saunders, than actual curiosity of the work.

"Walter's a goat, and *you'll* be helping me this week to extend the fencing around the large corral. For starters, I'll show you how things are run on a horse ranch. Then I'll put you to work next week on repairing the barn roof. Sound alright to you?"

"Yessir, sounds just fine. How many other hands are there on the ranch?"

"Well, I hire workers on a temporary basis during the busier parts of the year. No one else is currently pulling wages at this time."

Andrew unpacked his duffle and made up his bed with the hay and blankets Mr. Saunders had referred to.

Dinner was at six every evening, and as long as he wasn't late, Andrew could eat his fill. Unfortunately, Mr. Saunders was a private man with very little to say. The only words he spoke after grace were, "Please take your plate to the barn. I prefer to eat alone."

Without any argument, Andrew walked to the barn, where he ate by lantern light while cross-eyed Walter stared at his every bite, just waiting for him to drop something onto the ground. When Andrew went back for seconds, Mr. Saunders piled on another two pieces of chicken and a good amount of dumplings as well. For a man who seemed a little ornery, he certainly wasn't stingy with the food.

The next day, Andrew woke before dawn to the sound of Walter chewing on the brim of his good two-dollar hat. Andrew tugged at the hat with one hand, while tempting Walter with some hay in the other. Walter was having nothing of it, and only when Andrew dropped the hay and pulled with both hands, did the hat come free. Surveying the ugly bite mark on the front brim, Andrew placed the hat on his head in frustration.

Walter ran out of the barn before any revenge could be had.

Andrew worked on the corral with Mr. Saunders from sunrise until sunset. He cut fresh cedar poles from a nearby stand of trees and loaded them onto the wagon. Mr. Saunders would then drive the load over to the corral, where Andrew would unload them. Mr. Saunders taught Andrew how deep to dig the posts and how to build the corral fencing so it was sturdy, but also make it so a section could be replaced if necessary. Andrew worked on that chore for about a week, and when the corral was just about finished, Mr. Saunders rode in with a wagonload of shingles for the barn.

"Tomorrow you'll start on the barn roof. There's a long ladder in the back, behind the hay bales. Be sure you brace it good before you climb up there. The last time I shingled the roof was twenty years ago. Tied myself off to the weather vane in case I slipped. You might want to do the same."

Andrew looked up at the weather vane, which sat on the peak some twenty-five feet above the ground. He wasn't afraid of heights, but wasn't sure he trusted the old weather vane to hold him, should he slip. "I purchased a small keg of nails that should see you through the job, but all the same, it might be wise to save any nails that aren't too bent," said Mr. Saunders as he walked away.

The next week, Andrew spent most of his days up on the old roof. The first day he carried each of the seventeen bundles of shingles on his shoulder, up the ladder and onto the roof. Each day he'd haul his tools, his lunch, which usually consisted of deer venison and a piece of bread, along with a bucket of water up with him. When he needed to relieve himself, he'd just walk over behind the roof peak and piss a long stream into the dirt below.

It was Tuesday when he got revenge on Walter for taking a bite out of his hat, showering the goat as he ate the weeds on the back side of the barn. It was a hollow victory, as Walter was so stupid he had no idea what was happening and probably thought it was raining.

Andrew liked having everything he needed up on the roof. It kept him clear from Mr. Saunders' beckoning and gave him a feeling of freedom within his small world of hard work. The pitch of the barn wasn't as steep as it looked from the ground, and Andrew would often stop and lie on his back while he took a break. With scarcely a cloud in the sky, he'd stare up at the patch of bright blue until a hawk or buzzard would fly into view. Once in a while a breeze would blow and he'd feel the sweat on his body cool him a bit.

When Saturday came, he was done with the barn and was almost sad it was completed. The bright, unweathered cedar shingles had a warm glow to them, and he wished his pa could see the work he had accomplished.

As he stood with hands folded in front of him, marveling at his handywork, a whinny came from the far corral. The gray mare shook her head as Andrew looked over to her, as if she wanted some attention. He felt bad that she was all alone in the small corral, while the other horses Mr. Saunders had separated out were in the larger, expanded corral. Andrew walked over to see her, and she took a few steps to the side, moving away from him as he approached the fencing. He folded his arms on the cedar rail and spoke gently to her.

"Hey gal, I'm just payin' you a visit. That is what you wanted, wasn't it?" The gray just stared at him with her big, dark eyes. Andrew held out his empty hat in front of him, brim side up, as if offering something to her. As she slowly walked over and sniffed at the hat, Andrew slowly reached with the other hand and gently stroked her forehead. She pulled back and gave a small snort, surprised at the feeling of being touched by a human.

"I'll be back tomorrow," he said, as he walked over to the house. "You and I have unfinished business."

As he approached the house, Mr Saunders, who was obviously watching from inside, swung open the front door at the exact moment Andrew's foot hit the porch.

"All done with the barn roof, are ya'?" he asked as he rubbed the back of his neck as if he was sore from working. "I'll start you on branding some of the horses in the large corral."

"What about the gray?" Andrew asked. "Has she been broken yet?"

"One of the hands that worked here last fall tried to break her. He didn't get very far. I don't go near her, other than to feed and water her. Might be best to get rid of her. Just too mean spirited."

"She doesn't seem mean spirited to me," said Andrew.

Mr. Saunders stared at Andrew from head to toe, measuring him up for the task.

"Well son, if you think you can handle her, then you just go ahead and give it a try, but your daily work will need to be done beforehand. I've got an extra saddle in the barn you can use. But just remember, you break a leg and you can't work."

"Thank you, Mr. Saunders. I'll be careful," answered Andrew in a confident voice. "And I'll make sure my daily work is done first. You saw the good work I did on the barn, didn't ya'?"

Mr. Saunders took another step and leaned forward, his hands on his hips as he stared at the barn. 'Well... we'll see if it's a good job when we get some rain."

Chapter VII

Mr. Saunders watched from the window of his house, as Andrew used his rope to lasso the high-spirited gray mare and haul her in close enough to cover her eyes with his coat. Andrew wrapped one end of the rope around the center pole in the corral to give him leverage against her spirited strength. Only when he had pulled the gray to within a few feet of the center pole and tied off the rope, did he remove the coat from her eyes.

Andrew had worked with horses on a limited basis as a blacksmith, but it was with horses that were already saddle-broke and needing new shoes. He told Mr. Saunders he had experience with them, but that was before he knew he was going to be asked to break them. Afraid of going back on what he said he could do, he relied on his instincts, rather than looking green to the chore.

As soon as the coat was off, the horse began to pull and rear back. She whinnied as the rope stretched taught in Andrew's hands. He gradually let out a little more rope at a time, as she simmered down. She began to learn that the less she reined up, the more rope he gave her from the center post.

"That's the way, Cloud," he said to her. He had been toying with the idea of naming her since he had seen her. Mr Saunders didn't seem to be the type that would show the sentiment needed to name a horse; and the one time he had referred to the gray with Andrew, he had used the term "hell-bitch". Cloud was a fitting name, as she was as gray as some of the afternoon clouds he remembered seeing back home, right before the rains came. Out here, it was as dry as the back side of a dutch oven.

He hadn't seen rain once since he arrived, and had to carry every bit of water needed for drinking and washing from the stream past the house. Andrew continued to speak to Cloud in a calm voice, as he slowly worked the halter around her head. She stamped and whinnied as he set the bit in place. Her tongue wandered over the strange piece of metal as she shook her head from side to side.

Within a few days, Andrew had Cloud walking around the corral with her bridle on, as he held the rope in both hands with no assistance from the center post.

The gray would look at him out of the corner of her eyes as he led her around the large circular corral. After a half hour or so of this work, Andrew would gently reel her in close and talk to her softly as he removed the bridle and bit. He could sense her beginning to trust him. He thought: "A few more days of this, and you night be ready for the feel of a saddle."

It was a Tuesday afternoon after he had completed his chores, when he met Cloud with the bridle and a saddle blanket in his hands. He no longer needed to rope her in order to get close, and she would softly whinny when she saw him coming. Andrew held out his hand as he approached her. Her eyes seemed to light up when she saw the two large wedges of apple he offered her.

She nibbled at them from his hand and crunched on them with her large molars. She prodded him in the chest with her nose as if asking for more. "Sorry gal, that's all I have," he said as he patted her cheek. He slowly moved his hand down her left flank and gently placed the blanket on her back. He expected her to jerk to the side, or run to leave the blanket behind her, but she didn't. She turned her head and looked back as if to say, "I'm not exactly sure why you are placing that on me, but it doesn't hurt, and since I am curious, I shall let you."

Andrew placed the bridle on her as well, and walked her around the corral as he had done the past few days. It wasn't until that afternoon, when he placed the weight of the full saddle on her back, that she reared up, letting the saddle slide up and off her back onto the dusty ground before Andrew could thread the strap through the buckle. The second attempt went no better than the first. So the next step was to cover her eyes with his coat as he had done in the beginning, which seemed to calm her. Eventually, he was able to cinch the saddle down around her mid-section and walk her around the corral with ease.

Everything was going pretty smoothly up to this point for a man who had never broke a horse in his life, but he knew there was much to be done before he could ride her. Cloud trusted Andrew. She needed to get to the point where she could work through those new, different and awkward sensations, so she could tell herself, she was in fact okay, and neither the blanket, nor the saddle could hurt her. She was starting to learn that the man with the reddish-brown hair who often brought apple slices, was her friend.

The next day, as Andrew walked from the barn with Cloud's bridle and saddle, Mr. Saunders walked past Andrew and into the barn, only to reappear minutes later with a shovel and pickaxe. He walked over to a clearing, thirty yards in front of his house, and proceeded to draw a six-foot-wide circle in the dirt with the pickaxe. He then threw the tools into the center of the circle. "Here's where you're going to start digging the new well," he said, as he pointed his finger at the ground emphatically. "You can use the spare rope and timber in the barn to build yourself a frame and hoist. If you dig around toward the back of the barn, I believe there's an old pulley somewhere in there from when old man Baker's barn burnt down."

"I'll get to work on it, right after I finish breaking Cloud," replied Andrew.

"Who the hell is Cloud?" shouted Mr. Saunders.

"She's the gray from the small corral that I've been trying to break. I think I'm pretty close to doin' it, too."

"Well, that's as close as you're gonna to get to her for some time. You're to start on the well today and nothin' but, until it's done!"

"But I'm so close to..."

"You'll dig that well, son, and that's that," Saunders interrupted. Andrew softly mumbled under his breath, "I'm not your son," as he walked over and picked up the shovel. He was about to start digging, when he stopped and called out to Mr. Saunders. "About this job, when do I get paid?"

"I'm payin' ya' by feeding you every day and providing you with a place to hang your hat. You'll draw wages after I figure your worth and where you'll fit in when the other hands arrive next month. You wanna find another job, you're always welcome to climb back on that train."

Andrew stabbed the earth with the shovel and took out his frustration on the hard, dusty ground. By evening, he had dug down roughly six feet. Using the ladder from the barn, he climbed out and walked down to the stream to wash for dinner.

For three days, Andrew worked at digging the hole for a new well. He longed for the type of work he had done on the barn roof, when he could lay back and look at the endless blue sky. At fifteen feet down, the six-foot-wide shaft only gave him a small view of the sky above. Once in a while he'd wipe his brow and look up, only to see Walter gazing down at him with his creepy eyes. "Maaaaaaa," Walter would bleat, and then he'd run away, with the ringing of his bell growing fainter until it was gone. It seemed as if it wasn't Walter peering at him, it was Mr. Saunders. He'd say nothing, but watch his progress. As soon as Andrew would look up, Mr. Saunders would walk away.

The rest of Andrew's world was rusty-brown. The clay-rich dirt clung to his body, which was drenched in sweat in the ninety-degree heat, and gave his skin a darker than normal appearance. He had stopped washing his pants in the stream, for they would be just as dirty the next day. It made no difference how dirty he was anyhow. He saw no one other than Mr. Saunders and Walter each day.

When he was no longer able to throw the dirt up and out of the hole, he started filling four buckets at a time, which were tied to a rope. The rope was thread through a two-foot-diameter iron pulley, which in turn was attached to a wooden frame he had constructed above the hole. The eight-foot ladder from the barn he started out with, would no longer serve his needs. Each time he needed to empty the dirt, he would climb out of the hole by using another long rope, which was knotted every few feet for grip, and attached to the wooden frame.

It was slow work, for the buckets did not hold more than five or six shovels full of dirt each. For every three buckets of dirt, a fourth would be filled with rocks and stones he had unearthed with his pick. The deeper he dug, the slower the process became. Sometimes the rocks would be too large to even fit in the bucket, so he needed to tie a rope around them and haul them up individually.

Each day, after several hours of this back-breaking work, he could feel his arms aching from hauling himself repeatedly out of the hole, along with the hundreds of buckets of dirt. His experience working as a blacksmith served him well, as his forearms were sinewed with muscle and better prepared for hard work. But this job pushed his entire body to even greater limits.

When he had finished his digging each day, he would then start removing the unearthed dirt from the well site, by shoveling all of it onto the flat buckboard and driving it down to the stream. There, he would shovel it off the buckboard, onto the ground. He put most of the stones aside for the outside of the well, which he would build later. Even though he was exhausted at the end of each day, he knew this work would make him even stronger over time. The one saving grace was that Mr. Saunders fed him well. Sometimes he would just walk down to the stream with his meal if there was enough light in the sky left to see by. Only minutes after he finished his dinner, he would be asleep in his bunk in the barn.

It was early morning after two weeks of digging, Andrew's shovel rang out as it struck something very hard. He used the edge of the shovel to search for the width of what appeared to be a great rock. When he had confirmed it was about four feet wide, he switched to the pick in order to pry up one edge, but the stone ran too deep to pry up. He dug deeper around its edge for over a foot, and still its bottom was not to be found. He drove the pick into the center of the stone in an attempt to break it, or at least chip off a large portion, but the rock did not yield.

At twenty-five feet down, what was he to do? He panicked at first, thinking the ill-tempered troll would make him start a new hole from a different spot. He sat down on the stone with his elbows on his knees and his hands on his forehead. He remembered the sledge he had used to set the corral posts and climbed out of the hole to fetch it. Once back in the hole, he swung the sledge with all his might. Sparks jumped off the stone as the sledge ricocheted back from the mighty blow. After several consecutive swings, he had to stop for lack of oxygen down at the bottom. His face covered with sweat, the large stone only bore small whitish marks for all his effort. He sat down again and thought about what his father might do. Then he thought about what Mr. Hollings might do, and how he would sometimes creatively solve different problems in the blacksmith shop. Then an idea came to him.

He climbed out of the hole and ran into the barn to fetch the mule. Hitching up the harness on the mule, Andrew firmly attached a rope around the large farrier's anvil and led the mule out of the barn, dragging the large 250-pound anvil behind him. Once near the well, he untied the rope from the harness and fed it through the pulley system. He then reattached it to the mule's harness. Coaxing the mule forward, the large anvil dragged heavily in the dirt, as it approached the hole. Upon reaching the edge, the anvil went over the side and the mule gave a tremendous bray, as it stamped its legs to dig its hooves into the ground for traction. The rope held tight as the heavy anvil now swung back and forth over the deep open hole. Andrew pulled at the stubborn beast's harness, coaxing it forward. As the anvil appeared from the hole and rose up close to the pulley, it was now centered over the large stone below.

Feeling confident that the mule would hold his ground, Andrew ran to the hole and reached out to the rope, to slow the anvil's swinging. When it had finally come to rest over the center, he drew his knife and started to cut into the rope just above the anvil. Before he could cut through, the rope started to split and its fibers uncoiled and spun erratically from the great weight. With a loud snap, the rope broke. Twenty-five feet the anvil fell, meeting the stone with a loud bang!

Andrew peered over the side into the hole. When the dust cleared, he thought he could make out a crack, but he couldn't be sure.
At least the anvil looked to be in one piece. He lowered himself into the hole and not only found a four-foot-long crack in the mighty stone, but a wetness seeping up from the crack. He had done it. He had hit water!

After retrieving the anvil from the hole, Andrew watched as the water slowly filled the well. Foot by foot it slowly rose. When it reached seven feet from the bottom, it appeared to stop. Andrew hooked up one of the buckets to the pulley system and lowered it into the well. Hauling up the bucket, he swallowed several gulps before dumping the contents over his head.

Mr. Saunders appeared from his house and walked over to the well. "You'll need to be starting the stone base around this frame. We can't have any animals falling in. You ought to be able to get in a few hours of work before dinner."
Andrew couldn't believe it. Not a thank you, or any type of praise after all his hard work. He was starting to understand that not everyone was like his family. He wondered what happened to Mr. Saunders that made him so cold and unwilling to share a kind word. He missed the

feeling of being part of a family, the evening conversation exchanged at the dinner table, as he and his parents would recount the day's events. Sometimes a story would be told. Andrew liked it best when his ma would tell of her childhood, and how times were now so different from when she was growing up.

Throwing the bucket back into the well, Andrew kept his head high as he walked over to the pile of rocks and stones he had collected over the past few weeks. He could hear his pa's voice saying how proud he was of him for digging that well all by himself, and that he should probably forgive the old man for being so cross and without feeling.

Chapter VIII

During the next week, Andrew had finished the stone wall around the well. It was a great aid when it came time to water the horses or just get a drink himself during the hot days, although he still preferred to wash down by the stream. The peacefulness of the area reminded him a little of home. He was homesick, and with all the work he had been doing around the ranch, he hadn't spent the proper time to write a letter to post.

When Saturday came, he asked Mr. Saunders for a few pieces of paper, so he could write a letter to his folks. Mr. Saunders mumbled something under his breath about the cost of posting a letter, as he handed Andrew a few sheets of paper. "I suppose you'll be wanting a pencil and an envelope as well," he griped.

"Yessir, if it's not too much trouble," Andrew replied in a confident voice, as if to infer he'd earned the privilege through hard work.

"Well, I'll be heading into town for provisions later today. We've got hands comin' in on Monday. You're welcome to ride with me and I'll forward you the cost to post it. Just don't make it a regular habit."

"Thank you," said Andrew, as he headed down to the stream to write his letter.

When he reached the stream, he found a good log to sit on. Using a section of one of the old barn shingles he'd tucked into his belt as a flat surface, he began to compose his thoughts to his family.

Andrew used every bit of both sides of the two pieces of paper, and told his family about all his hard work. He painted Mr. Saunders in a brighter light than he deserved, but he didn't want his ma and pa to worry about him. He spent more than an hour writing his thoughts down by the stream. When he had finished, he folded the paper carefully, placed it in the envelope and tucked it away in his shirt pocket, making sure it was out of reach of Walter's ever-insatiable appetite.

Walking back to the barn, he noticed two horses, adorned with saddles, saddlebags, bedrolls and rifle scabbards, tied to the outside of the large corral. "Whomever these belong to, they rode a fair piece to get here," he thought to himself.

Andrew walked up to the house to return Mr. Saunders' pencil to him, and to see if he was ready to head into town. Upon reaching the front door, he held off from knocking, because the voices inside were growing in volume. "That's not what we agreed to," Mr. Saunders yelled. "If you can't make due with the wages I pay, you're both welcome to move on. " Andrew couldn't make out the reply, as it was spoken in a harsh, but stoic manner. He then heard his own name mentioned, as the old man presented his current situation to his guests. As he heard footsteps walking toward him, he backed away from the door and stepped off the porch, pretending he was just approaching the house. The door swung open quickly, and two men stepped out onto the porch. Both looked to be in their thirties and had obviously seen their time working under the hot western sun. Their faces had wrinkles, where Andrew's had none. Their clothes looked tattered in spots and their chaps well-worn. One of the men looked to Andrew and said, "You might want to wait a bit, son, before approachin' him. He's madder than a hornet right now."

Andrew stepped through the doorway and placed the pencil on the wooden table next to Mr. Saunders' rocking chair.

"I'm just returning this to you," he said, and then turned to walk out, not wanting to bring up the subject of riding into town just yet.

"Hitch up the brown gelding to the buckboard, Andrew. We're going to town," Mr. Saunders replied.

Andrew was not too surprised at Mr. Saunders' announcement, but he was taken aback by the soft tone of his voice. Andrew was used to Mr. Saunders barking orders and not addressing him at all by his first name. It was as if someone had taken all the wind out of his sails. Andrew merely replied with a "Yessir," and walked outside quickly to leave Mr. Saunders with his thoughts. After hitching up the wagon, Andrew climbed onto the buckboard, reins ready to head out to town. Five minutes later, Mr. Saunders walked out of the house with a Winchester lever action in his hands. Andrew had never seen Mr. Saunders with a gun around the ranch, and he didn't have one with him the time he picked up Andrew from the train station.

The two rode several miles until they came to the stream they had crossed on the day Andrew was brought to the ranch.
Mr. Saunders said nothing as he climbed down from the buckboard, walked down to the stream and sat on the bank with the rifle across his lap. Andrew didn't know if this was a good time to approach Mr. Saunders about what was troubling him. After all, Mr. Saunders wasn't very approachable on a good day, and this certainly didn't seem to be one of those. But something in the back of his mind, or maybe it was his heart, made him walk over and sit beside Mr. Saunders. He said nothing, but just watched the stream flow, the sunlight creating slight reflections on the water.

"Life isn't always fair, son," Mr. Saunders said aloud, as he stared straight ahead at the stream, tossing in pebbles from the ground and watching the concentrical circles expand across the water's surface. It was the second time he had referred to Andrew in that way.

"I really do appreciate all your hard work. I know I'm not the sunniest type of person you're likely to run across, but I haven't always been this way. Life's made me hard, son. I was married a long time ago. I had met a nice Irish gal, and the two of us were very much in love. We had dreams of building a cattle ranch together, settling down and raising a family. Well, we had us two sons, Ben and Jake. But life wasn't to be what I had envisioned. Ellen got sick and died just a few years after our second son, Jake, was born."

Andrew said nothing, but just listened to Mr. Saunders as the words began to flow from him, like a river long since due to overflow its banks. "I blame myself for not spending the necessary time raising them proper. Ben, who was two years older than Jake, went bad. Started hangin' out with undesirables in town. They were a lazy lot, and he wanted nothin' to do with the ranch. He'd often come home drunk and disappear for long stretches of time, comin' back only when he needed some money. Then one day, I found out from a friend in town he ended up gettin' killed trying to rob a bank in Billings, Montana. He's buried somewhere up there. Never been to his grave. Probably unmarked anyhow, seein' he was no good.

Jake started out working hard at the ranch. He's the one that rode in this morning with his friend, Luke Nettle. I made Jake foreman two years ago, and he was helpful bringing in additional hands when we needed them. But he didn't show up last spring, and neither did Luke or the other hands he hired. Now Jake's pressuring me to sell the ranch. He says he's due his share of what's his, and I should retire and go live in town. But I'm not ready to sit back and retire. When I do, it'll be from my front porch in a rocker, not in town. If he'd just come back and work for wages, we could make out just fine, and it would all be his someday. But he doesn't seem to want the sweat and hard work of running a ranch anymore. All he really wants is the money."

"Are you planning to sell?"

"Hell no! This is my way of life, and I'll fight for it if necessary."

"Why would you need to fight? He's your son."

"I'm convinced if something was to happen to me, he'd step in and sell this place. I'd make you foreman if you had more experience, son, but I don't think I'd be doin' ya' any favors. I'm hoping I can get us some honest hands for the next roundup of horses, when we reach town. The army is looking for good horses and we could make out fine if I can get two or three more hands to work for the ranch this summer. Hopefully, I can find what I need in Durango."

A few hours later, the two rode into Durango and pulled the buckboard up to the general store in the center of town. Mr. Saunders climbed down and reached for his rifle. He then looked at Andrew, who was still sitting in the buckboard staring forward down the street. "You comin'?" he asked.

"Yessir," he replied, glad to be included in the business at hand.

Mr. Saunders knew Abe Waterson quite well, as he'd purchased all of his goods from Abe over the years.

"Why, Red Saunders. What brings you to town?"

"Abe, I'm needin' some help to round up a few good hands to work on my ranch. Two or three ought to do. I'll pay top wages for good men. I hear the army is lookin' for good horses and I can give two to three months of steady work. I'd appreciate it if you could spread the word for me, and keep the request out of the saloon if you can read my tracks. Most of the men who hang out there don't agree with hard work."

"I'll spread the word to those who come in, and I'll mention it at this Sunday's service as well."

"I really appreciate it, Abe. By the way, this here is Andrew Thompson. If I had two more of him, we'd be set."

Andrew shook Mr. Waterson's hand, and the compliment by Mr. Saunders was not lost on him.

Mr. Saunders picked up some pipe tobacco, and then asked Andrew to wait for him as he went in back to see about some baling wire.

Andrew walked around looking at some of the newer items for sale in the shop. He stopped when he came to the gun case. The new Colt revolvers sparkled with their nickel silver finish. Beside the Colts, there were a few new knives and some custom tooled leather holsters. He then looked up above the case and saw what he thought was the prettiest shotgun he had ever seen, hanging on the back wall. It was a brand new model Winchester 1901 pump-action shotgun. He had used his father's Henry rifle many times growing up, but this was a weapon that could adapt to different types of hunting. With this gun, he could picture himself hunting everything from grouse to deer. All one would need to do is carry different types of shells. It would also be great protection against the big cats he had heard about in this part of the country.

He marveled at the deep blue color of the barrel and receiver. The polished walnut stock was outfitted with a fine leather sling. The hang tag said: 10 gauge, 2-7/8 chamber, 26-inch barrel, Brush model with take-down feature - $25.00.

Andrew's eyebrows raised slightly and the smile left his face as he let go of the price tag. Mr. Saunders and Abe walked back into the room.

"Anything you'd like to see?" asked Abe.

"No thank you, sir. I was just admiring the shotgun."

"Yes, she's a real pretty gun; 1901 model. Comes with a sling and a saddle scabbard too. I ordered two of the same model several months back, and just got them in a few weeks ago. Probably the only two in ten gauge this side of the Mississippi. Takes a while to get a nice gun out here, all the way from New Haven, Connecticut. Sold one to a rancher, who lives a few miles north of town. I had a deposit on this one here, by one of our stage drivers. Then he decided he couldn't afford it. Must have had a turn of bad luck at the card tables. So... there she hangs."

Mr. Saunders walked over and looked at the tag. "Hoo-wee... that's about two weeks pay, top hand wages, wouldn't you say, Abe?"

"Yessir, that's what she goes for. About the same as a new Colt revolver," answered Abe. "Pretty much why she's been sittin' there."

"I'll take her," said Mr. Saunders. "As long as you throw in a few boxes of that bird shot and a box of double-aught buck."

"Done deal," said Abe.

Abe walked into the back room for a moment and then appeared with the boxes of ammunition, the saddle scabbard and a piece of literature on the gun. Mr. Saunders picked up the shotgun from the counter, worked the slick action a few times and then placed it in the scabbard. He then handed it to Andrew.

"I figure this squares us," said Mr. Saunders.

The surprised expression on Andrew's face was quickly replaced by a huge smile. "More than square, I figure!" replied Andrew. "I don't know what to say... thank you, sir."

"Well, don't just stand there, son. Load that wire onto the buckboard while I settle with Abe here. We got work to do back at the ranch." Andrew rushed out the door with all the enthusiasm of a young boy.

The ride back was much more pleasant than the ride up. Andrew and Mr. Saunders shared hunting stories, and the tips and tricks that accompanied them. Each of them learning something from the other. Mr. Saunders was amazed at how much Andrew knew about tracking, hunting and the woods in general.
"I suppose your pa had something to do with all those good stories?" asked Mr Saunders.
"Yessir. My pa was a scout for the army. Well, he's not my real pa. My real pa was killed in an accident when I was young. But I've known James for so long, well, it feels like he is my real pa. James taught me just about everything I know of the woods, camping, tracking, hunting and all sorts of things about the weather and animals too, you name it."
"Sounds like quite a man," replied Mr. Saunders. "And how about your ma, is she back home, too?"
"Yessir. She helps teach at the local... Oh, no! I forgot to post my letter back in town!" Andrew exclaimed. He reached into his shirt to confirm it was still tucked inside.
"Don't worry," said Mr. Saunders. "We'll make another run to town next week."

As the sun was getting low on the horizon, the two men decided to stop at the familiar creek and make camp for the evening.
"I can take care of gathering some kindling and makin' a fire, if you'd like to scare up a grouse or two for dinner," hinted Mr. Saunders.
"I'll give it my best try," said Andrew.

Taking the new Winchester from its scabbard, Andrew loaded the tubular magazine with four of the birdshot shells, and then put one in the chamber. He tilted the brim of his hat low on his brow and walked down to the creek. He worked the west side, hoping to shoot away from the sun, and then slowly made his way along the willows, bushes and rocks that bordered the creek bed.

About thirty minutes had passed as he pushed through the brush, when a flurry of wings flew up in front of him with a surprising whistle. Two prairie chickens shot straight up and flew toward the north, one directly behind the other. Andrew swung the gun up toward the birds and pulled the trigger, just as the barrel intersected their flight path. A loud boom echoed along the creek bed as the walnut stock pushed back into Andrew's shoulder, and both birds fell into the surrounding bushes. He was surprised to fell both birds with one shot, an experience that could never have been matched by the Henry. He found one bird immediately, as it had fallen into a thick bush and was being supported by its branches. It took a little more searching to find the other bird, which had landed on the inside rim of the creek bed among some rocks. Andrew held both birds by the feet in one hand as he made his way back to the camp. He could see a small column of smoke rising in front of him, just above the willows.

As the sun set, Mr. Saunders slowly turned the birds over his makeshift cooking spit. The two exchanged more stories, as they shared a good meal.

The next morning the two men arrived at the ranch, eager to get started on rounding up a herd of wild horses, which they would eventually break and sell to the military. They still needed to find a few good hands, and hoped Abe Waterson could drum up some help by spreading the word in town.

"I know you've taken a shine to that gray, the one you call Cloud," said Mr. Saunders. "Go ahead and finish breaking her. In the meantime, you can saddle up the chestnut and we'll head out to the western edge of the valley where the grass is greenest close to the river. I'll still need you to use some of that soft wire to mend a few spots on the corral. Then we'll head back out early evening and see if we can cut a few of them out and run them back here before sunset.

The following week, Andrew and Mr. Saunders had managed to round up twenty-two horses by themselves. It was slow going with just the two of them, but the wild herd had held to where the sweet grass and water was plentiful. Andrew used his evenings to work with Cloud, and he now had her to the point where he could ride her around the corral. It wouldn't be long before he planned to have her out on the plains among the other mustangs.

Two days later, at the end of a long day of riding, a young man rode up to the house. Andrew watched from the barn as the man climbed down from his sorrel and walked up to the front porch. His hat looked well-travelled and sweat-stained, and his shirt and chaps told the same story. The sorrel bore a bedroll, saddlebags, a saddle-ring carbine and a coiled rope. A well-rounded outfit, to say the least. Walter walked over to the sorrel and was sniffing around its haunches, when the big gelding launched a rear hoof in Walter's direction, sending the goat kicking up dust as he ran back into the barn.

Andrew, who was still eating his dinner, brought his plate of chicken and biscuits outside and sat on a chopping stump, keeping watch on

Mr. Saunders' front porch. Finishing his dinner, Andrew pulled out his mouth organ and began to play a soft ballad. After twenty minutes went by, the man stepped outside of Mr. Saunders' house, climbed aboard his sorrel and looked over at Andrew. He tipped his hat to him, before riding back the way he came.

Putting his mouth organ away, Andrew walked back to the main house and gave a knock on the door.

"Come on in, son," answered Mr. Saunders.

"The chicken was exceptionally good, sir," said Andrew. "Um, who was that who came to visit?"

"Says his name is Pete Lewis. Rode in from Antelope Spring looking for work. He says Abe mentioned the job to him after he arrived in town. He's got some experience around horses and is willing to start day after tomorrow. If you have no objections, he can take the extra bunk in the barn."

"Sure, it's fine with me. With the three of us, we ought to get some real wrangling done. Goodnight, Mr. Saunders," said Andrew as he walked out the door.

Mr. Saunders returned the sentiment as he slowly stood up with his hands on the table, which he used for support as he rose. He stretched backwards and let out a soft moan as his back ached after a long day in the saddle. He hadn't done this much riding in several years.

Rolling a cigarette, he walked out onto the porch and watched the sun go down as he slowly inhaled the tobacco from his rocking chair. When the sun had set below the sage grass, he went inside and blew out the kerosene lamp.

The hooting of an owl woke Andrew from his sleep. It was the kind of noise that suggested a hunt was taking place, but it was also a comforting sound that reminded him of the woods back home. Many a night he had fallen asleep listening to the calls of a Great Horned Owl or a pack of coyotes filling the night with their high-pitched howls. Plumping his pillow with one of his fists, he gathered the blanket around his shoulders and chin, with just his eyes and nose peeking out from the thick wool.

Then he heard something that made him sit up in bed with a fright. A loud boom of a gunshot echoed in the night. He had to challenge his own senses at first. Did he dream it, or actually hear it? He reached over to the bale of hay where his Winchester sat. He kept the gun empty, for that is how his pa had always instructed him to keep his firearms when at home. He stood up and quickly ran over to where he kept the boxes of ammunition. Opening the breech, he quickly loaded four rounds of buckshot, cycling one round, and ran toward the door of the barn, wearing just his long-johns. Opening the barn door just a crack, he peered out into the night, which was faintly lit by a waning crescent moon.

He waited for three minutes, which felt like fifteen, before he decided to approach the main house. He still wasn't sure if the shot he heard was real, or if he dreamt it. Perhaps someone was out hunting coyotes, or maybe it was a signal that someone needed help. A flurry of ideas came to his mind as he approached the front porch. He kept bent over, trying to stay below the line of the front window panes, should Mr. Saunders also be at the ready with his rifle.

"Mr. Saunders?" Andrew called out, loud enough for him to hear should he be on the other side of the front door.

"Mr. Saunders?" he called again, but this time louder.

With no response, Andrew walked up the steps of the porch and slowly worked the latch on the door, which was unlocked. It creaked slightly as he pushed the door with enough force so it swung open to give him a clear view of the kitchen, but he saw no one inside.

He called again to Mr. Saunders, but got no reply. He then walked inside, and reached over for the box of matches on the kitchen table. Pulling a match out of the box, he lit the kerosene lamp and adjusted the wick so it lit up the room with a flickering glow. There was a metal tin that Andrew remembered being on top of the stove mantle, lying open on the floor. He picked it up, confirmed it was empty and placed it on the table. Looking over toward the bedroom, he could see the door was ajar, and what looked to be the legs of a man on the floor inside. Andrew took the lamp from the table and slowly walked closer to the bedroom, shotgun ready and crossed over the arm in which he held the lamp.

It was when he stuck his head past the door frame, that he saw Mr. Saunders lying on the floor with what looked to be a large shotgun wound in his back. Andrew felt a chill go through him and he gasped aloud at the sight of the body, which lay facedown in a pool of blood. The wound had torn the clothing from the back of the nightshirt he had slept in, and blood was also on the bed and wall. A single empty shell lay on the floor.

Breathing heavily, Andrew spun around, thinking someone might be standing behind him, but no one was there. He then heard the hoof falls of a single rider, heading off into the night. He ran to the door, but with the clouds passing in front of the sliver of moonlight, he could only make out the rider's faint silhouette, as he sped north.

Andrew sat down on the porch, placing the shotgun down beside him. He was feeling sick to his stomach as he tried to push the gruesome image from his mind. He needed to calm down and think of what to do.

After several minutes, he knew he needed to ride to Durango and retrieve the sheriff.

Running to the barn, he threw his clothes on over his long-johns, stuffed what possibles he had in his saddlebags and then filled his canteen from the rain barrel. He took his saddle and blanket from the barn and ran out to the corral to saddle up Cloud. She stomped her front hooves into the dusty ground, showing signs of being spooked. "Easy, Cloud, it's okay. No one's going to hurt you," he whispered to try to settle her down. No sooner had he thrown the saddle and blanket over the top rail of the corral, when a voice spoke behind him, clear and loud.

"Throw your hands up mister, or I'm gonna' shoot you down."

Andrew did as he was told and gasped out a pleading reply.

"Please don't shoot me, mister. I work for Mr. Saunders and sleep in the barn. I had nothin' to do with him getting shot. I just discovered him. I heard someone ride off. I think to the north, but I can't be sure."

"All I know is that you're gonna pay for killing my pa!" said the gruff voice.

That's when he remembered hearing the same voice the day the two men rode in and argued with Mr. Saunders in the kitchen. It was Jake Saunders.

He shivered with the thought of being shot in the back. After all, why should Jake bring him to the law? He certainly looked guilty enough with a loaded shotgun and attempting to saddle a horse.

"Listen, Jake. I didn't do it. I swear," Andrew pleaded. Just bring me in and we can clear all this up!" Turning around slowly and looking past Jake, Andrew could see Walter on top of the three-foot-high wall that circled the well, quietly chewing on the rope tied to the bucket, which was resting on the well.

Even though he was scared to death, he could almost laugh inside at the thought that his last glimpse of life just might be dumb, old Walter.

"I don't need the law," said Jake, his eyes narrowing as he raised the rifle from his hip to his shoulder.

Andrew's thoughts raced through his head, trying to come up with anything to say that might stop Jake from pulling that trigger.

"You can't shoot me with the new hand who rode in yesterday just over there in the barn."

"What hand would that be?" Jake challenged.

Andrew searched his thoughts, trying to remember the hand's name Mr. Saunders had mentioned, but nothing came to him.

It was in that brief moment, that Walter managed to chew through the last strand of rope that was attached to the bucket. It rolled off the edge of the stone wall and hit the ground with a loud "clank".

Jake spun halfway around, keeping the rifle pointed at Andrew while glancing quickly over his shoulder.

Andrew found the courage to act. He seized the rifle barrel in his left hand, pulled it straight past his left side and swung his fist into Jake's face. Jake hit the ground with a dusty thud, his rifle falling from his hand as it landed on the other side of him.

Andrew quickly picked up the rifle and tossed it into the well.

Jake, who had managed to get to his feet, leaped at Andrew with both arms outstretched, his hands making their way around his neck.

Andrew fought to breathe as he looked into the crazy eyes of a man prepared to give no mercy. Being pushed backwards against the well and unable to break Jake's grasp, he reached blindly beside him, hoping to find a large stone.

What he found, was the handle of the metal-clad bucket. With all the strength he could muster, he swung the bucket, catching Jake upside of his head and knocking him face down onto the ground, rendering him unconscious. Walter gave a bleat, hopped off the stone wall and cocked his head as he looked at Andrew, then ran back into the barn.

Andrew quickly saddled Cloud, keeping a close eye on Jake, who was still lying unconscious next to the well. He placed his saddlebag around the front saddle pommel and tied his Winchester in its scabbard to the saddle ring. As he threw his leg over the saddle, he realized he couldn't just leave poor Mr. Saunders lying dead in his bedroom the way he was. He rode Cloud over to the house, tied her to the front post and went inside. He approached the bedroom with remorse and fear, as he did not want to see the awful, lifeless body again. Yet he felt respect for the man who lay there and wanted to at least put his body on the bed before leaving to fetch the law.

Andrew pulled the top sheet from the bed and was able to wrap Mr. Saunders in it. A lot of blood had already soaked into the dry wooden floor of the bedroom and made the floor slippery in spots. He carefully lifted the sheet-wrapped body and placed him face up on the bed, covering him with his wool blanket and placing his bible from the nightstand by his side. He felt that was the right thing to do. As he took one knee beside the bed, he said a prayer for the old man, so that he may rest in peace.

"Old man, I had just started to get to know you. You were a man who was often strict with words, yet you had a tender side underneath all that pain. You taught me what hard work really was, but also how to be forgiving. I hope you rest in peace, and that the good Lord opens the gates of heaven for you and your son, Ben. Amen."

When he walked back outside, Jake was nowhere to be found and the faint glow of dawn was beginning to lighten the sky. He quickly scanned for Jake's horse and discovered it, too, was gone. Cloud was still tied to the post in front. Andrew climbed into the saddle and whisked the reins to the side as he turned and cantered toward the barn. "Good-bye, Walter," said Andrew, as he rode past the opening of the barn. Walter managed a bleat as he chewed on some hay.

Andrew rode toward Durango, following the only trail he knew. It was hard to get the image of Mr. Saunders from his mind. He was still in shock over the act, and wondered if Jake himself had done the killing. He thought that if Jake did ride straight to the law, he would surely arrive before him, and who knows what story he would tell, as he wouldn't put it past him to lie. He kept thinking of the argument between Jake and Mr. Saunders and how he wanted the old man to sell. But to murder one's own father was too much for him to believe. All he knew was, he needed to get into town and tell his side of the story as quickly as possible. The only other person he knew in town was Abe Waterson. Maybe it would be best if he rode there first, and have Abe fetch the sheriff back to his store in order to avoid Jake.

The sun was rising higher in the morning sky when he reached the stream he and Mr. Saunders had stopped at during their trip to town. He scanned the horizon in several directions before climbing out of the saddle. He could see no sign of trail dust or riders. Cloud slowly walked down to the stream and drank from the clear flowing water. A hare, spooked by the big gray mare, jumped from the bank and hopped into some sage grass.

Andrew refilled his canteen and patted Cloud on her neck as she drank. Being alone, he now realized what a beautiful and peaceful spot this truly was. He liked how the stream made little noise and how the small blue and yellow flowers lined its banks, like something one might see in a painting. He took his handkerchief and soaked it in the cool water. As he ran it over the back of his neck and chest, he felt the letter he had tucked inside the pocket of his shirt. He never had gotten to post it, and so much had happened since he wrote it. He thought how his parents must be worried by now, not having any word from him. He hoped they would be forgiving, and that maybe he could post a new letter after he cleared up his story with the sheriff. He watched a hawk that flew high in the sky, riding a thermal to scan the ground below. It flew in a pattern of what looked to be overlapping circles, gradually getting closer to where he sat. Then, in one graceful movement, it seemed to roll over slightly before diving down, close to where Andrew sat. Just yards away, the hawk plummeted, before pulling up at the last second to grab the hare that had jumped from the stream bed. Only a slight squeak was heard and the hawk cowled its wings around the dead hare. Andrew's stomach growled with hunger, but there was no time for a morning breakfast except to grab a few bites of jerky. Andrew left the hawk to eat its meal in peace and rode off toward town with a slightly faster trot than before, eager to get the whole incident over with.

It was mid-afternoon when Andrew approached town. Still a few miles away, the buildings in town were warmly lit by the sun as it worked its way into the western sky. Just outside of town, puffs of smoke could be seen billowing from a freight train. The smoke rose high into the sky and then dissipated as the engine pulled its eight cars and caboose out of Durango and made its wide turn toward the north.
When he turned his gaze back toward town, Andrew spotted what looked to be a group of riders from the north cutting southwest and

heading in his direction. They must be riding fast, he assumed, as a good sized dust trail could be seen kicking up behind them. Andrew began to feel nervous and gave Cloud a slight kick. She jumped into a canter as he pointed her nose toward the western part of town. The riders in the distance were closing fast, and they had now cut across in front of the town and were heading straight toward him. He counted three in all. Andrew needed to make a decision. He knew Cloud was fast, but the riders had clearly taken an intentional angle to cut him off from town. He shifted the reins to point Cloud even further to the west, as he tried to circumnavigate the riders. A rock kicked up beside him, followed by the sound of a rifle shot, and then another. There was no mistaking their intention, they meant him harm and he needed to act fast.

He kicked Cloud again and slapped the reins hard on her neck as he called to her. "Come on Cloud, ride!"

Cloud thrust into a full gallop, her gray mane and tail now fully extended back against the wind. Andrew sat forward and low in the saddle, as he tried to outflank the riders. As he cut west, the riders also turned. Two more shots were heard, as he kept his body behind Cloud's neck, shouting and kicking for all the speed she had. He could still see the train pulling away, now a few miles away from Durango. Fearing to be shot from the saddle before he could reach town, he widened his path and pointed his mare toward the train with hopes he might catch it. He heard a bullet hit the back of his saddle, with remarkable luck, not striking him or Cloud. Another whizzed past his head, so close he could actually hear the buzz of it cut through the dry air.

He doubted these riders could be the law, for there was no warning given. These men were shooting to drop him from the saddle. Now only a half-mile or so from the train, he pulled his Winchester from its scabbard and fired one shot blindly at the group. One horse went down and the rider along with it, tumbling into dirt and stirring up a huge cloud of dust.

The other two were still coming, and fired another two shots at Andrew. Unable to work the rifle's action with one hand, Andrew slung the shotgun sling over his head and shoulder, holding onto the reins with his other hand.

He was now almost alongside the train, and the riders behind him had stopped shooting for the moment.

Cloud was now starting to tire. Riding her as fast as she could go, Andrew reached for one of the side ladder rungs on the rearmost boxcar. It seemed just beyond his grasp, as the train continued to pick up speed. He hated to leave Cloud, but it was either this, or be shot or hung by those vigilantes. He attempted to swing the front saddlebag with his ammo and food over his other shoulder, but it slipped from his grasp and was lost behind in the trail dust along the tracks. Again, he kicked at Cloud's ribs to get every last ounce of speed from her as he focused on the boxcar rungs. With one last effort, he leaned as far forward as he could in the saddle and grasped one of the iron rungs. As Cloud slowed, the train's momentum pulled him from the saddle, his legs dangling beside the fast moving train. Twisting himself to face the ladder, he grasped another rung and slowly pulled himself up the ladder. As he stood on the rungs, leaning toward the side door of the boxcar he reached over to pull the latch. After a few attempts, he was finally able to work the latch and slide the door open enough to swing himself into the dusty, dark refuge. With a loud thud, he landed on his back and then rolled a few times over the floor of the car, which was littered with remnants of hay and dried dirt.

The door behind him slid closed and the latch engaged with a loud click. A low, raspy voice spoke out from the partial darkness. "Now that's what I'd call an entrance!"

Chapter IX

As the dust in the rail car started to settle, Andrew could see a form seated opposite him on a burlap sack of grain. The few shafts of sunlight that shone through the cracks in the car walls illuminated portions of the man's bearded face. A knapsack lay beside him and a Kentucky long rifle rested across his lap.

"Took me several tries to get it right, myself," the man said in a rough, but welcoming voice. "First time, I was ass-over-elbows in the dirt. Plumb lucky I didn't break nothin'. Of course, I wasn't riding no mustang neither. I Iad to run to catch up to the car. Always best when a train's chuggin' uphill. She slows quite a bit, especially with full cars." The man lit a match against his rifle stock and held it close to his pipe as he puffed rapidly, the light from the match fully illuminating his face for a few seconds. "Name's Jeb Slate, from Missouri," he added with the "Missurrah" pronunciation used by the state's natives.

"I'm Andrew Thompson, from Altamont, New York."

"Glad to meet ya'," said Jeb, as he reached across and offered Andrew his hand. Andrew shook the hand and was surprised to feel such strength in a handshake from a man who looked so old and run down. At the same time, Jeb admired the strong grip and calloused hands of a man who looked so young.

"You done some work, you have," said Jeb, as he nodded his head with approval.

"Mostly blacksmithing and ranch work," Andrew answered. "Where you headed, Jeb?"

"Oh, I figure I'd head west of the Rockies and see if I could live the life of a trapper. I hear they have deer the size of bears out that way."

"I've read about those myself," replied Andrew as he laughed. "They're called elk. I also hear they have grizzly bears the size of a small stage coach." Andrew moved a few of the grain sacks that were stacked up in the back of the car and placed them across from Jeb so one was flat on the floor and the other set as a back rest. Sitting down, he turned to work out a few spots with his fist before leaning back again.

"How about yourself?" asked Jeb as he leaned back against the slotted car wall and puffed on his pipe.

"I've got family back east, but I came out here several weeks ago to see the west. Had a job doing ranch work, but that fell through. In fact, you could say I was encouraged to leave."

"Steal somethin', did ya'?" asked Jeb, eluding to the gray mustang.

"No, honest. I stole one time when I was younger, and learned my lesson. If you're meaning that gray, I broke her from green and then got her as a gift. Problem was, I witnessed something I shouldn't have... a killing. I'm pretty sure the ones that did it, have already pinned that on me. So I guess there's no going back."

"There's always a way to go back, son. You should clear your name after the smoke has cleared. After all, every man has only two things he's born with, his name and courage.

The first one's easy to find. It's right out in front of ya', and everything you do your whole life will be tied to it. The second shows up when it's good'n ready. Sometimes it takes years, but it's there. Believe me. Sometimes it don't seem like it, but it's there."

"You sound a little like my pa. Trying to teach me something, are ya'?"

"He's right. You're never to old to learn somethin' new. If it suits you, we can travel together, since this here train is takin' us in the same direction."

"Sounds good to me," said Andrew.

With nothing but the clack of the rails as background noise, Andrew told Jeb all about his family back east and how his real father had died in a logging accident when he was very young. He went on to tell how his new pa, James, was a scout for the U. S. Army before moving back east, where he met and married Andrew's mom. Jeb shared some of his past with Andrew as well. He described how he left home at an early age after his ma died of smallpox, and how he joined the army himself when he was young. They seemed to have a lot in common, and Andrew was feeling glad he fell into Jeb's company. The two drifted off to sleep after talking for several hours.

During the night, the train made a stop in Idaho Springs to load up on wood and to fill the large steam tank with water, which Andrew slept straight through. Late the next morning, he awoke to the sound of a wagon being driven by two men who were sent to start unloading the cars further down the train.

"We should be goin'," said Jeb, as he shook Andrew's leg, making sure he truly was awake. "I think we're over the border of Wyoming, judging by the sign over there," he added, as he peered through one of the slats in the wood car. The sign read "Laramie Station" in white letters painted on a red background. "You slept through breakfast, but it don't matter much, since I only had some left-over biscuits that I'd cooked in bacon fat the other day. I won't blame ya' if you don't ask for seconds," said Jeb, as he handed Andrew a biscuit and a flat piece of jerky.

"Much obliged," said Andrew, as he shoved the biscuit in his mouth and placed the piece of jerky in his shirt pocket for later.

"If I was to share somethin' with ya', would you promise to keep it under your hat?" asked Jeb.

"I can keep a secret til' hell freezes over," answered Andrew as he picked up the few small crumbs of biscuit that were caught in the front folds of his shirt and placed them in his mouth.

"Well, I come across this map back aways. It clearly marks the location of some sort of mine, but I'm not sure what type of mine it is, or exactly which state it's in."

Jeb unfolded the piece of leather and showed it to Andrew.

"See. This here marks the mine and the closest town to it is this Phillipsburg." He shook his head and rubbed his bearded jaw as he studied the other towns, just as he had dozens of times over, hoping one of them would ring a bell. He looked up at Andrew, who was also studying the towns. "So, whatta-ya' think? Any of them sound familiar?"

"Not to me. Up until now, I never traveled anywhere. Most of the towns we studied in school were state capitals and such. Never heard of these towns."

"When I asked the telegraph man about this here Phillipsburg, he said he knew of one in Kansas and one in Montana. "I'm figurin' we'd only need to cross the corner of Colorado to get into Kansas. But we'd need to cross all of Wyoming to reach Montana. Not sure which way to head."

"You probably should have asked about this town called Anaconda. There can't be two of them in the whole country."

"I didn't think of that," said Jeb as he rubbed his chin again. "Figures. I was concentratin' on the town closest to the mine."

"I rode the train through most of the country east of here," said Andrew. "I remember it being pretty flat. This map shows rivers coming down from the mountains."

Montana is full of high peaks, and I'd be willing to bet that this town Anaconda has something to do with a winding river. After all, an anaconda is a snake."

"I ain't never heard or seen any snake called that, mostly rattlers and such around here."

"That's because it's not from this country. Anacondas are supposed to live in the jungle, like in Africa."

"Well if this here mine is in Africa, they can just keep it."

Jeb lit up his pipe, lowered his eyebrows and puffed it in a hasty manner as Andrew smiled and laughed inside, slowly shaking his head back and forth. "The mine's not in Africa, but it could be in this town called Anaconda, perhaps in Montana."

"Okay!" Jeb exclaimed. "We'll confirm your guess, that this here Anaconda is in Montana. But if it is in Montana, we're going to need a few horses, a good mule, camping equipment, and a lot of grub. Heck, we might even be able to build us a homestead."

"I would think that would cost quite a bit of money," said Andrew, shaking his head as he looked over at Jeb. "I've got nothing to throw in. I had a few dollars, but the train I was on was robbed. They took my money and the watch that my pa gave me. I just lost the horse that I broke from green, and all I have left is this shotgun that poor ol' Mr. Saunders bought for me. I'd rather not part with it, if it's all the same to you."

"Now settle down, son. I wouldn't make you part with a gift, especially one that might provide meat for the stew pot. I've recently come into a few dollars and should be able to get us each a horse and some grub for travelin'. We'll worry about the rest when we get further up north. Right now, we better get off this train before they find us out."

Jeb slid open the door and waited for the men further down the train to climb back into the car they were unloading, before giving Andrew the sign to jump off.

The two men walked hastily down the boardwalk, past the engine and onto the town's main street, looking in either direction to see if anyone had caught a glimpse of their quick departure from the car.

After they'd walked a good ways down the street, Andrew remembered something he needed to do. "I've got to post this letter to my folks," said Andrew. "I'm way overdue writing them and they must be worried sick."

"You go on then. I'll be in the saloon getting somethin' to wash down all the car dust I swallowed last night."

"I thought you were going to get us some horses?"

"I am, son, but I'm gonna need more than what I got with me."

"So how are you going to get more?"

"You just leave that part to me, son. Now you best go post that letter and I'll catch up with you a bit later."

Andrew walked on as Jeb pushed through the swinging saloon doors. When he found the post office, he sat down in front on the wooden side walk. Pulling the letter from his pocket, he began to rework his thoughts onto a fresh piece of paper he had folded in his pocket. A lot had happened since he had first written alongside the stream on the ranch, but he thought it best not to include anything about the train robbery or the incident with Mr. Saunders. He simply mentioned wanting to leave the ranch to seek other work, which was not really a lie. He had always asked for help when he needed it in the past, but something inside made him feel that he needed to tackle the problems by himself, and not worry his parents any more than he already had. He ended the letter with:

"The ranch job was good for a while, but I needed to leave. I found new work prospecting in Montana. Heading there with a friend that I met along the way, name of Jeb Slate. Jeb is an interesting fellow to say the least, and looks to be a little older than you, Pa. At times, he has me laughing inside. This could be my chance to earn some real money if the mine works out. Besides, traveling with a friend is safer and more interesting than traveling alone. I'll write again before we're settled.
All my love,
Andrew"

Twenty minutes later, Andrew entered the Laramie Hitch N' Post saloon. It only took him a second or two to locate Jeb at a back table, set up in a poker game with two other men. One of the men looked to be dressed pretty dapper, with a fancy waist coat and bowler hat. The other man looked like he had just climbed out of the saddle. His shirt and hat were sweat-stained, and he wore a single gun rig. Andrew knew very little about the game of poker, but from the amount of coins and the small stack of bills piled in front of Jeb, it looked as though he was doing alright.
He could catch parts of the conversation as he sat down at a table, several feet away.
"I'll see your five and raise you ten," said Jeb to the man with the bowler, as he polished off his beer. The small beads of moisture glistened in his beard, until he dragged his shirt sleeve across his mouth to remove them.
The cowboy threw his hand face down on the table. "I'm out!" he yelled in disgust, as he folded his arms in front of him and watched the hand play out. The man with the bowler looked down at his cards and then back at Jeb, hoping to catch a tell of whether or not Jeb was bluffing.

But there was nothing to gather, as Jeb raised the small tin plate from the table above his head without looking backwards and shouted: "Bar maid, some more of those peanuts please!" The floor around him was already littered with the shells of the previous batch he had devoured. Neatness and courtesy were clearly not among Jeb's strong suits.
"So, what's it gonna be, fancy Dan?"
"The name's Dave," replied the man, before throwing back the remainder of the whiskey in his glass.
"Sorry, Dave. Takes me a while to remember a name. You gonna sweeten the pot or call?"
"I'll call," said Dave. He placed the three red jacks and two black eights in front of him. "Full house!" he exclaimed with part confidence and part frustration at being rushed.
Jeb slowly flipped his hand over onto the table. A single queen looked up from the table, flanked on either side of her, by two pairs of twos.
"Four of a kind," answered Jeb.
He reached into the center of the table and gathered the loose bills, before scraping the coins to the edge so they could fall into his hat.
It was the third hand Jeb had won. And unbeknownst to his playing partners, Jeb usually wasn't that lucky when it came to cards.
That, and the eyes of Andrew affixed on him with all the worry of a mother hen, gave him cause to call it quits, while lady luck was still on his shoulder.
"I thank you gentlemen for the game, but I need to be getting along, as I have business elsewhere," he said motioning to Andrew who breathed a sigh of relief after watching Jeb gather the winnings.
The cowboy rose without saying anything and walked over to the bar to spend his remaining money on beer and women. Dave stared at Jeb, trying to figure how he had enough dumb luck to best him, or was he

truly a card player of equal caliber. "Surely, you must give me a chance to win some of my money back?"

"Sorry Dan, uh, Dave. Like I said, I gotta be movin' along."

All Dave could do was watch Jeb leave with the sixty dollars he'd won from him, plus the thirty he had won from the cowboy.

Chapter X

The large horsefly landed on the hitching post outside the saloon. It walked slowly across the long, sun-baked rail, waiting for its next meal to ride up. After a few minutes, it could see the blurred image of a rider approaching. It waited patiently as the rider came closer and closer, until at last he had arrived. The horse made a snorting sound and then proceeded to dip his mouth below the waterline of the murky water trough. He drank as the rider dismounted and tossed the reins over the rail, wrapping them one additional time.

The rider had a dirty-blond mop of hair and a large scar on his left cheek. The horsefly seized the opportunity while the horse's head was down, and landed on its left ear. It sank its tubular mouth into the horse's ear and drank as the flow of blood released. The horse continued to drink and could only twitch its ear as the horsefly fed. WHAP, went a pair of worn leather gloves across the horse's ear, and the horsefly fell dead into the watering trough.

Luke Nettle stepped onto the boardwalk in front of the Laramie Hitch N' Post and pulled a watch from his leather vest pocket. Studying the front and back of the silver timepiece, he pressed the top spring to release the front of the case. Noting the time, he turned his head to look up and down the boardwalk as if expecting someone. He closed the watch with a click, tucked it back into his vest, and decided to get himself a room until that someone arrived.

The next day, around two o'clock in the hot afternoon sun, a young man entered the saloon and ordered a beer.

He took his hat off and placed it on the bar next to him as he addressed the bartender. "You know of a Luke Nettle, from the Triple Fork?" he asked.

"That I do," answered the bartender. "Who would be asking for him?"

"Pete Lewis," the man replied.

"Nancy, go upstairs and fetch that man in room six. Tell 'm Pete Lewis is here to see him.

A few minutes later, Luke Nettle appeared from his room and slowly made his way down the stairs. The young man had gotten himself a table and was working his way through a second beer.

"Jake Saunders hired me. Said I was to meet you here," he said as he pushed out the chair opposite him with his boot.

Luke sat down at the table and pulled out a small leather sack from his vest pocket. He threw it just in front of the young man. The pouch jingled as it hit the table. "Jake said I was to give you that. The remainder would be paid when you help find his father's killer so justice can be served."

"Well, I'm a damn good tracker and fair with a rifle and six-shooter both. I've done some work as bounty hunter for the railroad as well."

"That's good," said Luke as he asked for a bottle of whiskey from the bar. "He had to make it to this town 'cause the train had no other stops before this one, and I've got a feelin' he jumped off here.

"What makes you think that?"

"Because I arrived just after the cars were unloaded and searched every one. He must have already gotten off. My guess is that he's either gonna catch the next freight outta here tomorrow or look to buy a horse, and I doubt he has the money to buy a horse and saddle."

"If he needed money, he just might wire or send word home."

Minutes later, Luke and Pete approached the telegraph station. The man behind the window was sorting letters at his desk, the top of which was partially illuminated by the strong sun that beat through the open window of the station. Finishing what was left of his sandwich, he washed down the last bite with the remains of his cherry soda pop and donned his leather visor.

"Excuse me," said Luke. "I was hoping you could help me locate a friend of mine. His name is Andrew Thompson. He's about twenty-two years of age, with reddish-brown hair. Stands about six-foot or so. We were wondering if he stopped by within the last few days to post a letter or perhaps send a telegraph."

"Now let me think a minute, here. I get quite a few people in here every day wanting to post letters. Young man standing over six feet, you say. Well, I couldn't speak for the hair color or the name, but I did have a young man fitting that description who stopped by last week to post a letter."
"Could you tell us where he posted it to?"
"Well, I don't recall exactly where, but I think it was back east. Maybe Massachusetts or New York. That's all I can tell you. I hope you find him."

The two men next walked to the livery. The ringing of the anvil could be heard up and down the street as Luke and Pete approached the blacksmith shop.
"Good afternoon, sir. We're looking for a young man standing about six-foot, answers to Andrew Thompson. It's real important we find him." Luke tipped his hat to the man, trying to remember the manners

he only pulled out of his memory when he needed something from someone.

"Why you askin?"

"We're from the family farm back east. His ma's real sick and we were sent by his pa to fetch him home. We tried sending a wire to a ranch he was working at, but the lad just keeps movin' around."

"Well, I did have two men come in about a week ago. The younger one fits your description. The old man looked about sixty or so; looked like he'd been livin' out of a saddlebag for most of his life. They purchased two horses and a mule from John Rollings, who lives just outside of town. They brought the bay and buckskin here, and asked that the horses be reshod 'cause they'd be travelin' a long ways up north. I believe they took the mule over to Grover's to fill their supplies.

"How'd you know they just bought them horses?"

"I recognized the brand on them, and knew they were from John's ranch. That's how. When I see strangers from out of town asking to have new horses shod, I always inquire about papers of sale. Sheriff Bloom hung a man just last year for horse thievery. Hell, you never..."

"They headed north you say?" Pete interrupted. "Are you sure you meant north? Maybe they were heading back east?"

The blacksmith scratched his beard as he thought, spit into the hot coals and confirmed his memory.

"Nope, they definitely said they were headed up north."

"Thanks for the information." Pete flipped the smithy a silver coin, which the man caught in his large coal-stained hand, then nodded in return as he tucked away the coin into his shirt pocket.

Luke walked around the corner and stopped to fix a cigarette. He rolled one of his own as he thought about what the blacksmith had told them as he lit up. "You buyin' what that smithy said about them headin' up north?"

"I don't see why he'd lie," said Pete. "Besides, it should be real easy to pick up their trail once we're outside of town and the tracks thin out. What I'm more concerned about is now he's got a friend. It's gonna make it a might harder to bring that boy in."

"If the old man gets in the way of justice, that's his problem. We have the right to use whatever we need to get the job done."

Luke took one last drag off his cigarette and flicked it into the middle of the street. "Let's find this Grover's. We best fill our own saddlebags if we're gonna hit the trail."

Eighty miles to the northwest, Jeb and Andrew had stopped for the evening. They had decided to set up camp at the edge of a stand of pines, which overlooked the hills and plains below. They were only a few miles from Iron Mountain, a small town where they could restock their supplies. For the past six days they had been riding north, following a trail that wound through the mountain pass. The trail looked like it was used just enough to keep it slightly worn. In places it would seem to disappear. When it did, Jeb and Andrew would simply make their best guess, until they could pick it back up further north. So far, that plan had worked fairly well.

Jeb Slate stirred the beans in the cook pot, adding in the cut up pieces of salt pork.

"Is that dinner just about ready?" asked Andrew, who had just finished stretching the canvas tarp above their sleeping area.

"You can't rush perfection, son," answered Jeb, who couldn't keep himself from tasting the beans every few minutes. "I make the best damn beans this side of the Rockies," he exclaimed, as he poured a generous splash of whiskey into the pot, before tasting them again.

"That's probably because no one east of the Rockies will eat 'em," Andrew answered.

"Ha!" was all Jeb could think of to shoot back. Another spoonful went in his mouth. "We should make the town by midday tomorrow. I sure hope the prices on them possibles won't be too high."

"How much money do we have left?" Andrew asked, trying not to put too much emphasis on the word "we".

"Oh, about four dollars, give or take a bit. We'll be fine, as long as we only buy what we can't do without. We can shoot some grouse and maybe even get lucky and bag us an elk."

It had been a while since Jeb bagged anything larger than a coon with his muzzleloader, and he wondered if he still had the skill to shoot an animal at the distance needed to take an elk. Surely he would need to make a hundred-yard shot, maybe more.

"You do any long-range shootin', Andy?"

"No, not much. Unless you call seventy yards long-range. Most of the hunting we did back east was in thick woods. We usually took deer at twenty to thirty yards. I wouldn't mind giving it a try, though."

"Well, I might be lettin' you try just that, with ol' blue here. That is, if we see any of them elk." Jeb tasted the beans one last time and took the lid off of the small dutch oven. "Mmmm. Corn bread looks ready, too. Let's eat!"

After dinner, Jeb and Andrew laid back on their wool blankets that were set next to the fire and looked up at the sky.

Andrew had never seen so many stars before. The bright canvas before him filled his entire field of view. There were sections so bright and so full, it was as if a luminescent river was flowing across the dark sky. He closed his eyes and pulled the wool blanket up about his shoulders as he shifted his body closer to the fire.

Jeb's voice broke the silence of the night. "You figure we made the right decision to come out this way?"

"Sure. I suppose the worst thing that could happen is if there is no such mine to be found. Or even if there is and there's nothing to mine, we can always look for work wherever we are. You still interested in becoming a trapper?"

"Yeah, that was the plan until I found this map. Now I've got my heart set on finding this place. Having money would be nice, but I'm tryin' not to get myself worked up too much over somethin' that ain't a sure thing... but it sure is nice to dream about it. Goodnight, Andy."

"Goodnight, Jeb."

Andrew closed his eyes again as his thoughts turned to poor old Mr. Saunders. As much as he wanted to enjoy the thought of finding the mine on the map and the possibility of finding whatever riches might be in there, part of him felt uncomfortable with the way he fled the posse, even though he didn't do anything wrong. He lay awake looking up at the stars, and wondering how he might ever clear his name.

It was both Jeb's snoring and being downwind from the random loud toots bugling from Jeb's britches that woke Andrew just as the sun was coming up.

Andrew reached over and placed several sticks of wood on the fire to battle the morning's chill. Jeb, still asleep, turned from his left side to his right, pulling the blanket about his shoulders and his knees up toward his stomach, so his feet wouldn't stick out from the end of the blanket.

"Come on, Jeb, we've got miles to go today."

The rekindled fire felt good to Jeb, who muttered something in a low, hoarse tone, which couldn't be comprehended.

Andrew remembered the time his pa, James, tried to wake him for school while he pretended to be asleep. James' solution was to whisk the blankets off the bed in one quick motion, startling Andrew and leaving him exposed to the cold room.

Trying the same tactic with Jeb crossed his mind, but he decided it was wiser to place a cup of coffee within a short distance of Jeb's head and let the aroma do the work.

"What time is it, Andy?" asked Jeb as he yawned, scratching his beard.

"Couldn't tell you. My watch was stolen, remember? But judging by the sun, I'd guess seven."

"Mmmm. Thanks for the coffee."

"You're welcome. About time we got packed up and moving, don't you think?"

"What about breakfast?"

"Breakfast is coffee and the corn cakes you cooked up yesterday."

A few seconds later, two corn cakes landed on the blanket, which lay across Jeb's lap.

It was late afternoon when Jeb and Andy started down from the pass trail and reached the open plains below. The prairie grasses moved in unison as the wind blew from the west.

"How long you think until we get there, Jeb?" asked Andrew. "I've got a terrible growling in my stomach, and we're all out of corn cakes."

"Judging by that map, we should be in Iron Mountain just before dark," said Jeb. "But we might get wet before we get there." Jeb looked up at the dark clouds rolling in across the sky. Faint rumbles of what was to come could be heard off in the distance. Andrew turned his gaze from the sky and looked across the prairie grass, thinking he saw something move. He reined his horse to a slow walk and looked carefully at the ground around him. He could make out the tracks of a small animal. "Maybe a rabbit or ground squirrel," he thought to himself.

As he climbed down from the saddle, he scared a jack rabbit from its hiding place. It jumped quickly out to the side of him and then dashed off into thicker brush. "I'm going to get us some dinner," said Andrew, as Jeb finally turned to look back at him, from several yards out in front.

"If you can catch that rabbit, Andy, I'll clean and cook it!" shouted Jeb. Andrew climbed down from his horse and removed his Winchester from its scabbard. He fed a few shells from his pocket into the shotgun and stooped over slightly as he stealthily made his way through the brush. He picked up the rabbit's tracks in the loose sand and scanned the area, ready for another outburst.

"Probably went down his hole!" shouted Jeb.

"Quiet," Andrew shot back.

Jeb laughed, as if the rabbit cared how much noise they made. Just then, the rabbit jumped out from a sage bush to Andrew's right. It hopped erratically back and forth as Andrew took aim and fired. The rabbit tumbled head over heels and came to rest in the sand. The mule brayed at the report from the loud gun.

"Nice shot, Andy!" Jeb shouted, as Andrew picked up the jack rabbit by the ears and carried it over to him.

"Here ya' go, partner, he's all yours."

As Andrew handed the rabbit to Jeb, he heard something else off to the side of them. Thinking it was another rabbit, he readied himself for another shot. He moved to the rear of Jeb and stood behind the mule, looking to catch a glimpse of what lay in the sage brush. He stamped his foot hard, hoping to flush any rabbit or bird that might be in the brush, but nothing moved. "Just my imagination," he said as he racked the extra shells from his shotgun. Just then a crack of lightning sounded and the sky lit up. Startled by the sudden display of light and noise, the mule kicked out in defense, catching Andrew in the side just above his belt. Andrew dropped the shotgun as his body shot forward and fell to the ground. He lay there holding his side with a terrible grimace on his face, as Jeb tried to get the skittish mule under control.

"Damn mule," Jeb grumbled. "Andy, are you okay?"

Andrew could not speak. He hurt so bad he thought he might be sick. He tried to get up, but felt a terrible sharp pain and thought it better to stay still for the time being.

Jeb jumped off his horse and knelt at Andy's side. "Let me take a look boy," Jeb insisted. Andrew moved his arm away from the side of his ribs, and Jeb could see an angry red mark and partial slice in Andrew's skin made from the shoe of the mule. When Jeb gently felt the area, Andrew cried out from the pain.

"Looks like you got somethin' busted inside, Andy. We need to get you to a doctor." The rain started to fall and Jeb covered Andy with his coat, being afraid to hurry him onto his horse. He looked around for any trees or long branches to make a travois, but the scrub bushes and prairie grass were of no help. "I know you don't feel like travelin' right now, Andy, but we best get movin'."

Andrew groaned as he sat upright, and Jeb gathered his hat from where he had fallen and placed it on his head. "You let me know when you're ready, and I'll help you into that stirrup."

Andrew just nodded his head affirmatively, and Jeb helped him stand. On the second try, Andrew got his foot in the stirrup and with another groan, swung the other leg over the saddle. Jeb tied the reins of Andrew's horse to a rope, and then to his own horse. The mule was led last. Andrew slumped in the saddle and said nothing as the rain came down harder. Two miles down the trail, Jeb saw what looked to be a small house up in the hills. "Any port in a storm, Andy. That's what they say, ain't it? Let's make us an entrance."

Chapter XI

The whistle from the tea pot gave off its high pitched call, then faded away as Helen Downing lifted the kettle from the stove to pour herself a cup of afternoon tea. She took the warm cup in her wrinkled hands and walked outside to her bench, which overlooked thousands of acres of prairie land.

Her husband, Ben, had the foresight to purchase the forty-acre property back in 1842. This home and the land it sat on was to be their great adventure together. She remembered how he carried her over the threshold of the cabin on their wedding day. It seemed just like yesterday that they sat on this bench together overlooking the lake. She remembered how they used to walk down to the river together and how he teased her over not wanting to swim in the cold mountain water. She smiled, remembering when she finally gave in, she jumped in with one great effort and the splash fight that soon followed.

But that was over sixty years ago, and Ben had long since passed away.
He was only thirty-two when he died in a mining accident.
They had never had the children that they had so desperately wanted, and Helen never remarried.

When the Indian Wars came, she often volunteered in town to assist when wounded came through on their way back to Fort Laramie. Now she got by with the chickens, pigs and the one cow, who seemed to be giving less milk these days. She sold fresh eggs in town and slaughtered a pig every now and again, which she would process and hang in the smokehouse to preserve. During the summer, she would fish along the river for trout.

She had also become quite the gardener over the years, with her green thumb winning a few ribbons at the local fair every fall.

As she sipped her tea, she listened to the squirrels chasing each other through the fall leaves. The light from the river in the distance sparkled, and the fir trees blew in the breeze ever so slightly, silhouetted against the bright body of water. Helen had seen so much here, but the feeling of loneliness never left her. Her later years blended together, season after season of solitude and reflection. She felt no more comfort now at eighty-four, then she did when she was seventy-five, or fifty-two.

Even with arthritis in her hands and feet, she was in fairly good shape for a woman so late in her years. The hard work that her property required had made her strong and fit. But she felt as if the strength of her body was now outliving her will. All her family and friends had also passed on, and she was the last figure remaining in all of the old photographs in her picture box.

With the call of a hawk far off in the distance waking her from her daydream, she decide it was time to go for a walk. She had wanted to climb that peak off to the west. The one that caught her gaze every morning. She dressed in her polka-dot Sunday dress with two front pockets, one in which always had one of Ben's folded white handkerchiefs. She put on her black lace up shoes and her knitted shawl, which she wrapped around her snowy white head, more out of habit now than necessity, and headed out the door.

She took no food or water with her, only her walking stick, which she had carved from an aspen sapling years ago. Slightly stooped over, she walked down to the river and turned north to climb up the mountain trail.

The sky started to change as she walked. The light breeze which had moved the pine trees, had now picked up and the gray clouds started to roll in upon the lake. She hastened her pace as she climbed the path, ever becoming steeper as it cut back from one side to the other, navigating around trees and boulders like a snake.

Two hours into her walk and halfway up the mountainside, she felt a small drop of rain hit her nose. Then another.

Within seconds, the sky had opened and down fell the sheets of rain soaking her clothing as she pulled her shawl further over her head. The path turned slick with running rain water, and she slipped a few times, catching herself against her walking stick to regain her balance. Suddenly, thunder sounded and she could see the bright flashes of lightning in the distance, which looked to be coming her way.

She pushed on against the rain and wind until she was only a hundred or so yards from the top. The vegetation was smaller this high up. With her legs growing tired and her body starting to shiver, Helen sat down under the largest pine tree she could find, which stood only twenty feet tall.

Her heart grew weary as she watched the thunder and lightning move in. She wondered if it would be painful if she was struck, if it would all be over quickly that way. But the thunder and lightning passed overhead and continued to move off into the distance.

Helen closed her eyes and tried to fall asleep, knowing that with the bitter cold night would come her release from this lonely world. But her constant shivering from her soaked clothing and the strong winds made it difficult to do so. Thirty minutes later the rain stopped, and she again tried to fall asleep with the day's light starting to fade.

It was then that she heard a noise from down the trail. It was the calling of a voice and for a moment she thought it might be her husband or her heavenly father calling her home. But as she tuned her ears as best she could to its direction, she could see two riders on the trail below, riding toward her house. The first rider seemed to be calling out and waving his arm over his head, to draw the attention of anyone who might be inside the home. The second rider was clearly draped forward over the neck of his horse, which was being led by the first rider.

She felt the will to live seep back into her as she watched from a distance, feeling quite helpless. She wanted to tell them why she couldn't come to the front door, and had wanted to yell back, but her voice was weak due to her being exhausted. Gripping her staff with both hands, she slowly lifted her stiff frame from the ground and started to make her way back down the mountain trail.

It was over an hour later that Helen opened the cabin door to find one of the two men inside. He was trying to get the stove lit to make some coffee, when he turned around, surprised at her sudden appearance.

"Is this your house?" asked the man.

"Yes, it is," she quietly replied.

"I'm terribly sorry to walk in on your place, but I shouted out loud for help. My name is Jeb, and my partner Andy was kicked by a mule, and he's hurtin' somethin' fierce. I placed him in your bedroom to lie down and covered him with one of your blankets ma'am." Helen just nodded and walked into her bedroom to find the man, clearly only in his twenties, lying with his eyes closed and moaning softly. She placed her hand on his head and whispered, "My God, boy, you are burnin' up." Opening her small closet, she stripped from her soaked garments, and wrapped her robe around herself before assisting Jeb with lighting the kitchen stove.

"That boy's got a bad fever," she said to Jeb. "It's too dark for me to ride now, but come first light, I'm going into Iron Mountain and fetch the doctor." Helen looked up at Jeb, who was soaked to the bone.

"You best go into my bedroom and get some of my husband's old clothes. He's been gone now more than fifty years, but I couldn't seem to part with his things. You look about his size."

When Jeb came back out from the bedroom, he looked as dapper as he had in years. The checkered flannel shirt and gray wool slacks did, in fact, fit him well. "I hope you don't mind that I borrowed one of your husband's belts. I haven't worn one in years. Grown too accustomed to suspenders, I guess."

"You look just fine," said Helen. "And you can keep the clothes. I've really had no use for them until now. I have some chicken soup in the ice box. Warm some on the stove if it suits you. The pans are in that cupboard and there's a loaf of bread I baked yesterday, too. Goes good with soup."

"Don't mind if I do, ma'am. We haven't eaten for most of the day."

Helen took Jeb's soaked clothes and laid them over a chair close to the stove before going back to check on Andrew. She went to her dresser and took one of her late husband's handkerchiefs from the top drawer and held it to her face for a moment before soaking it in the cool water of the wash basin on her dresser. She neatly folded it and brought it to Andrew, placing it on his forehead.

He opened his eyes just enough to get a glimpse of her old, but gentle, smiling face standing over him. He didn't know where he was, but even through his pain, he felt comforted. Upon lifting Andrew's shirt, she could see a large black bruise on his side where he had been kicked. She couldn't tell the extent of his injuries but dared not move him, although he was badly in need of a bath. Instead, she used a wash cloth to gently clean his chest and arms. Exhausted, Andrew closed his eyes and slept. Caring for the young man brought back memories of cooking and caring for her husband when she was younger. She wasn't much older than Andrew when they were wed. She moved her rocker close to the bed and turned down the lamp, so it only kept a slight flame. She folded her quilt and placed it across her legs, as she sat by his side, gently rocking. As Andrew slept he dreamed of a thick forest, full of conifers. As he was drawn toward one of the pines, he could see there was a small bird on one of the lower branches. It sang to him as he walked closer. When he put out his hand, the bird landed on it and continued to sing. Then the bird flew away into the pines. Andrew followed it through the pine needle laden floor of the forest. Then he lost sight of where it had flown. Looking around, he saw a man in the distance. He was carving something into one of the trees with a pocket knife. As Andrew walked closer, he could see the man was his father. He had carved a large crescent moon into the bark. The man turned and smiled at Andrew, and placed a hand on Andrew's head. It felt comforting. "Dad, stay with me," he pleaded. His father smiled and then walked away into the pines.

Andrew woke to Helen standing over him. She changed out the cool cloth on his forehead, trying to keep him as comfortable as possible as his body fought the fever.

Throughout the night Helen stayed close, keeping the cloth on his forehead cool, and holding Andrew's hand when he woke shivering. When morning came, Helen asked Jeb to hitch up her small wagon, so she could ride for Doc Shepherd in the town of Iron Mountain.

She instructed Jeb to try and get Andrew to eat a little chicken broth while she was gone. Without delay, she would be back by mid-afternoon. She snapped the leather reins against the mare's back, and the small wagon sped off down the trail, leaving small wisps of dust in its wake. The sun shone on her face, and the feeling of loneliness and despair seemed to have left her. She smiled to herself, as she rode toward town. It felt good to once again have a purpose.

When Helen reached the doctor's office in town, she found a note on the door that read "Gone to lunch". Not wanting to waste time, she decided to walk across the street to the only place in town to get lunch, the town saloon. Dr. Shepherd was a good man and a fine physician, but he often enjoyed a good beer with his lunch. Helen was known in town as a strong-willed woman, who was not to be trifled with when she meant business. Doc Shepherd pretended not to see her as she walked into the saloon, a place most woman dared not set foot in. Finding him, mid bite into his steak, she pulled out the chair opposite him and sat down.

"I've got two men at my place Ben, and the younger one has been kicked bad by a mule. I need you to come out to my place right away."

"I'll see if I can get out that way later this afternoon," said Doc Shepherd, as he lifted his mug to his mustache-covered mouth.

"Ben, I need you out there now." Helen's hand clasped the glass mug and removed it from his hand, placing it back down on the table. "He's got a bad fever and maybe broken ribs. I can only do so much for him."
"Oh, alright. I'm coming. Just let me grab my bag from my office and I'll follow you back home."
As Doc Shepherd hastily shoveled a last forkful of steak into his mouth, he grabbed his hat and followed Helen out the door. Neither of them noticed the two men at the bar who had overheard their conversation.

When Dr. Shepherd examined Andrew's ribs, he discovered that two of his back ribs were broken. The mule's shoe had broken the skin and infection had taken hold. He asked Helen to bring the lantern close as he drained the cut and applied hot towels over a series of a few hours to help draw out the infection. Andrew woke a few times during the procedure, but was delirious with fever for the most part.
"I'll need to wrap this, Helen, and you'll need to make sure he stays off his feet for five days, and no riding for at least two weeks. I'll head back this way in a few days to see if that cut is better."
"He's welcome to stay as long as he needs," Helen said warmly, as she wiped Andrew's brow with a cloth.

It wasn't until noon the following day when Andrew woke, feeling a little hungry. Helen brought a bowl of soup into the bedroom.
"I feel sore all down my left side," said Andrew. "I remember someone standing over me. A man with a worn, waxed coat. I remember smelling pine needles."
"You were very feverish last night. That was probably me or Jeb standing over you, son," said Helen.

"Thank you, ma'am. I'm grateful for you staying by my side."
"No, Andy. It is I who thank you," she said, as she smiled. "I haven't felt this needed in years. Now how about some of this rabbit stew? Your friend Jeb said you took it the other day down on the flat."
"Yes; thank you, ma'am. I sure am hungry. Is Jeb nearby?"
"You can call me Helen, Andrew. Your friend is out back chopping wood for the stove. He must have checked in on you half a dozen times last night. You had a serious fever, son."
Andrew winced as he tried to sit up to take the stew from Helen's spoon. "Take it easy, I'll bring the stew to you," said Helen. "That's them ribs talking. Dr. Shepherd said that mule broke two of your ribs when she kicked you. Broke right through your skin, too. You'll need time to mend. That means no riding horses for a couple of weeks. Dr. Shepherd will be back tomorrow to check on you."
Helen smiled as she fed Andrew the stew. She felt a warm, comforting feeling, the kind that comes only from being a woman. She wondered if she should have remarried and had children when she was younger. Why had she felt so dedicated to Ben, living by herself all those years? When Andrew finished the stew, she helped him to the outhouse and then walked him back to bed. From her dress pocket she pulled out a small leather-bound book, not much bigger than a deck of cards. She handed the book to Andrew. He opened it up, and at first was surprised that every page was blank. Then he saw the small yellow pencil that was tucked into the spine. "This is so you can write down your thoughts and keep track of your travels."
"Thank you, Helen, that is very generous of you."
"Well, a man should keep track of his thoughts. It's often the things that are simple, like this, that we look back on and wish we had done when

we were younger. I'm just givin' you a head start so you have something to tell your grandchildren about some day," she said with a smile. Then she pulled up the covers around his chest and drew the shade on the window, which covered the room in a half-darkness. "I'll wake you in time for dinner," she said as she softly closed the bedroom door behind her.

Over the next few days, Andrew's cut had nearly healed. He no longer needed assistance to use the outhouse, and took his meals at the kitchen table with Jeb and Helen. But most of the days he rested, as Helen was quick to scold him if he didn't. It was difficult to be indoors when the sun shone so brightly outdoors, reminding him when he was younger and sick in bed. Writing in his journal kept his mind busy, but he could never seem to bring himself to write about Mr. Saunders' accident. One afternoon, he watched Helen through the window as she prepared dinner. He peeked through the drawn shade, observing as she rounded one of the chickens from the fenced-in run. She gently stroked its neck with her wrinkled hands as she spoke to it, softly. He could hear her muffled voice through the glass. Not enough to make out the words, but enough to know she was calming the bird down, perhaps feeling troubled herself for what must be done. What she had probably done hundreds of times over the years. She took up the hatchet from the weathered pine stump, and with one swift blow, the chicken's head came off.

The bird flapped a little under her tucked arm, spilling a few drops of blood on her apron, and then stopped. Somehow, the blood from the dying bird brought back memories of Mr. Saunders. Perhaps it was the helplessness of the victim, or his own guilt for not being able to help the old man when he needed him most. He slowly released the shade and climbed back into bed, staring at the cobwebs that attached themselves where the wooden beam met the ceiling, thinking of how he would ever be able to make amends.

In the days that followed, Helen and Andrew would sit and talk together at the kitchen table. Usually around ten in the morning, she'd put the tea pot on the stove. A few minutes after the whistle of the pot stopped, the conversation would start. Helen talked mostly about her life out in the west and asked about his back east. She stressed to Andrew the importance of a good marriage and the blessing of children, wishing she herself had given birth to several... or at least one. Andrew told her about how his biological father died when he was very young, and how he gained a new father when his mom married James Riley. He complimented Helen on her strong work ethic and gentle manner, and told her how it reminded him of his mother back home. She laughed as he told her about Jeb and how they met in a box car, and how he snored so loud he felt assured no coyotes or bears would stray too close to where they camped. But he never mentioned anything about the awful incident back in Colorado. He just summed up his whole time at the ranch with a few sentences, and then changed the subject to something else.

On the tenth day of staying with Helen, just before their usual cup of morning tea, two men approached the house on horseback. Jeb, who was helping around the house by chopping his usual stack of wood for the stove, stopped and sunk the axe into the stump. He gathered a handful of kindling and walked inside, closing the door behind him. He placed the kindling down beside the stove and looked at Helen, thinking of how he wanted to phrase his next words. "You get much company out this way, Helen?"

"No. Just Dr. Shepherd, and he's not due back until Sunday."

Jeb stood next to the window, only exposing his right eye and part of his cheek as he peered out at the path which led up to the house. The two young men stopped and got down from their horses. One pulled the rifle from his scabbard and the other, who carried a Colt rig, walked behind him, off to the side. Helen could tell Jeb was a little nervous. She peeked out the window and saw the two men walking up the path. Telling Jeb and Andrew, who was seated at the kitchen table, to stay inside, she walked out the door and closed it behind her.

"Good day, gentlemen. How can I help you this fine day?" she asked as she dried her hands on her apron, as if she'd been baking.

"My name is Luke Nettle and this here is Pete Lewis. We've heard you might have a young man by the name of Andrew Thompson stayin' with you. He's wanted for the murder of a ranch owner back in Colorado."

Andrew peeked from behind the curtains at the two men. One of them had a long scar on his left cheek. Andrew knew he had seen that scar before and searched his mind for the man. Images of each new person he had met over the past several months came into his mind's eye, but he knew it was none of them. Then it must have been someone he didn't know well but saw in passing. As the man took a step closer, he could see a silver chain catch the light from the sun as it sparkled. At the end of the chain was a deer head fob. Suddenly Andrew gasped, and Jeb looked over at him. "What is it?" he asked.

"That man... the one with the watch chain. He's one of the men that robbed the train I was on, back in Colorado. I'm sure that's my watch in his pocket."

"Have you ever met him before?"

"Well, I think he was at the ranch the time Jake rode in and they argued with Mr. Saunders. But I never got a good look at his face then."

"Then chances are he never got a good look at yours either."

"I can't be sure Jeb. He saw me plain as day when he robbed the train. But he probably didn't know who I was."

Outside, Helen continued to question the two men. "You'll excuse me, but I find it very hard to believe the boy would hurt anyone," she shot back. Helen's tone quickly changed from inviting to challenging. "Of course you have paper on this young man?" she asked.

"We've been hired by the deceased ranch owner's son, ma'am. We've come a long ways and we don't need any papers."

"I beg to differ," said Helen, her tone now quite sharp. "You boys head on into Iron Mountain and bring back the sheriff, and then we'll talk about what needs to be done."

"I think we'll just have a look inside for ourselves," said Luke.

As he reached forward as if to brush the old woman aside, a shotgun barrel protruded from the slightly open kitchen window, and the slide could be heard racking a shell into the ten gauge chamber.

A raspy voice came from inside. "I'd head back toward those horses of yours, unless you want to be feed for the pigs!"

Luke withdrew his arm and slowly took a step backwards.

The expression on his face changed from one of confidence, to sudden shock, being only a few feet away from the business end of the shotgun.

"You can't stay in there forever!" Luke yelled out as the two men walked back to their horses.

As they rode away, Helen kept watch at the window for several minutes, making sure she could follow their dust trail as a sign they didn't turn back. She poured the tea into three cups and sat at the kitchen table. "I think you owe me an explanation, Andrew," she said in a stern but slightly disappointed voice. Andrew went on to tell Helen about the train robbery and how he was sure that was the man who stole the watch given to him by his father. He told her about the ranch he worked at and how he remembered Mr. Saunders telling him that Luke was a friend of his son, Jake. He went into detail about the night of the killing and swore he had nothing to do with it, but was at odds with clearing himself of the situation. "I had no idea they would follow me this far west. I just thought I'd wait a while and then ride back to speak to a lawman about the whole thing."

"When?" Helen asked.

"I don't know. I was heading into town to find a lawman, when a group of men started shooting at me. I was scared."

"Usually the law doesn't shoot at someone, unless they are shot at first, Andrew."

"I know that. That's why I ran. I had the feeling that I couldn't trust anyone back there, like they were out to get me, without even letting me have a chance to speak. I just need to give it more thought."

"What you need to do, Andrew, is clear your name."

Andrew sipped his tea, knowing full well, Helen was right.

Chapter XII

Pete Lewis sipped his coffee as he started to have second thoughts on working with Luke to bring in Andrew Thompson.

"Let's ride into Iron Mountain and wire for those papers, Luke. That old woman can't hold them once we get those papers."

"We can't do that," said Luke.

"Why not?" Pete asked and emphatically tossed the remainder of his coffee onto the ground.

"Because we're working for Jake Saunders, not the federal marshall, that's why! This is ranch business, Pete. Jake wants Andrew Thompson brought in for the murder of his father, dead or alive. We'll head back toward town, but keep an eye on the main roads and railroad. Sooner or later he's going to try and leave the area, and that's when we'll get him. We'll put him on a train back east and be done with this."

"What if he resists?"

"If he does, we'll just say he drew on us first. We won't need any papers to claim self defense."

Back at Helen Downing's place, Jeb was finishing up some chores. During the past couple weeks, Helen had cooked for Jeb and Andrew, and had given them a good roof over their heads. In return, Jeb felt obliged to chop and stack several cords of wood Helen had near the house, and felt confident it would see her through most of the year. When he saw the fencing that held the pigs needed repair, he asked Helen where she kept any spare fence wire and set out to make the repair. Two of the three pigs she kept came over to watch Jeb work. Rigging the wire to a green branch he had cut, he twisted his newly made tool in a circle. The tighter he twisted, the more taut the wire became. The pigs tried to push their noses through the small openings in the wire as he worked, snorting at him and distracting him from his chore. "Hey, you pigs," Jeb called out. "Don't you have better things to do than gawk at a fella?"

Jeb made the final twists of the wire that held the branch in place, and looked happy with his work. "That oughta' hold you boys for quite a while." As he stood up from his seated position, he heard the sounds of ripping fabric. He looked over at his arm as his elbow protruded slightly from a brand new hole in his shirt. "Dog-gone you pigs!" he yelled, knowing it wasn't the pigs' fault for his own clumsiness. Helen heard his frustration and walked over to Jeb.

"Looks like you might be in need of a repair, Jeb?"

"Yes ma'am, I guess those pigs had me a little distracted from my work."

"Well, since you repaired my fence, how about I take a needle and thread to your shirt?"

"Thank you, ma'am, that would be very nice, especially with it being a gift from you." Jeb untucked the shirt from his pants, unbuttoned it and handed it to Helen. Helen laughed inside at how immodest Jeb was, as he stood there with his belly hanging slightly over his belt. "I'll be back soon," said Helen. "Won't take me but a few minutes."

Helen carried the shirt into her bedroom, and laid it on her bed as she brought over her sewing kit, which she kept on her dresser.

As she sat on the bed and worked the sleeve inside-out to stitch it, a thin, folded piece of leather fell from the front pocket of the shirt and onto the floor. She picked up the scrap and thought nothing more of it than a handkerchief of sorts. She place the scrap on top of her dresser and set about mending the shirt. When she was finished sewing, she walked over to the dresser and was about to place the leather scrap

back in the front pocket, when she paused and smiled to herself in the mirror. Opening a small top drawer of the dresser, she pulled one of Ben's folded white handkerchiefs from it, and tucked it neatly into the front pocket of the shirt. She then presented Jeb with the newly repaired shirt. "You boys can wash up if you'd like, I'll be serving dinner soon. Roast chicken with mashed potatoes."
"Sounds wonderful, ma'am. And I'm much obliged for fixing that sleeve."
"You can call me Helen, Jeb. Makes me feel younger." She giggled and gently touched Jeb on the shoulder in a motherly manner.
"Well, you've certainly made Andrew and me feel like family, Helen. We thank you for that, too."

That evening Dr. Shepherd came back to check on Andrew and confirmed him fit enough to travel. Helen asked the doctor if he'd spotted any men along the trail to town who might have seen him head over, but the doctor had seen no one.
Helen invited him to stay for the chicken dinner and stay in the spare bunk, as payment for services rendered.

After the sun had set, the four of them sat around the table enjoying one last cup of tea and a few cookies Helen had baked. Jeb and Andrew figured to be heading out at first light.
"I packed you boys some biscuits for the road and a few of Ben's shirts in case you need a change of clothes along the way."
"We owe you a lot, Helen," said Jeb. "We won't forget you neither."
"It will be quite a change without you two around, but I hope you find what you're looking for in Montana, and please be careful you don't run

into those two men. I have a feeling they weren't planning to come back with the sheriff, so you know they're up to no good."

"Hmmm...," Jeb mumbled. "They're sure to be waiting for us in town or along the trail west."

"They most certainly will. You two be careful," replied Helen, and with that, she went to turn in for the evening.

The next morning, the rooster in Helen's coop fluffed his wing feathers and crowed just as the sun peeked above the horizon. Both Andrew and Jeb said their good byes and headed out the door.

It was only an hour past sunrise when Luke Nettle sat up on his bedroll and checked his pocket watch. The two men had camped out on the trail for the past week, only heading to town when they needed supplies. As he held up the watch in his right hand and glanced at the time, he could see a wisp of trail dust out in the distance, the kind made by running horses. He nudged Pete with the side of his boot to wake him. Pete rolled over quickly, with the palm of his hand on his Single Action Army. He glared at Luke, but didn't say anything after he realized where he was and who woke him.

"They're making a run for the trail," said Luke. "We need to break camp now!"

Pete had his bedroll on his horse and tied down in just over a minute. Luke double-checked the rounds in his revolver and the two rode down the steep slope, their horses kicking up loose rocks along the dry ground. Like a predator chasing down game, the men rode on an intercepting course, but were a good fifty yards behind when they hit the main trail. They kicked the sides of their mounts to gain speed as they rode, slowly gaining a few yards at a time. The trail rose and fell over small hills as the chase went on for several minutes.

When they got within thirty yards of the riders, Luke suddenly pulled his revolver from his holster and fired a shot at one of the riders.

"What the hell are you doing?!" shouted Pete above the sound of the hooves galloping on the compacted dirt trail.

One of the riders slumped slightly in the saddle, and the two then slowed down to a trot, still keeping their backs to their pursuers.

Pete and Luke quickly caught up to them and circled the riders.

The face of an old man looked up from under his hat, his hand firmly pressed against his right arm. "I hope you have a good reason for shooting me," he said in a strict tone. "It's a damn good thing it's only my arm you hit."

Luke's face turned from an expression of confidence, to one of shock. "You... you're... you're not him," he stuttered.

"Were you looking for someone else?" spoke the other rider, removing her hat and uncovering a head of white hair, which fell down around her shoulders, once released from under the hat.

"Why the hell were you riding so fast, old woman?" Luke Nettle accused.

"I think you better worry about yourself, young man. You and your friend here are going to have plenty of explaining to do. The town sheriff is going to want to know why you fired at two helpless riders without any warning. The sheriff doesn't take kindly to bounty hunters."

Helen's words had the desired effect she was after, as Luke nodded his head toward the trail and the two men rode off with great speed.

"I can still ride, eh Doc," she said, patting her horse on its neck.

"Come on, Helen," said Dr. Shepherd. "We'll ride back to your place so I can get this arm taken care of."

Back at the house, Helen helped Doc clean and dress his wound. Later, with Doc's arm in a sling, the two sat at the kitchen table drinking a cup of tea.

"You think we bought them enough time?" asked Doc.

"I know one thing is for sure," said Helen. "Those two won't be showing their faces in town anytime soon."

"It was a misfortune of sorts; having a mule-kicked boy stumbling upon your home and you having to deal with the likes of those two bounty hunters," said Doc.

"Oh, I wouldn't say that at all, Doc. I feel lucky having met Andrew and Jeb. They're good folk. And to tell you the truth, I haven't felt this alive in a long time."

After they finished their tea, Helen helped Doc Shepherd back on his horse and rode with him back to town. They weren't gone but a few minutes when two familiar men came out from behind the barn and walked quietly up to the house. The front door burst from its latch as the lead man threw his shoulder into it. The other man immediately swung into the kitchen with his rifle ready. They expected someone to be home, but heard or saw no one. The man with the rifle searched in the bedroom as the other sat himself at the kitchen table and poured himself a cup of tea. Within a few minutes, the man with the rifle came back into the kitchen and threw a piece of leather on the table in front of the man drinking tea.

"Whatta you suppose this could be?" he asked.

The man at the table placed his tea cup down and picked up the soft, round piece of leather, holding it up toward the kitchen window to catch better light.

"Looks like a map to me, Pete. I think we just found where our two friends are headed."

Eight miles away, Helen's small wagon rolled into Iron Mountain. Jeb Slate climbed down and wrapped the reins twice around the small hitching post in front of the railroad station. "Well, this is where she said to leave it. Sure was nice of her to let us borrow her rig."

"I'm going to head inside and see about the train schedule," said Andrew. "Helen said this line goes all the way to Casper, and we could resupply there and then ride north to pick up the Bozeman Trail again."

"I'm just glad we don't have to ride with the cattle or in some pile of soiled hay this trip. Sure was nice of Helen to pay us for the horses and mule. Although, I am going to miss that mule."

"We can get you another mule once we're settled in Montana. Now don't go anywhere. I'll be right back."

"Where the heck would I go?"

"Perhaps the saloon..." Andrew answered sarcastically.

Minutes later, Andrew returned to the wagon and handed Jeb his ticket. "They said it should be leaving at ten a.m. It takes about four hours, with the one stop it makes in Douglas." Andrew studied the railway map he had picked up in the train station.

"Looks like the Bozeman Trail turns northwest just north of Casper and then moves along side of the Big Horns."

"Then what?" asked Jeb.

"Well, it looks to be about a hundred and thirty or so miles to the Montana border, which means if we cover twenty miles a day, we should be in Montana in six or seven days."

As Andrew climbed aboard the train, he scanned the faces of those already in the coach, looking to see if he recognized anyone. Feeling fairly secure with his assessment, he and Jeb headed to the rear of the coach. Jeb tried to place his backpack in the overhead rack, but it seemed to be a tight fit. Slamming both of his fists against the side of the pack caused it to squeeze through the opening with a loud thump and a rattle of a few plates moving around inside. He plopped himself down hard in the seat, startling the woman who sat in front of him.
"Heck, first time I ever PAID to ride a train," said Jeb. The formally dressed woman turned around and gave a snobby type of glare at him. Jeb gave her a big closed-mouth smile back, so the whiskers on the sides of his cheeks stood out farther than normal.
"Quiet, Jeb," said Andrew. "You don't need to advertise it."
"Well, I suppose I'll just take myself a nap." He tipped his hat down over his forehead and adjusted his posture so he leaned slightly to the left. His big head rested against the window, causing the brim of his hat to fold upward. He then gave a yawn, stretched his legs out below the seat in front of him and accidentally broke wind at the same time. "Sorry," he quietly said from under his hat.
As the train conductor yelled "All Aboard", the steam engine jolted forward and started chugging down the tracks.

Two hours later, the train jolted to a stop in the town of Douglas. Jeb woke mid-snore and abruptly sat up in his seat, getting his bearings, as he had forgotten for a second where he was. He looked across at Andrew, who sat staring out the window watching a few people step off the train as the engine puffed intermittently on the tracks, as if it were catching its breath after the long trip.
"What you thinkin' bout, Andy?"

"I keep hearing Helen's voice in my head, telling me to go back to Durango and tell my part of the story. But the last time I tried that, I nearly got killed when I approached town."

"Maybe someone don't want you to get back to town. Someone who figures you saw somethin' that night. You told me that you heard Mr. Saunders arguing with his son Jake the day before he was killed, didn't ya'?"

"Yes, but I just can't see a man killing his own pa."

"You also said you saw a rider heading away that night."

"I did, but why ride away only to ride back minutes later? It doesn't make sense."

"Look here, Andy, whether he done it himself or thinks you done it, bottom line is he wants you dead. Why else would he send a few hired hands to track you down instead of just sending the law?"

Jeb took his pipe from his front shirt pocket and stuffed a wad of tobacco in it, compressing it with his thumb.

"I have a feeling you wouldn't have made it a mile down the trail with those two," he said as he spoke out of the corner of his mouth between puffs.

"You best stay with me, Andy. We'll find a good, safe spot to settle near Anaconda."

As the train made its way toward Casper, Andrew wrote a letter to his parents. He told them about how he was kicked by a mule, downplaying the extent of his injury, and how he and Jeb were lucky to run into Helen and Doc Shepherd. He wrote about Helen's good cooking and how they nursed him back to health. He even wrote about Jeb's first time inside the passenger car of a train. But no matter how he tried to work his words into an adventurous and positive picture for his parents, his mind never was far from the thoughts of losing his watch or being pursued by the two men who meant to take him back for the murder of Mr. Saunders.

Chapter XIII

Willow Gaithers swept the wooden walk in front of her father's general store just as she had every morning for the past several years. She had a knack for being meticulous and liked to get up early so she could have the sweeping done before too may people were out and about. It also gave her some time of her own before the store opened at eight. She always used a bandana to knot her long black hair behind her head, which created a pony tail that she would tuck into the back of her shirt so it didn't interfere with her work. When she was done sweeping, she walked over to the stable behind the store to see her chestnut gelding, which her father had bought for her on her thirteenth birthday. It was a generous gift, and one her father had set aside money for over several months. The horse perked up as she walked close, and stuck his head over the railing of the stall so Willow could rub his forehead. "Good morning, Star," she said as she reached into her front jeans pocket for a sugar cube. Star took the cube in his mouth and nuzzled against Willow's cheek.

This was Willow's favorite time of the day. She liked the clean smell of the fresh hay and hearing the sounds of the blacksmith as he started his work down the street. She loved watching the rising sun's rays shine through the cedar trees just outside of town, casting long shadows over the flowing grass.

She fitted Star with an old worn saddle that her father had obtained from a neighbor by trading it for an overdue payment on some store goods. Taking the reins, she walked the horse outside to enjoy the morning sun. Double-checking her saddle belt cinch and stirrups, she climbed up and gave Star a gentle hick with her heels. The response was instant and Star dashed down the dirt trail and then up into the prairie grass.

When Willow had ridden over a hill and cleared the line of sight from town, she reached behind her head with one hand and pulled the knotted bandana from her hair and placed it over the saddle pommel. Her long black hair flowed past her shoulders and rippled back and forth like a flag, mimicking Star's mane as they rode. The sensation of her horse moving swiftly, the wind in her hair and the smell of the prairie flowers stirred something inside of her that could not be attributed to memory. It was something she couldn't put her finger on, but perhaps it came from a part of her ancestry. It was something she felt that would always be with her.

Willow was adopted by John and Lucile Gaithers from a local orphanage when she was five. John and "Lucy", as she liked to be called, came west from St Louis to open a store on their own in the ever expanding west. But that wasn't the only difference between Willow and the other girls in town. Because Willow's real mother was full blood Shoshone, she was never truly accepted by the other children. She was never invited to a birthday party or asked to an afternoon tea. If it bothered Willow inside, she never let it show. She had always said to her father she'd rather be out riding in the hills or fishing at the stream which ran behind town, than sitting around playing with dolls. She never knew who her real father was, and when she asked John, he could only tell her that it was rumored he was a soldier in the army. Willow's blue eyes were the only visible tie she had to her original father. Her memories of her real mother were mostly lost. She could only recall a pretty woman with dark skin and hair, who was often sad. Her faint visions were of the day her mother brought her to the orphanage and left her there. Willow could only guess it was because she could no longer care for her. She remembered the orphanage as a lonely place, where other children could be quite cruel to someone who was different from their own color of skin and hair and wore the beaded leather clothing of the Shoshone.

She stopped her horse to drink at a pool, which formed from part of a stream that flowed down from the hills. Taking a blanket from behind her saddle, she opened it up and with one long flip of her arms, spread it on the prairie grass under the shade of a tree. Making sure no one was around, she removed her boots, shirt and jeans, and lay them on the blanket. Taking a bar of lilac soap from her saddlebag, she slowly lowered herself down from the bank into the cold water. Her long hair floated on top of the water, spreading like a shawl around her, until she dunked herself under. She loved the smell of the soap and how it reminded her of spring. Her father stocked several bars in the store on a regular basis, as they sold well to ladies who shopped there. Lavender, rose, lemon and vanilla filled the wicker basket on the counter, but it was lilac that was Willow's favorite. While she washed her hair, she looked across to the far end of the meadow where a mother elk walked, with its yearling trailing just behind. She thought of how wonderful it might have been to have spent more time with her own mother. To learn all there was to know about their family and traditions. Lucy was a good mother, who could not have children of her own. She had loved Willow very much and never made her feel any different than if she was her real daughter. She taught Willow how to cook, bake and sew, and although Lucy understood very little of the Shoshone culture, she never kept any truth of her heritage from her daughter.

Willow took one last dunk into the pool and then walked up onto the bank. Twisting her long hair with her hands, she wrung out the remaining water and then laid down on her blanket to watch the clouds pass overhead.

Willow was only ten when Lucy passed away from pneumonia. After Lucy was gone, John did the best he could to raise her. She attended school in town until she was fourteen, and then decided to work in the store full time for her father.

John ran a fairly successful business, but he didn't make enough money to send his daughter to a private school or university. So he started teaching her as much as he could about running the store.

Willow knew everything from the right price to pay for a dozen large eggs, to the best muslin to sell by the yard for a Sunday tea gown, and even how many shingle nails would be needed to re-roof an outhouse. She found it rewarding to have learned all these things, but it never felt the same as riding through a meadow or watching the sky at night to pick out the constellations of stars. She felt as though there was so much more to learn, which was somehow a part of her from the past. Now at the age of eighteen, she wondered if she would ever find a husband or would she just live with her father for the unforeseeable future. She often day-dreamed of getting married, living on the open prairie and having several children of her own. Children who would always know who their parents were and how much they were loved. When she saw the climbing sun start to filter through the leaves on the overhanging tree branches, she knew it was time to dress, climb into the saddle and ride back to the stable. The store would be opening soon and there was another day's work to be done.

Chapter XIV

It was four-thirty in the afternoon when the Union Pacific 1242 pulled into Casper Station. Jeb and Andrew decided to see if they could purchase two horses, a mule and supplies with the remainder of the money Helen had given them. At the Adams livery, Andrew picked out a spirited young dapple gray horse and Jeb selected a more mature buckskin. The gray reminded Andrew of Cloud, and he wondered what might have happened to the horse he had spent so much time breaking. The livery only had one mule, and it looked to have seen better days, but the men needed another animal to haul goods, so it would have to do.

They paid the owner for the animals, receiving the papers in return, and then headed to the local store to stock up on provisions. The two men would have a good day's ride ahead of them toward the Bighorn Mountains, before they could pick up the Bozeman Trail, which led into Montana.

As they left town and headed up into the hills, Jeb reached into his front left shirt pocket to pull out the leather map, only to pull out a clean white handkerchief in its stead. "What the heck..!" he called out in disbelief. "Andy, did you borrow the map from my pocket while I slept on that train?"

"No, sir. I figure that's your property. Besides, I pretty much have that thing memorized by now."

Jeb opened up the linen cloth and held it up to the sun, as if still trying to figure what had just happened.

"That's a good thing, Andy. 'Cause this isn't what I had in my pocket yesterday, and there aren't any markings on this here cloth."

Andrew, who rode a few yards ahead, stopped his horse and turned towards Jeb. "What exactly are we talking about?"

"The map. I'm positive I had it in my shirt pocket yesterday, and today it's just a hanky."

"You must have lost it somewhere back at Helen's place. She did give you one of her husband's shirts, didn't she?"

"Yes, but... I thought... Oh, heck. Maybe it's in my pack."

"We'll look for it later," said Andrew. "We have a ways to go before we reach the Bighorns."

Just before sundown, the two men set up camp just south of the Bozeman Trail. Before them, still miles away, the Bighorn Mountains rose up toward the clouds, capped in white snow. Andrew had made a fire for dinner and Jeb had dumped all his belongings out on his bedroll, looking for the leather map. "It's just not here, Andy. I went through my pants, the shirts Helen packed and everything in my saddlebags. I'm not sure how I lost it."

Andrew walked over to the fire and picked up a stick from the wood pile they'd made. He traced in the dirt what he remembered from his mind.

"Look, Jeb, here's the Bozeman Trail. Here's the town of Phillipsburg and here's Anaconda. The mine was marked about here, northwest of Anaconda, along this ridge. Now is that the way you saw it?"

"Yes, I believe that was it, Andy. I guess your memory is a lot better than mine. I don't feel so bad now."

"We're going to find that mine with no trouble at all, you'll see. We'll get ourselves a map of the state when we get to the next town. Now how about you fix up some of those biscuits and beans you are so famous for?"

Andrew didn't tell Jeb that he was a little unsure of his markings, but it didn't matter now. He knew the marked towns and the general direction they needed to go in relationship to them. That and a bit of luck would have to do.

As the two men ate their dinner, a lone figure approached them from the south. His gate was slow and methodical, and he used a walking stick to steady himself. He rode no horse and looked to be a Native American Indian of some sorts, but his clothing was different from any Andrew had remembered seeing in any newspaper or dime novel he had read.

He wore a leather frock coat with a button-front shirt under it, and carried a leather pack on his back with a bedroll tied to the bottom. His bow and arrow quiver were tied to the side. The brown felt hat which sat low on his head, looked like it had no style of its own, since the brim was perfectly flat and the crown had no dents in it, but rather a simple rounded top. The hat bore one feather in the band, which looked to Andy like it came from a turkey.

His hair was mostly gray, with a few remaining strands of black, and was bound with a thin strip of leather behind his head, stopping a foot below his coat collar. When the man stopped just shy of walking up to the camp fire, he called out in a voice that was very hoarse and rather high in pitch. It sounded to Andy more like an old woman, than a man.

"May I join you beside your fire?"

There was a brief moment of silence as Andrew looked toward Jeb to answer. "Yes, yes. Come sit down, friend," said Jeb. He casually glanced to where he might have placed his rifle if trouble ensued.

"Is it possible that I might share some of your meal?"

"Sure... well, if ya' don't mind using a cup. We're plumb out of plates." Jeb ladled a generous scoop of beans into one of the coffee cups.

The man reached into his coat pocket and pulled out a spoon that looked as if it had been hand-carved from a piece of wood, and quickly started eating the beans.

He said nothing as he ate, and Jeb nor Andrew thought to interrupt him as he focused on the cup of beans. He only paused a few times to look up at his hosts from under his hat. When he was done, he made sure the spoon was licked clean and then placed it back in his coat pocket.

Jeb would have offered more, but there was none. He took the cup from the man's hand and placed it by the other dishes.

"What part of the country are you from, friend?" asked Jeb.

"I come from the west." The Indian pointed over his shoulder from the direction he had travelled. "Wind River Reservation. Many of my people were moved there by the white man's army over thirty years ago."

"Well, what's your name, friend?" asked Jeb.

"Dugumbaa'nna kai daka'bi is my name in Shoshone," he said. There was a pause and a slight laugh before he continued. "Sky With No Clouds, would be how you say in your tongue."

"Well, that's a damn proper ten-dollar name," said Jeb.

"Why were you named that?" asked Andrew.

"My father said on the day I was born, the brutally cold winter had finally broken, spring had come to the valley, and the sky was clear and blue."

"My name is Jebediah Slate. You can call me Jeb; and this here is Andrew Thompson, but I call him Andy."

"It is a good evening," answered Sky With No Clouds, which Andy interpreted as his way of expressing approval with their company. Sky reached into his bag and pulled a tobacco pouch and pipe from it.

He packed in the tobacco up to the top and lit the pipe. A strong, earthy aroma floated around the men and Sky passed his pipe for the other two to try. "It is good to smoke with those who share food and fire, yes?"

"Absolutely," said Jeb, who was about to pull his own pipe from his pocket, but thought better to just share what Sky was offering. Andrew looked a little uncomfortable as Jeb passed the pipe his way. He didn't want to insult Sky With No Clouds, and since this was the first time he had met a genuine Indian, he decided to take a few puffs. He coughed into his fist once, then passed the pipe back to Sky.

"I have walked for five days. Tomorrow I travel north to the Crow Reservation in Montana," said Sky between puffs. "There is a woman living there who I must see."

"Going to get hitched, are ya'?" asked Jeb.

"No, I am looking for my granddaughter. My daughter left our people many years ago, because she had loved a white soldier. I now believe that for some reason she had gone to live with the Crow."

"Montana's a long way. Why don't you ride a horse?" asked Andrew.

"I was not permitted to take a horse when I left Wind River, and I cannot afford to buy one. So I walk alone," replied Sky.

"Well, we don't have an extra horse, but you're welcome to travel with us since we're headed up to Montana ourselves. We plan to make Powder River by tomorrow evening. We're hoping the trout are biting, since we can only pack so much food."

"I make do with rabbit and grouse," said the Shoshone, patting his hand on his weatherworn bow and quiver. "Now I will sleep; goodnight." With that, he excused himself from the conversation, laid out his bedroll several feet from the fire and lay down.

"I guess we'd better turn in, too," said Jeb. "We have a long way to go tomorrow."

The next morning, the three men packed up camp and started north. They reached the Bozeman by late morning. As the trail turned northwest, a view of the Bighorn Mountains rose up in front of them. After a few hours, Andrew offered his horse to Sky to give him a break from walking, but Sky refused and said it was good for him to walk this path. He had been walking for so long, he was starting to feel a stronger connection to the earth beneath his feet.

Up ahead, Jeb led the mule with all their supplies tied to its back. Andrew kept a slower pace beside Sky. He was especially interested in him, since he had never met a real Indian before. Awkwardly, he jumped into a conversation, not quite sure how to speak to the man who was so quiet and said very little.

"So you think you'll find your granddaughter at the Crow reservation in Montana, do ya'?"

Sky looked up at Andrew for a moment, then stared straight ahead before speaking. "Yes. When my daughter left our people, she was carrying a child inside of her. I had a spirit dream that my daughter gave birth to a girl."

"What do you mean by spirit dream?"

"Have you never had a dream so strong and full of life, that when you woke, it was as if it were real?"

"Actually, yes. I often dream of my father. My real father, that is. You see, my real father died when I was really young, and my memories of him are limited. My stepfather lives with my mother back east."

"Is a stepfather like a grandfather?"

"No. It's uh... Well, my mother married another man, who loves her very much; so he is my stepfather."

"I understand now. What do you dream of your first father?" asked Sky.
"I dreamt of him working as a logger before his accident. I also dreamt of him rising up to the clouds after his accident, as if he were alive again. I know it sounds strange, but that's how the dream came to me."
"I do not think it strange at all. Many warriors go to the spirit world after they die," said Sky. "Your father must have been very brave."
"I'm sure he was. I only wish I had more memories of him."
"Don't lose hope. Maybe he will come to you again in your dreams."
Andrew took a sip from his canteen and offered it to Sky, who gladly accepted it for a lengthy swig. Sky wiped the corner of his mouth and handed the canteen back to Andrew. "In my dream, I saw the death of my daughter's soldier husband, and then I saw her strength failing as she grew sick. So I think she is also in the spirit world. I had visions of her living with the Crow people and giving birth to a small child. That is why I know my granddaughter must be there."
"What will you do when you find her?"
"It was over eighteen years ago when my daughter was cast out from our people. I never wanted her to leave, but it was not my choice. The elders made her go. They said there was no room for a Shoshone who cared for a White soldier. If I find her, I will ask my granddaughter to come back to the Wind River Reservation and live with me, where I can share stories about her mother and teach her the ways of the Shoshone. I will also give her this."
Sky reached under his shirt and revealed a medallion on a woven leather necklace. The medallion looked to be made from antler, and on it was carved a small bird. "It is a meadowlark, which my daughter was named after. Hiitoo' is how we say it in Shoshone."
"I hope you find her. I'm sure she will love it," replied Andrew.

By the time the sun had sunk far enough to touch the tops of the Bighorn peaks, the three men had reached the Powder River. They set up camp among the flowing grass, close to the small trees, which seemed never to wander too far from the precious life-giving water. Unfurling their bedrolls under the shade of the cottonwoods was the best they could do in the hot summer sun. Soon the sun would set, and the evening air would turn quite cool due to the high elevation. Andrew cut himself a cottonwood switch and started making a pole to try his luck at a few trout for their dinner. Sky walked along the riverbank, in and out through the cottonwood trees, in search of a rabbit.

Not long after the time it took for Jeb to get a small fire going, both men had returned from their endeavors with bounty in hand. They shared their catches and ate well under the canopy of bright stars. Andrew kept note of the special day in his small, leather-bound journal so he could describe the scene to his parents in his next letter.

"...When I left home several months ago, I had no idea I'd be eating rabbit and fish under the beautiful night sky with an old war veteran turned hobo, and a gray-haired Shoshone brave who seeks what remains of his family. It seems ironic to imagine that they could have fought against each other at one time had their paths crossed, but now each seeks to find himself in the twilight of his years. I must remember the importance of what I have seen, as each has lost loved ones and has shown signs of the remaining scars. I have not yet decided if this new west is right for me or if I should build a life here. But whether I stay or end up going back east to live my life, I will keep in my heart the importance of family."

For the next two days, the three men walked and rode along the eastern side of the Bighorns, slowly making their way northwest toward the Montana border. When they noticed their supplies running low, they cut off the Bozeman Trail to stop for provisions at the next town. The sign posted at the outskirts read: "Big Horn City, established 1882." The silhouette of the town looked like many they had seen from a distance. Andrew and Jeb waited near the sign as Sky caught up with them. "Maybe I should wait for you here?" asked Sky.

"Nonsense," said Jeb. "We'll all go in together and look around."

The two men rode in slowly with Sky walking close behind them. Sky felt slightly uncomfortable with the glances passersby cast his way. Less than twenty-five years had passed since the Great Indian Wars took place, and many of the locals had lost brothers, uncles and fathers to an Indian rifle or bow. Andrew could feel Sky's uneasiness, as he walked with his head turning from side to side to avoid the glances from people on the boardwalks. Perhaps, he thought, Sky wore the clothes of a white man to avoid conflict; but it seemed to have more to do with submission to a change of life, than from acceptance.

As the men entered the center of town, a large hotel named The Orient stood out on their right. Across the street was the Big Horn Mercantile. As Jeb took his horse down to the livery to check on what he thought might be a loose shoe, Andrew and Sky went into the mercantile to resupply. The shopkeeper was filling the order of two other men, but stopped to glare over at Sky from the corner of his eye as Sky poked through a few of the folded shirts on display. He was amazed the softness of the shirt but could not read the hefty price.

"Can I help you sir?" asked the shopkeeper as he looked over at Andrew, but continued to glance over at Sky.

"Yessir," Andrew replied. "I'd like to get two pounds of flour, four pounds of bacon, four pounds of beans and a pound of lard. Oh, and a map of Montana if you happen to carry one."

"I have a map of Wyoming, but not Montana," said the shopkeeper. "If you travel just five miles north, you'll find the town of Sheridan. There's a railroad station there. They should have a map of Montana."

A tall thin man at the end of the counter, who was overhearing their conversation, spoke aloud to his partner. "Look at this fancy injun, Zeek, I ain't never saw an injun wearin' a white man's coat and jacket before."

"Unless maybe he killed for it," said his partner, loud enough for all to hear. "Come on, Sam, let's get outta' here before he shoots you with his bow." The two men walked out of the store still snickering as the door closed behind them.

Sky didn't enjoy the comments, but he ignored them anyway, as he was used to hearing such slights, and knew when to walk away. He approached the counter and stared at the six remaining eggs from that morning, which sat neatly arranged in a basket lined with cloth.

"We'll take those six eggs, too," said Andrew, who looked over at Sky who was now grinning back at him with the thought of fresh eggs.

Ten minutes later, the shopkeeper had wrapped up Andrew's supplies and totaled up the order, which just about took the remainder of Jeb and Andrew's money. Andrew handed the bag of eggs to Sky to carry as they walked out the door, and carried the rest of the goods himself. As they walked down the boardwalk toward the horse and pack mule, the tall thin man, who was now leaning against one of the walkway railings, stuck his foot out in front of Sky, catching him on the shin. Sky stumbled forward, just catching himself from falling on his face, but losing their bag of eggs in the process. The two men laughed hard at the expense of the old Indian, who still showed little emotion on his face. Sky stood up and slowly walked up to the man who tripped him. "You owe us for the cost of the eggs you broke."

"I what?" asked the man.

"You owe us ten cents for the eggs. Was it not your foot who tripped me?"

"My foot? I think you tripped over your own feet."

Andrew watched closely and placed his armful of goods on the boardwalk next to the store front. "I saw you trip him, mister," he said.

"You owe us ten cents for those eggs."

"You saw nothin'," said the thin man's friend, who looked to be the bigger of the two and the same height as Andrew. The thin man just laughed aloud, knowing his bigger friend was there to back him up. The few townspeople who walked past the men quickened their pace, as if to steer clear of any ensuing confrontation. A few other people watched the scene from across the street. Neither of the two men wore a gun, and Andrew wanted no part of a confrontation, but he couldn't stand being bullied, and the more the thin man laughed, the madder he became.

Reaching down and picking up the bag of eggs, he walked over to the thin man. "Since you have broken them, they are now yours." He then turned the bag over and with one quick move, splattered the runny eggs all over the front of the thin man's shirt. The thin man stopped laughing and raised his fist in anger. That was all Andrew needed to see as he caught the thin man's wrist in mid-swing. When the man swung his other fist, Andrew caught that one too. He squeezed the man's wrists as hard as his blacksmith-hardened muscles could. The man could feel the strength of Andrew's grip start to turn his hands numb, and all he could do was call out to his friend, who also was no longer laughing. "Zeek," he cried out in a panic. "Do something!"

Zeek tried to grab Andrew from behind, but Sky was ready, and in one swift movement had swung his bow off his shoulder and had captured the large man's arm between one end of the bow and the string. He spun the man around as he jerked the bow back and then crouched so low, that he flipped the approaching man over his back and onto the street. He hit the ground hard with a thud and a small wisp of dust was produced in the process. The thin man cried out, "I've had enough," and Andrew released his arms. The man rubbed his wrists as he walked off the boardwalk and stood by his friend who slowly stood up and collected his hat from the street. As the two men walked away, they glanced over their shoulder with empty scowls. The owner of the mercantile burst out the front door. "I saw the whole thing; glad you stood up to them. Town bullies, those two are. They cause more trouble than they're worth. I'll have more fresh eggs in the morning if you'd like to stop by. On the house, of course."

"Thank you," said Andrew. "But we'll be moving on after our friend gets his horse's shoe fixed. Can you tell me where to post a letter?"

"Post office is closed on Sunday, but I'd be happy to post it for you tomorrow if you leave it with me."

Andrew handed the man the folded letter from his pocket. "I don't have an envelope for it."

"Not to worry," said the owner of the mercantile. "I'll be happy to take care of that, too. The least I can do for you after running off those two. Maybe they won't hang around here botherin' my customers anymore. Good luck to you both."

"Much appreciated," Andrew replied, as he and Sky collected their goods and headed down the street to the livery.

After meeting up with Jeb, the three men camped just outside of town and were back on the Bozeman Trail at first light. Around noon, clouds had rolled in and the rain had start to come down. First it was light, but within another hour, it had changed to steady a steady, hard downpour. The men stopped in Sheridan long enough for Andrew to find his map of Montana, then continued northwest. For two hours, the men walked and rode through the hard rain. They made do with their hat brims pulled down and coat collars buttoned up for a while, but then stopped short of a river to deliberate their crossing.

"I'm as wet as a muskrat, Andy, and Sky don't look too keen on continuing either. Looks like he's havin' a tough time keeping up on this slippery ground. We should stop and make a fire."

"Agreed," said Andrew, as he looked over at the tall pines to the west. "Let's move over to those timbers and set up camp. We'll dry off if we can find any dry tinder, then cross the river tomorrow."

The men were in luck, and dried their clothes by the fire and slept on pine boughs under their tarp. When they woke the next morning, the rain had stopped, but there was another noise, which rose from the northeast. They broke camp and walked down to the rocky bank. The river had risen during the night, and the usual fifty-foot width of stream was now a one hundred-foot span of rushing water. Jeb was the first to approach it, and carefully waded up to his boot straps with a long stick in hand. "It's pretty fast, Andy," he called out. "Fast, but not too deep." Andrew walked up the horses and mule. "We'll cross on horseback," he called out to Jeb. "Sky can ride the mule in tow."

Sky shook his head at Andrew's suggestion. "I cross on foot," he said. Jeb gave Andrew a long stare and Andrew knew that Jeb was against any of them crossing the fast moving river on foot. "I highly suggest you ride the mule, or take the horse if you'd like and I'll ride the mule." Sky still shook his head. "I will look downstream to cross on foot," he answered back, and just walked away without arguing the point further.

Jeb and Andrew rode into the stream with the mule roped behind and slowly made their way across. When they reached the other side, they looked downstream for Sky, but neither could see him.

"Did you see him cross?" asked Jeb.

"No, I was too busy with my horse to look for him."

"Damn," said Jeb, spitting onto the ground. "Wait for me here." He climbed off his horse and walked down the length of stream past the tall pines, looking for any sign of Sky. He thought he might have heard a voice, but could not be sure with all the rushing water around him. Walking his horse along the bank further down, he came to a spot where he could see Sky's footprints in the mud, which lined the banks. He could understand why Sky might have chosen to cross here, due to the lower water level, but knew it was deceptively fast-moving. A pine tree had been swept down stream and was been wedged between two large boulders, along with various sticks and grass. He climbed back on his horse and waded in, making his way slowly toward the tree until his boots were just above the surface of the water. Then he saw the first sign of despair. Sky's bow, which he might have been using as a walking stick was hung up on the other side of the fallen tree, but there was no sign of Sky himself. Jeb thought he might have lost his footing and been swept around the bend in the river. Perhaps that was the voice he had heard. Guiding his horse back to the bank, he rode further downstream, rounding the bend.

By now, Andrew was quite worried. Why was Sky so stubborn about not wanting to cross on horseback? He took out his journal as he waited and painted a story of what was before him, and what might lie ahead. He had only written a few paragraphs, when he looked up to see Jeb riding back, with Sky lying across his saddle. Jeb shook his head out of frustration and a chill came over Andrew, as he feared the worst had happened. "His leg was wedged between two rocks Andy. The water wasn't that deep, but he couldn't stay above it for long with the fast current. It's a damn shame."

Jeb slowly lowered Sky's body to Andrew. As he gently cradled Sky's head, as if he were asleep on his back, Andrew saw the outline of the carved antler medallion Sky wore under his shirt. He reached behind the man's neck and untied the leather necklace.

"We can bury him with it or use it as a marker," suggested Jeb.

"We can do better than that," replied Andrew. "We can deliver it to his granddaughter." Andrew tied the medallion around his neck and then walked back to the mule to retrieve a shovel.

An hour later, Jeb placed the last of the large stones the two had gathered from the river, on top of Sky's grave. "We hardly knew the man, but I believe he'd like it here under these tall pines. May his soul be at rest."

"Amen," answered Andrew, placing his bow and quiver atop the grave. Andrew noted in his journal the passing of Sky:

"Sky was an interesting man who's people had settled here long before we arrived. The strange accident that took him, causes one to wonder about their own fate, and just how quickly life can leave any of us at any time. He was a complete stranger who had arrived in our camp only a week ago, and now has gone on to be with his ancestors. I wonder if there was some reason beyond our knowing, of why he had crossed our path for such a short visit. I could have learned more from him and his past, but we know how special his family was to him, and Jeb and I will do our best to deliver the gift he had brought north for his granddaughter."

As he tucked the journal away in his saddlebag, he pulled out the map of Montana. He lightly marked the area on the paper map where he remembered the mine was located from the old leather map. He couldn't be sure of the exact location, but gave it his best guess. He then packed it away and saddled up.

The two men rode north past the Big Horn Mountains, and crossed the point where the Bozeman Trail intersected with the Union Pacific line. They decided to ride a few miles more and make camp just south of the Big Horn River. Unknown to them, they were already on Crow Reservation land. Andrew showed Jeb the map of Montana. They took notice that while the Bozeman Trail turned northwest and then west into Anaconda, so did the railway.

"I know what you're thinkin' Andy. I have no desire to sell our livestock again, just to jump back on a train," said Jeb. "Besides, I've grown accustomed to this here mule."

"I tend to agree with you Jeb, but it looks to be about two weeks to Anaconda by horse and mule."

"I'll admit, it sure would be nice to be out of the wind and rain. My old bones ache in this weather." Jeb looked up at the clouds rolling in from the west and then looked in his pocket at the few dollars he had remaining. "I don't think we can afford passage all the way to Anaconda, Andy."

"Look, we've got enough supplies to easily make it up to Billings, all we have to do is follow the tracks. Once there, we can get us a job and earn the money to ride the train and pay to keep our horses and mule in the livery car. I got most of it figured out. I'm going to sleep on the details."

As the sun started to set, they could see the firelight from a camp about a mile up ahead. "Let's ride on up, Andy. Whoever they are, maybe they have dinner in the soup pot."

As Jeb and Andrew rode under the moonlit sky, they could start to see the outline of three teepees illuminated by the firelight. Jeb could smell the food cooking in one of the kettles, which overhung one of the fire pits. A few dogs barked as they grew near to the camp. A woman ran into one of the teepees, only to return with two men beside her. They wore the traditional clothes of the Crow. "I believe we're on Crow land now," Jeb said to Andrew.

The older looking of the two Indians walked forward. In his left hand was a rifle, which he used as a walking stick. "Welcome," he said in a voice that sounded deep, yet soft. "Let us go inside and get warm." Andrew and Jeb ducked as they entered the small entrance of the teepee. The inside smelled like smoked meat and leather. "My name is Small Fox, but the people here know me as Grandfather. Perhaps because there aren't many braves left my age. Please, sit down," said the Indian as he motioned with his hand at the area on the other side of a modest fire, which was in the center of the teepee. "Have you travelled far?" he asked.

"A fair piece," replied Jeb. "I take it this is the Crow Reservation we are on?"

"It is," answered Grandfather. "We were allowed to keep this land after the Whites made war with us. They said we were given the land, but I could never believe someone could give that to us which we already lived on. Besides, the land is not a thing to be owned by one man or another. We simply pass through it on our life's journey."

"We were traveling with a Shoshone Indian by the name of Sky With No Clouds," said Jeb. "He was on his way up to this reservation, but he died while trying to cross a flooded river. He had mentioned that his daughter had come to live here many years ago. He said her name was Meadowlark. He also believed his daughter gave birth to his granddaughter. Said it came to him in a dream."

"I'm sorry for the loss of your friend. Sometimes we are called home by our fathers when we least expect it. His name is not familiar to me, but I do remember a woman named Meadowlark. She came to live with us for several years, but then left several years ago. I think she feared that she would not be able to provide a good way of life for her daughter here. Many things have changed since the days of the war."

"You say she gave birth to a daughter?" asked Andrew.

"Yes. There is one woman here who might recall her name."

Grandfather motioned to one of the women who sat further away from the fire; she stood up and exited the teepee. A few minutes later she returned with another woman. Grandfather spoke to the old woman in their native tongue for several minutes, and the woman replied in a soft voice.

"This is Sad Woman. People began calling her that because she lost all of her children to White man's fever. She helped bring Meadowlark's daughter into this world about eighteen years ago. She says Meadowlark left us soon after her daughter was born. Meadowlark named her daughter Willow, after the trees that grow near the water and remain flexible in the strong wind. Sad Woman says Meadowlark knew her daughter would need to also be flexible in a life between Indian and Whites. It was rumored she took her daughter and went west to find her husband, who was a white soldier. When she learned of his death, she brought Willow to an orphanage in Anaconda. She does not know where Willow is now. Meadowlark was not seen by our people after that."

"Thank you, Sad Woman," said Andrew.

Grandfather said something in Crow to Sad Woman and she nodded to Andrew with a half-smile and left the teepee.

"We have a necklace that Sky With No Clouds wanted Willow to have," said Jeb. It just so happens we're on our way to Anaconda and we'd like to deliver it to her, given she's still there and we can find her."

"If you decide to head west, we will provide food to take with you. Anaconda is many days ride from here."

"Thank you," said Jeb. "We accept your gift."

Jeb and Andrew rode north toward Billings the next morning, and arrived just south of the town before sunset. After enjoying a meal of smoked fish provided by Grandfather and biscuits, which Jeb baked in a dutch oven, the two rode into town.

Jeb stopped in front of the Golden Belle saloon and climbed down from his horse. "Come on Jeb, we don't have time to play cards with what little money we have left," said Andrew.

"Who said anything about playing cards?" replied Jeb, pulling a paper posting from the hitching post. I can't read much, but I can make out the words "For Hire". Here, you go ahead and read this, Andy."

Andrew took the tattered poster from Jeb and read it out loud.

"For Hire... Two railway guards needed for Union Pacific freight line. Four days a week. Top dollar paid. Inquire within Sheriff's office."

"There you go, Andy, as if it just fell in our laps. Ha!"

"Jeb, I've never been a lawman of any sorts, and this job may be dangerous."

"Where's your sense of adventure, Andy? We can work the job for a week or so, and then quit and ride the train west after we get paid."

"Still sounds dangerous to me, but we can inquire if it makes you feel any better. Judging by the age of this paper, the job has probably been filled anyhow."

Twenty minutes later, Andrew and Jeb walked out of the office with papers in hand. "Wahoo, Andy! That was right smart of you to ask for a week's pay in advance."

"I was trying to not get hired, Jeb. I had no idea he was going to say yes."

"I feel like celebrating! Let's head down to the Golden..."

"Now wait a minute, Jeb. We start our work tomorrow, bright and early. Sheriff says we report to the bank at seven. We can hold off on celebrating until we get a few runs behind us, at least until we work off our week's pay in advance."

Chapter XV

The train headed for Livingston contained five cars full of livestock, three with grain and two with passengers heading west. But there was another car two down from the engine, that carried a different cargo. In the corner of the nine-by-twelve-foot car where Andy and Jeb rode, there stood a steel safe with a combination lock only the banker in Livingston could open. It contained coin and cash money to be transferred to the Livingston bank, one hundred miles to the west. Andrew sat on the same small stool he had sat on for the previous two weeks. Made of metal from an old tractor seat, and barely large enough to cover his backside, the tiny stool faced a small window on the side of the car, which was paned in glass, which in turn was covered by iron bars. Andrew's Winchester shotgun lay across his lap, filled to capacity with double-ought buckshot. In the corner, Jeb tinkered with the combination lock on the beautiful steel safe. For the past two weeks, he had tried his hand at opening it. Andrew would just roll his eyes at Jeb's feeble attempts, reminding him that he was no safe cracker. Painted like a piece of art, pinstripes and all, the squat, heavy cube sat in a corner like some quiet little elephant. Jeb ran his hand over the smooth, cold metal surface. "Imagine, Andy, over five thousand dollars inside this safe. I believe this is the largest amount we've guarded yet. Ain't never heard of so much money in one box."
"I'll be happy when we're in Livingston," replied Andrew, who double-checked his coat for extra shells. "You think they could at least have a stove in here or something. It's darn chilly in this box car."

"Aw, it ain't that bad. You could be riding with our horses and that damn mule in the livery car."

"At least they got hay," said Andrew. "I'm just glad this is our last run."

"Did Mr. Peabody say he'd wire our last payment into Anaconda?" asked Jeb.

"Yeah, he said we could ride the train all the way into Anaconda and he wouldn't even deduct the price of travel from our pay. Pretty nice guy, if you ask me."

With a jerk forward, the train started west, picking up speed and raising the tempo of the click and clacks with the passing rails.

Several miles into their trip west, Jeb sat back on his stool, slightly tipping its rear legs backward and propping his feet up on the safe. He searched his pockets, finding his pipe and lighting it up with several heavy puffs.

"Great, now you have to fill this sealed box full of smoke."

"You know I relax better when I have my pipe, Andy."

"Yeah, I know."

"Better a pipe than chewin' tobacco. Some guys, they just spit and spat that stuff everywhere. I knew one guy who used to play cards and just spat it under the table every few minutes. The only time he didn't spit was if he was nervous about a bad hand. One time he had such a bust hand, he just swallowed the whole..."

"I get the picture, Jeb. Glad I ain't had my lunch yet."

"Speakin' of lunch, what did you bring us, Andy?"

"Two sandwiches from the Golden Belle. Both ham."

Suddenly, there was a jolt. Then another. Then a third, so hard that Jeb's stool slid out from under him, causing him to spit out his pipe and whack the back of his head on the side of the car as his backside slammed onto the floor. Andrew started laughing so hard, he nearly fell off his own stool, but suddenly stopped when the sound of a gunshot rang out, followed by another. Andrew held his Winchester firm as he peered out the small window through the iron bars.

"Holy cow!" yelled Andrew. "There's four riders with rifles following alongside the train. I think we're being held up, Jeb!"

Jeb stood up and caught his balance, then pulled out his 1860 Colt from his belt, which was loaded with six .44 caliber bullets. "As long as they don't stop, Andy, we'll be okay. They must have barricaded the tracks with tree trunks, an old trick we used in the Civil War to stop Yankee trains. Engineer must have been given orders to smash through it."

Andrew kept his watch out the window and saw one of the three riders jump from his horse and then disappear from his view. "I think they're boarding us, Jeb."

"Damn." Jeb looked up at the small square vent on the roof. If they make it past the other guards, they're bound to get inside here, Andy. We've got to get outta' here. Help me move this safe."

"Jeb, we gotta stay and protect the money, like we signed on to do. Besides, the car door is locked from the outside. They only open it when we get to Livingston."

"The hell with that. During the war, I seen men burn a boxcar with the guards inside, just to get to the safe. Another time I seen 'em use dynamite. If we make a fight of it, I'd rather do it from horseback and not locked in here. Now help me move this safe!"

Andy helped Jeb by putting their backs to the car wall and pushing with their legs until they were both red in the face. The safe moved just enough to line up slightly with the roof vent. Jeb then stood on the safe and pushed up on the small square vent. "It must also be locked from the outside, Andy."

"Let me try, Jeb," replied Andrew, who traded places with Jeb.

Andrew pushed up on the door, but could only get it to move a fraction of an inch. He could see the steel hinges on one side of the vent door. He aimed his Winchester at the opposite side and fired a shot up at the door, then another. Chips of wood shot back as the small door sprang open. Andrew then handed Jeb his shotgun as he reached up and slowly pulled himself upwards until he could get his arms up and out of the opening. He then pulled himself up through the small vent door and onto the roof of the car.

"Heck, Jeb. I don't know if you can fit through this," said Andrew, as he looked back through the opening into the car. "Hell, I'll fit. Give me a hand!" Jeb handed the shotgun up to Andy, followed by his own revolver, and then proceeded to stick his arms up through the opening. Andrew pulled on Jeb's suspenders to help, as Jeb's arms protruded through the opening, followed by his head. "Jeeeezuus!" proclaimed Jeb. "Couldn't they make these damn things bigger?"

Andrew pulled harder on Jeb's suspenders, but they snapped, sending Andrew falling backwards. Jeb's torso seemed wedged, with every part of his stomach filling even the corners of the small square space.

"I got nothin' to push against!" shouted Jeb. His legs dangled from the ceiling inside the car. "Pull, Andy!" Andrew pulled on Jeb's arms until his mid-section finally popped through, sending Andrew once again backwards on the roof of the car, this time almost losing his Winchester in the process.

As Andrew and Jeb slowly crawled along the roof toward the rear of the car, they looked back and saw one of the men who boarded the train making his way forward toward the engineer's car. Just as a railroad guard from the car behind the engine took position to fire, he was shot down from behind. The two men then dropped down between the cars to gain access to the engine compartment.

"We're gonna have to jump to the livery car, Andy," shouted Jeb against the wind blowing in his face.

Jeb stood up long enough to make the jump across the cars, then squatted down quickly. Andrew followed behind and the two men kept crawling rearward.

As they reached the end of the livery car, Jeb grabbed hold of the ladder and climbed down to access the door. It slid open and he stepped inside, with Andrew right behind him. They could see two other riders from the window about a mile back. They looked to be gathering the other two men's horses and were following far behind.

With a loud screech, the train suddenly jolted and started to slow rapidly, causing Andrew and Jeb to almost lose their balance.

"My guess is they got to the engineer. Let's get them saddled," said Jeb, referring to their livestock. Within minutes, both Jeb and Andrew had their horses saddled, with Jeb fumbling to control the mule's reins as it bucked and brayed.

"Those other riders are getting closer, Jeb," warned Andrew.

Jeb slid open the side door of the car and kicked his horse hard. The sorrel jumped out of the box car and hit the ground with Jeb holding tight to the horse's reins so as not to bounce out of the saddle. Andy followed on his chestnut mare. Jeb pulled his Colt from his belly with one hand and held tight to the reins with the other as he rode hard toward the front of the train. Andrew had never seen the old man so determined before. Mostly, Jeb was not the kind of guy that looked to move too fast. But Andrew saw a different man in front of him now. Not the fat old man who joked and snored at night, but a strong determined man. The man that lost his ma at at early age, joined the Army of the South and had fought in the war back east.

As Jeb approached the engine, he could see the engineer on the floor of the open car, his hat had rolled off onto the dusty ground with a blood red stain upon it. "Mister!" Jeb hollered out. The gunman in the engine aimed at Jeb, but Jeb was ready and shot him through the engine window. His body fell backwards, landing on top of the already dead engineer. The shot warned the dead man's partner who took position between the engine and boxcar. He fired at Jeb, sending a round whistling past Jeb's ear. Jeb kicked his horse and rode in front of the engine to meet the man at the other side. As Andrew rode up, he could hear several shots from the other side of the car. As he made his way around the other side of the engine, he found Jeb lifting a rifle from the dead man's hands. Jumping back in the saddle, Jeb said nothing as he rode straight past Andrew and down the length of train toward the two riders who were still approaching. Jeb let go of the reins of his sorrel as he rode within a hundred feet of the approaching men. Shots were fired at him as he raised his rifle in turn, dropping one of the men from the saddle, and just seconds later, the other.

He threw the rifle on the ground and rode back to the livery car, where he dismounted his horse. A remaining railroad guard emerged from the passenger boxcar and grabbed Jeb's hand as if to shake it. "Thank you, sir. Thank you," said the man. "You've certainly earned your pay today." Jeb merely said, "I reckon," and led his horse back onto the train. Andrew hadn't fired a shot, and he was just as embarrassed to have been no help during the fight, as he was astonished by Jeb's actions. After the dead men had been placed in the boxcar furthest to the rear and the horses were led back aboard, Jeb asked for the lock to be removed from the door on the car containing the safe.

He and Andrew rode on to Livingston with the door open a crack. Just enough for the wind to whistle as it blew through, as the train continued west. Andrew sat on his stool and slowly opened the paper bag containing his lunch. He chewed quietly as he ate his ham sandwich. Jeb sat with his back against the safe, puffing hard on his pipe, saying nothing, just staring blankly out the small opening.

Chapter XVI

Jeb and Andrew rode into Anaconda just before sunset, soaked through to the skin and chilled to the bone. The train that was to have taken them all the way into Anaconda, broke down a few miles outside of Butte. Their decision to ride the remaining twenty miles seemed to be a sound one, that is before they were caught up in a thunderstorm, which was followed by another day of hard soaking rain. Riding up to the saloon, Jeb slowly slid out of the saddle and swung his leather reins around the hitching post and then planted himself on the stairs just under the covered boardwalk. He removed his hat and wrung the water from it. Next, he took off his boots and turned those upside down to release a slow stream of water onto the stairs.

"Amen!" he said firmly, as he looked up at the sign just above and behind him. "Triple Dutch Saloon," he said slowly.
"I don't suppose we could stop at the bank and then get a warm bath and a shave first, Jeb?"
"Nope. Besides, the bank's probably closed by now. The Saloon on the other hand..."
"Alright then, I'm going to walk across the street to the dry goods store. They should know the best place where we can hang our hats for a few days."
"You do that, Andrew. I'm goin' to see to gettin' a nice bottle o' whiskey and a good cigar."
With that, he slapped his hat against his leg a few times, and walked up the stairs into the saloon.

Andrew let his horse drink for a few minutes before walking him across the street to the dry goods store. The bell above the door gave a jingle and Andrew approached the gentleman behind the front counter, who was wearing a shop apron and chewing on the back end of a pencil while going over his ledger. "Hello, sir," said Andrew. "Might you know where I could find room and board for the night? My partner and I just rode ... " Andrew stopped mid-sentence as the prettiest dark-haired girl he had even seen walked out from the back room and stood next to the man. Her hair was pulled back in a pony tail and her contrasting blue eyes looked at Andrew in a friendly, smiling manner.

"I'm John Gaithers and this is my daughter, Willow."

"Good day, miss," Andrew said as he nodded his head and tipped his hat. A trickle of water ran off the front of his brim, onto the floor. "I'm Andrew... Andrew Thompson. My friend Jeb and I just rode into town. Came all the way from Livingston. Well, actually Billings is where we started out from, but the train broke down in Butte and we got stuck in this downpour for two days." Andrew suddenly stopped, realizing the name of the beautiful dark-haired girl could very well be Sky's granddaughter.

"Nice to meet you, Andrew," said John. "You'll find there's an affordable boarding house down the street on the left. "The Mountain Inn is the name of the place. They serve breakfast and dinner, and have an indoor bath, too."

Andrew grew even more embarrassed, as he was now fully aware of his time on the trail without a bath, not counting the rain. He took a step backwards from the counter. "Thank you, sir. I'll be heading down that way."

He tipped his hat as he left the store and ran back over to the saloon to find Jeb. He didn't feel the time was right to discuss Willow's grandfather and needed time to sort out the right way to approach her, if she was, in fact, the girl they were looking for.

An hour later Andrew and Jeb had registered at the Mountain Inn. After a good hot bath, Andrew felt like a new man. Jeb, full of whiskey, seemed more like his old self as he sang "She'll be comin' round the mountain," over and over, enjoying his turn soaking in hot, soapy water.
"Did you hear the name of the store owner's daughter?" asked Andrew.
"I did indeed," answered Jeb. "I figure, I'd leave that up to you to handle, she bein' close to your age and all."
"Thanks," replied Andrew, looking at his clothes, which were drying next to the fireplace in their room. They were a bit tattered, and he decided it was best to buy some new ones as soon as the store opened in the morning. He wanted to make a good impression on Willow, and hoped he'd have the opportunity to speak with her before he and Jeb rode out to find the location of the mysterious mine. He tied the meadowlark necklace around his neck after he dressed, to ensure its safety.

The next morning after breakfast, Andrew and Jeb stopped at the bank and collected their payment from the Union Pacific Railroad. The railroad had doubled their weekly salary as a reward for stopping the men who had plagued the northern rail line. Andrew and Jeb walked out of the bank with one hundred and eighty dollars between them.
They stopped in John Gaithers' store to buy the necessary provisions for mining and restocked their food supply for the trip north. As Jeb paid for the goods, Andrew looked around the store, his eyes roaming to and fro above the shelves and racks of clothing.
"Something else I can help you with, young man?" asked Mr. Gaithers from behind the counter.

"I'd like to get a new shirt and pants while I'm here. We've been on the trail for a while." John helped Andrew pick out the correct size and allowed him to change in the back room to check the fit. Wearing his new clothes, he approached the counter to pay. He continued to look over his shoulder, as if looking for something. "Anything else I can help you find, Andrew?" asked Mr. Gaithers.

"Oh, I was just looking for Willow. Thought I might say hello before Jeb and I head north. We might be up north for a few days before heading back this way."

"She's gone out for her morning ride. Usually she's back by now. I'll tell her you stopped in and asked for her, Andrew."

"Thank you, sir," replied Andrew.

Jeb handed Andrew his share of the goods and motioned for the door with a nod of his head. "Let's get a move on, Andrew. We've got a ways to ride today." Andrew just smirked back at Jeb, as he had always called him Andy. No doubt a remark meant to call out his interest in Willow. As the two men stepped out onto the porch, Andrew caught a glimpse of Willow riding back toward the store. He placed his goods down on the boardwalk in front of his horse and made an obvious effort to step out onto the street where he could be seen. "Good morning, Willow," he said as he tipped his hat to her.

Willow pulled up on the reins of her horse. "Good morning," she replied. "How was your stay at the inn?"

"Very good, thank you. Jeb and I slept like logs and the breakfast was close enough to my ma's cooking, that I hardly noticed a difference. I stopped in at the store to see if you were there. Your father said you had gone out for a ride."

"Yes, I love to ride in the morning before the town gets busy and father needs me in the store. Are you leaving town?"

"We'll be heading up into the hills for a few days."

"A hunting trip?" Willow asked.

Not wanting the conversation to disclose their plans to look for a mine, Jeb spoke up before Andrew could answer. "Kind of. We're looking for a good place to set up camp for a while, and we hear there's great fishin' in some of those mountain lakes."

"Well, have a safe trip and good luck fishing."

"Thank you," said Andrew, waving as she rode behind the store to the stable.

"Jeez, Andy," Jeb whispered. "I thought for a minute there, you were going to tell her about the mine. We're not the only people in the streets you know. We got to find it first and then file a claim; and even then you never really can be sure someone won't claim-jump your goods when you're not lookin'."

"Sorry, I forgot where I was. I need to find the right time to talk with her about Sky."

"Well, maybe the opportunity will present itself at a better time."

Andrew sat down on the board walk and looked at the antler pendant. He shook his head, uncertain as to when that "right time" would be. Clearing his mind, he opened the map he had purchased in the store. He paid attention to where the rivers, valleys and mountains were located in relation to one another. He then tore a blank page from his journal and placed it on top of the map so he could see through to the markings. Drawing a simplified rendition of what he remembered in his head, he carefully aligned his drawing with the printed map. "I have a pretty good idea of where we need to head, Jeb."

He lifted the journal paper and marked the location of where he thought the mine might be on the printed map. "Right about here."

"Now you're thinkin' proper. Let's hit the trail."

Folding the map and placing it back in his pocket, Andrew stowed his goods in his saddlebags and the two men rode north. He couldn't help looking back on the town a few times as he and Jeb headed up into the hills.

The sky darkened before the two riders as they rode into the town of Red Lodge. "The heck with the livery. Let's just tie up here," said the tall blond-haired man with the scar on his cheek. "It's gonna open up any second. Besides, I could use a drink."

The two men entered the saloon and bellied up to the bar. Before they could finish their first beer, a fight had broken out over in the corner. It appeared one of the native Crow residents had caught a Scottish immigrant cheating at poker. Unfortunately for the Crow, he wasn't quite as fast with his knife as the Scotsman was with his revolver, who shot the Crow twice in the chest, killing him. Men gathered around to see the dead Indian. Other Crows who were in the saloon shouted at the Scotsman, who was threatening to do the same to them, until the ruckus was broken up by the appearance of the local sheriff, who hauled the lot of them down to the jail in the pouring rain to sort out what happened.

The two men at the bar turned to the bartender and ordered two more beers. "Like that in here very often?" asked the man with the scar.

"Five saloons in this here town," answered the bartender. "Some fight breaks out just about every night in at least one of them. Mostly it's to do with the rise in coal mining. The local Crows hate the immigrant workers, as this town was legally part of their reservation land. But that doesn't stop the owners of the mines from hiring the immigrants. You can read about the latest coal mine that opened in yesterday's paper, if you two are looking for a job."

The bartender tossed the paper in front of the man with the scar. He drank the foam of his beer as he read the article. When he flipped the paper over on the other side, he stopped for a minute, placing his beer down on the bar as his attention was captured by another article. When the man with the scar was done reading, he tossed the paper in front of his partner. There, at the bottom of the page, was a small article with a photo, featuring two men. The photo had a caption underneath that read: "Jeb Slate and Andrew Thompson stopped a train robbery on its way to Livingston."

The man with the scar smiled as he drank down the remainder of his second beer.

"Pete, I believe we're headed to Livingston tomorrow."

"Livingston? Where's that?" answered Pete.

"Further west, Pete. Further west."

Chapter XVII

Approaching the ridge of rock from the south, Jeb and Andrew rode parallel to the great cliff at a slow pace, looking for any sign of the mine. After riding twenty miles with much searching, the excitement of finding the exact mountain, after what they had thought sure to be what was exactly drawn on the map, had waned. Perhaps the mine had collapsed, or maybe it wasn't a hole in the mountain at all. Perhaps it was a covered-up shaft somewhere nearby that went straight down in the earth.

Jeb climbed down from his horse and stretched, as if trying to touch his toes. He fell short by half a foot, and groaned as he stood back up straight. He rubbed his beard several times as if searching for the right thing to say, but said nothing. He walked over to a nearby fallen pine and tied off his horse and the mule to one of the branches. Then taking his canteen from the saddle, he sat down on the moss-covered log. "I believe ol' Ben needs a rest," he said.
"Who?" asked Andrew.
"Ben," answered Jeb. "Our mule. I named him after Helen's late husband, God rest his soul. Mules got to have a name Andy, and Ben's as good as any."
"I suppose so. Just let me know when 'Ben' has had enough rest so we can move on."

Jeb wasn't getting any younger, and the thought of failing to find his place in life was becoming a reality. With all the wandering he had done, he had often wondered how he would spend his last days. He had reached the age where he knew he might have a few good working years left in him, but he wasn't the type to take a job in town. Settling down and finding a place where he could build his last home was becoming more of a priority - a cabin with a front porch, where he could sit in a rocker and look out on a stream with a few birch or aspen trees within his view. A half-smile appeared on his face, as the image filled his mind. He thought that maybe he could still have his dream after all, even if they never found the mine. He could hunt for his food and fish year-round. He could trap the river beds and sell his pelts.

He had heard that Montana was still offering 160 acres of land to individuals seeking to settle, as part of the Dawes Act of 1887. All he needed to do was stake a claim and register it with the nearest land office, which was in Helena. About two days ride east.

He thought of the piece of land that was just a mile back, where they had crossed the stream. The land was mostly flat, offered plenty of trees for a cabin, and he remembered it being fairly well sheltered from the wind. The stream fed into a small lake south of the trail, where he could hunt ducks in the fall. He envisioned a small cabin with a front porch, and a small shelter nearby for the animals.

"What are you thinking about?" asked Andrew, as he walked over to Jeb, who he wasn't used to seeing so quiet.
"Oh, the future, Andy. The future. A man needs to know where he's going to spend the rest of his days. I know that may sound funny to you. You've got family back east. But I ain't got nobody; and I'm kind of gettin' tired of movin' from place to place."
Jeb paused for a moment as he took a swig from the canteen and ran his shirt sleeve across his mouth and beard.
" I'm thinkin' of settlin' right here."

"Right here?"

"Well, back a little ways, where we crossed that pretty stream that opened into a pond near the birch trees and that large stand of spruce."

"But we ain't found the mine yet."

"No, we haven't. But I figure we could be looking for this thing for weeks and still not find it. I just can't see myself back in a town. I'd just as soon live here, mine or no mine."

Andrew sat down next to Jeb on the log. His eyes studied Jeb's hands that were clasped together as if he was trying to wring something out of them in his thoughts. He noticed how they were wrinkled and worn, kind of like how leather gets after exposure to rain and sun. He studied the gray in Jeb's beard, which had turned closer to a snowy white in a few spots. He looked down at his own hands in comparison and remembered the work he had done to dig out old man Saunders' well, and how he re-shingled the barn under the hot summer sun. He thought about old man Saunders, and how he died a lonely death, having neither the support or comfort of his flesh and blood to love him.

"So you're pretty sure this is the place, friend?"

"Yes, Andy. I'm sure. I had a place once, a little cabin by a stream back in Missourah'. I had a wife, too. She was a pretty young thing I had met working in a make-shift hospital during the war. Her name was Marie. Ya see, I had joined the Missourah' State Guard after the war started. I was wounded in the battle of Wilson's Creek. They brought me to the town of Springfield, where they had used some of the local buildings as hospitals. I was taken to a church where I met Marie. The doc took a Union ball out of my leg, and Marie looked after me and helped nurse me back to health. Well, when the war was over, I went back to that town and found Marie. We were married only three months later in that same church. Less than a year after that, I lost her to typhoid. I've been wandering ever since, Andy. Never could find it in myself to settle anywhere, but I'm gettin' old, son."

Andrew placed his arm over Jeb's shoulder.

"If this is where you want to live, then I'd be more than happy to help you build that cabin."

"You mean it?"

"We're partners, aren't we?"

"You bet, partner!"

Jeb shook Andrew's hand with all the life and spark of a man reborn. A man who had the look of hope in his face for the first time in a long while. He blew his nose into his handkerchief and stood up. "I'm gonna fix us a mess of beans and biscuits tonight!"

The next day, Jeb and Andrew made the trip to Helena to secure their claim on the property. They were happy to find no previous claims on the land. The following week, they began making the necessary trips to and from Anaconda, transporting the additional tools and other supplies needed to build their cabin.

They used a two-man crosscut saw to drop a stand of spruce and white pine in back of the cabin site, and then limbed the trees by axe. They then debarked the poles to make them dry quicker and become more resistant to insects that might bore into the wood. The spruce pines were soft and easier to cut than the large oaks and hickories Andrew remembered cutting back home. At the end of the week, Jeb and Andrew had cut, limbed, debarked and transported over forty trees. Jeb said it would be best to wait a few weeks, to let the trees dry and check before starting to notch and build the cabin walls. The two men had spent a great deal of time under their make-shift tent while traveling out west. A few more weeks wouldn't hurt them any.

Jeb started the morning off by hauling a load of stones from the nearby stream and then overlapping them into a rectangular shape, according to where he envisioned the fireplace would be. He then dug out a slight pit and gathered wood for their first fire, from which he baked a batch of biscuits. They enjoyed the warmth of the fire and kept it going into the afternoon and through the night, as the cool air spoke of the higher altitude.

When the cabin logs were sufficiently dry, the two men started measuring and cutting each pole according to their plan. Each log was notched with an adze before being set in place on top of the previous one. When the logs got too high to lift, Jeb rigged a rope and pulley, and used their mule, Ben, to pull each log up a ramp until it rolled over in place with a satisfying "thump". When they had the walls finished, Jeb worked on the front door, which he made from a few logs of white pine, which he and Andrew had cut into boards. The hinges were hand-carved from wood as well, and Jeb finished it off with a large sliding bolt on the inside. The next thing to do was to finish the roof, which would be covered with sod to help insulate the cabin during the winter months. Jeb made a travois with a few pine poles and Ben hauled load after load of sod from a nearby meadow. Andrew carefully placed the pieces next to each other, as if he were trying to complete a puzzle. Mostly due to the fact that Jeb couldn't seem to cut his pieces the same size, each load varied from one piece to the next. The only remaining task was to finish the stone fireplace and chink the walls. They hauled several loads of grass from the meadow and mixed it with the rich mud from the stream banks to create the mixture they used to plug the gaps in the logs. Jeb used a mixture similar to mortar, which he laid down between each layer of stones in the chimney. The heat from their evening fires dried the chimney well.

On the fourth week, when the cabin was complete, the two men stood back from it and took in the view of their new home.

"She sure is handsome," said Jeb. "Just look at her smooth walls and green roof. Best to take it in, 'cuz she won't always look this way."

"We'll take good care of her," answered Andrew.

"More'n likely, Andy, she'll take care of us this coming winter."

With several poles left over from the cabin, Andrew and Jeb started on building a food cache, which would keep their food off the ground. The two men dug holes in which the poles would sit. Then Jeb made a ladder out of one of the spruce poles and used it to work high off the ground, with Andrew steadying the bottom, in order to nail the boards in place for the walls and roof.

At fourteen feet off the ground, it would be hard for a bear to climb up and enter the cache without losing its grip on one of the poles. The cache would also keep the smell of smoked meat and fish out of their cabin.

"Well, Andy, the only thing left to do is to fill it up. If you're still set on using my old rifle to bag an elk, I say we head out tomorrow and see if we can spot one back in that big valley."

"You're on!" answered Andrew. "I'll pack up Ben and we'll head out first thing tomorrow."

The two men rode out at first light toward the valley. They reached the edge by mid-afternoon and set up camp where they could see any elk coming from the north or south end. For the rest of the afternoon they waited, trying to be silent and still. By the time the sun started to kiss the horizon, both of them were stiff from sitting still for so long.

"I don't think we're bagging anything today, partner," said Jeb.

"I'll get a fire goin' so we can get some food in our bellies before we turn in, if you'll set up that tarp across them alders."

By the time the fire was made and dinner was cooked, both Jeb and Andrew were pretty tired. They looked at the bright stars in the sky, which were starting to be obscured by a blanket of clouds blowing in from the west. They watched as it grew darker until there were hardly any stars left to see, then turned in for the night.

Andrew woke to the gentle, but cold sensation of snowflakes landing on the side of his forehead. He pulled his blanket up across his face, so that only his reddish brown mop of hair stuck out the top. The campfire had long since burnt down to just a few glowing coals and gave off a slow series of hisses as the snow flurries threatened to snuff it out completely.

Jeb snorted himself awake, as he often would do at the end of a series of long snores. He sat up, rubbed his eyes and mumbled something about coffee. Reaching over to the modest pile of branches the two men had stashed under their tarp, he grabbed the remainder in one large handful and placed them one at a time over the coals. Within a few minutes the fire was again burning, but did little to chase away the morning chill. It was several minutes later that Andrew sat up, after smelling coffee. The small pot hung from a hook on the iron tripod, whose three legs straddled the small pit. "You think this will keep going?" Andrew asked referring to the flurries.

"No, this is just cause we're up high, Down low it's probably rainin'," Jeb answered. "But I don't mind it as much as rain. I really hate bein' soaked to the bone. I'm gonna go get some more sticks, while they're still dry." Jeb grabbed his long, black powder rifle from beside him and used it like a walking stick to help pull himself up from his stiff position. He always kept powder and ball in the barrel, but rarely ever primed it to be fired.

"Remember, you said you'd come get me if you see any elk," said Andrew.

"Sure 'nuff," said Jeb, as he walked back-up into the alders.

It wasn't long before Jeb was back with a large armload of sticks from the alder thicket. The two men placed more wood on the fire as the snow continued to fall. Jeb taught Andrew how to fix up a batch of biscuits and then pulled a beat up deck of cards from his pack.

"You ever play any poker?"

"No, never had a reason to, I guess."

"Well, I'll be happy to teach ya'. It's a good game to pass the time, and an awful tempting game, when you have a pocketful of money."

Jeb dealt the first few hands face up, showing Andrew the combinations to look for. Then he shuffled the deck and pulled the brim of his hat down to meet his brow. "Okay, this here's a serious hand."

Jeb dealt the cards and peered at Andrews face. "Now don't go looking so disappointed! You're not supposed to show me what you might or might not have through your face. Here, look at me. This here's my poker face." Jeb squinted his eyes and tried to look serious; his bottom lip jutted forward slightly.

"Looks like you do when you're about to pass gas."

"Now is that a nice thing to say to your teacher? Pay attention to your cards. Whatta' ya' have?"

"Hmmm... Uh, I'll take three," said Andrew as he impishly copied Jeb's face and placed his discards down.

"I'll take two myself," said Jeb. Then he shifted to one side and expelled some of the gas from last night's beans.

"Ha! I told you that was your gas face."

"I just did that for effect. Whatta' ya' have in your hand?"

"I've got two sevens," answered Andrew.

"Got ya' beat, son, I got two... elk."

Jeb slowly put down his cards as he stared past Andrew into the valley below. "By golly, there's elk down there."

There, in the valley below them, a small herd of elk had come into view. Jeb estimated the distance to be about four hundred yards. Much too far to shoot from their camp, especially with the slope of the ridge making the distance harder to judge. He knew they'd need to close the gap to about a hundred yards, hoping to flank the herd as they drank from the stream and keep the wind in their favor.

Jeb grabbed his powder horn and uncorked the end. Reaching for the brass measure, which hung around his neck, he poured in the dark powder until it barely overflowed the measure. He then poured the powder down the barrel of his rifle and re-corked the horn. Taking one of his self-made lead bullets from his leather pouch, he showed Andrew how to place the end of it inside a thin layer of cloth before ramming the projectile down the barrel. A second small pouch held the copper caps, of which he took one and carefully, but firmly placed it on the firing nipple of the gun and gently lowered the hammer down on it. "She's ready to go now," said Jeb, as he handed the rifle to Andrew.

Andrew was surprised to feel the weight of the weapon. It was noticeably heavier than his shotgun.

"We'll leave the horses here," said Jeb. "They're close enough to pursue on foot, and with any luck from the wind, they may not have smelled us yet."

The two men used what cover there was, as they slowly made their way down the ridge into the valley below.

As they came within a few hundred yards of the herd, they could see there were two bulls. One noticeably bigger than the other. There were several cows and two calves that looked small enough to have been born just last spring. Every so often, one of the bulls would raise his head, trying to catch wind of any potential predators. The herd fed on the remaining sweet grass, as if they knew it wouldn't last once winter arrived. A few of the cows drank from a creek that flowed into a nearby pond.

"Once we're close enough, I'll give you a signal and you aim for one of the younger cows," Jeb whispered. "We ain't after no trophy bull, and they're much better eatin'."

Andrew and Jeb crawled on hands and knees through the waist-high grass and alder trees, as they flanked the herd. Andrew could smell the pungent odor of the herd, now just a hundred yards in front of him. The direction of the wind held as if ordered, blowing slow and steady in their faces. Jeb said nothing as he tapped Andrew on the shoulder and pointed at him, then motioned to a beaver-downed tree just a few yards in front of them at the edge of the small pond. He knew Jeb wanted him to move forward alone and use the log for cover and as a gun rest to steady his shot.

Andrew slowly made his way to the log and peered over the top of the end that was raised up higher, and was partially concealed by grass and goldenrod. He lifted the heavy rifle and rested the barrel on the highest end of the log, where it was barely attached to the pointed stump. He could see the hundreds of teeth marks left by the beaver on both stump and log. Slowly sliding the rifle forward, he felt the weight of the barrel balance between the breech and muzzle. Reaching his thumb up onto the hammer, he pulled the lever back past the first click, and then to the rearmost position. He held his breath, as if that might soften the noise of the hammer, fearing the great bull would hear the unnatural sound. The bull's head rose up again, but not able to catch Andrew's scent, he went back to feeding along the creek.

Andrew felt excited, but also nervous. He remembered his father, James, telling him where to aim on large deer, and how a smooth, steady pull on the trigger was important. He took aim on one of the smaller cows, as Jeb had instructed, lining up the front bead with the rear buckhorn sight. He slowly pulled the first of the two triggers, which clicked ever so softly. With the set trigger pulled, he moved his finger slowly to the rear trigger. Andrew knew the softest of pulls would cause the great gray barrel to erupt in a fury of noise and smoke.

Before he could pull the second trigger, the large bull elk suddenly started mating with one of the cows. This caused the other cows to move several yards from where they fed, as if trying to get away from the disruption of their meal. Andrew turned slowly to look back at Jeb, who merely shrugged his shoulders in admission to nature's drama set before them.

When the bull moved back to feeding, the small cow Andrew had targeted was now several yards to the left, and partially obscured by a much larger cow. He waited patiently as the wind held, keeping his finger clear of the second hair trigger. Finally, the young cow took a few steps forward and Andrew drew a bead on her flank. He barely felt the trigger under his finger as he planted the stock firmly into his shoulder. With slight pressure on the second trigger, the hammer came down on the cap. A slight crack was immediately followed by a loud boom! All the elk jumped in place, their muscles taught under their hides, as they all ran forward except one. The bull had turned, and ran head down at the log, which was Andrew's only shelter. The bull's great rack locked onto the log and broke it free from its pointed stump, sending the mass of wood up and over onto Andrew's legs. He knew he had little chance of jabbing the barrel into the great bull's face, to keep the thousand-pound animal from goring him with its great antlers.

As the bull bore its head forward, one of the antler tines jabbed into Andrew's lower leg. He screamed as the tine broke skin, but could not be driven deeper because the bull's antlers were bracketed by the log. Just as the bull freed his antlers from the log, a loud boom filled the air, and the great head of the bull rose to meet the new threat. Again, the loud noise echoed and the bull backed off. A third time, and the large male ran off, following the herd past the stream and up into the hills. Jeb worked the action of the Winchester one last time to expel the spent shell casing from the shotgun. "Hoowee... That was the last one in the chamber. I was about to use this ol' gal as a club."

Andrew, pinned on his back from the log that lay across his waist, looked up at Jeb. "How about getting this log off of me?" He could feel his ribs hurt as he spoke, and hoped none of them were broken. Jeb managed to lift one end of the log, so Andrew could slide out from under. Andrew moaned as he sat up and assessed his leg. It wasn't as bad as he feared, as the bone wasn't broken.

About sixty yards away, they could see the small cow on its side in the grass. Andrew's aim was true, and they would have enough meat for several months. They would celebrate with the best steaks they had eaten in a long time. Some meat could be smoked into jerky. Most of it would fill their food cache, promising meat throughout the cold winter. Jeb made two additional travois for the horses that were similar to the one pulled by Ben. Between the three animals, they would haul out roughly six hundred pounds of meat.

Jeb lashed all the meat on tight and covered it with the skin of the elk to further protect it from the sun.

Ben was first in line as they headed across the meadow and through the woods on the trail back to the cabin. Jeb would pat him on his rump every so often, so he wouldn't slow up too much.

Andrew led the other two horses behind Jeb. He carried an extra forty pounds of meat in his own pack, wanting to leave as little behind as possible, in case the remains were discovered by a predator before they could return.

Chapter XVIII

The grizzly sow moved up the slope of the mountain, looking back at her cub every few minutes to make sure he didn't fall too far behind. She had borne the cub the prior winter in the security of their den. The past eight months she had spent nursing her cub with her rich milk. Towards the end of that time she had shown the cub how to feed on particular grasses and berries, salmon from the river and the occasional deer or young elk. Only during the past week had she begun to ween her cub entirely off of her milk, and start him on the diet that he would follow for the remainder of his days.

The two took their time as they walked up the slope, looking for the Miller moths, which were a high calorie treat, and could be found underneath rocks, which they turned over with ease. There would be much more to teach her young cub over the next year-and-a-half they would spend together.

Vulnerable to predators, such as wolves, mountain lions and especially other male grizzlies, the sow paid extra close attention to the cub's whereabouts and would stop to smell the air, making sure they did not accidentally get too close to the territory of a rogue male.
As they worked their way along the rocky slope that ran adjacent to the valley below, the big sow suddenly stopped and caught the odor of something that smelled promising. She knew the scent all too well, but could not see where it was coming from. She stood up on her hind legs to better see what might be in front of her that carried on the breeze.

The scent she smelled was elk. Not just any elk, but an elk that had been recently killed or maimed.

The scent of the blood triggered a hunger in her that needed to be addressed. With the winter months coming soon, an elk down would be an easy meal she might be able to claim. She looked at her cub and was challenged by the decision of whether to proceed or veer away. The kill might be guarded by wolves or even another bear.

Again the breeze blew the scent toward her, and she realized that the animal was not still, but in fact, was moving. Perhaps the wounded elk was just up ahead of her, which would be an enticing meal for her and her cub.

She walked her cub up the slope, past the scree of rocks and into the woods filled with pine, fir and aspen. She quickened her pace as the scent grew stronger, with her cub trotting at her heels. Again she stood up on her hind legs, quietly peering toward the cliff face ahead, her face framed by the cone-laden branches of a Douglas fir.

It was then that she saw where the scent was coming from.

A short distance away, Jeb and Andrew moved their horses and mule up the path along the bottom of the rocky cliff face.

Only a mile from the cabin, they had just to cross the stream up ahead and they would be filling their cache for the winter.

Jeb patted Ben firmly on the rump to keep him moving forward, and then turned and walked back down the trail to help Andrew with the two horses.

Just as Jeb reached Andrew, the two men heard Ben bray from up ahead. Andrew quickly grabbed his Winchester and ran ahead of Jeb to see what the commotion was about. As he rounded the corner of the rocky slope in front of him, Andrew could see Ben had broken free from the travois. He seemed to have been clawed on his right rear quarter, and was running around the corner of the cliff face, out of view. The travois had snapped off its leather harness after catching on the base of a fir tree. Only forty yards away stood an adult grizzly with its cub only feet from her. She clawed at the cotton canvas which covered the elk meat, exposing the fresh haunches of skinned meat. She circled the travois, as if claiming it hers. Andrew knew best not to advance on the sow and her cub. He slowly backed down the trail until he was around the corner and out of view, where Jeb waited with the horses, his rifle loaded and ready.

"Lost the first travois of meat to a grizzly," said Andrew. "We best not head back that way. She's more than either of us can handle and she has a cub with her, too."

"Did she kill Ben?"

"No. I seen Ben run off around the rocky bend up ahead. Looks like she might have got a paw on him before he broke free. I've never seen Ben move that fast before."

"We best look for him later or we risk losing all this meat. We'll head south for a bit, and cross the stream further down, then head north to the cabin."

It was hours later that they reached the cabin. With only four hours of daylight remaining, Jeb carried each of the remaining haunches and both sets of ribs up into the cache. The cool night air would preserve the meat well, and they could build their smoking racks tomorrow.

Jeb insisted on using the remaining daylight to ride back and look for Ben. Andrew offered to stay at the cabin and start cooking up some elk stew over their new fireplace, so they could have dinner upon his return. Jeb asked to borrow the Winchester and loaded it with double-ought buck, just in case he was surprised on the trail by the big bear. When Jeb reached the stream, he crossed and rode west toward the base of the cliff face; being extra careful to approach the area slowly where Andrew had seen the grizzly. Jeb could see the shape of the travois up ahead. As he rode up very slowly, he could see the remains of the meat covered with dirt, pieces of branches and pine needles. Clearly the bears had eaten quite a bit and moved on, partially burying their cache before they left. Jeb listened for a moment before trotting away. The last thing he wanted was to run across a sleeping bear with her cub.

The sun was lower on the horizon, and in the woods the lack of sunlight was further pronounced. He could barely make out some of Ben's tracks, as they rounded the base of the cliff face and headed northwest. Jeb climbed down from his horse and walked ahead slowly, so he could better make out the tracks. He could judge the straddle of the tracks, noting where Ben had slowed to a walk. As he followed the trail that wound left then right, following the base of the cliff face, he noticed a large section of rock that must have slid down the mountain hundreds of years ago. The giant slab, which must weigh several hundred tons created an A-frame shape as it leaned against the existing portion of the lower cliff face. Moss covered large sections of it, and a tree grew out from the top of the A-frame. The tracks Jeb followed seem to go straight into the opening made by the large slab of rock. Jeb could not see in too far, due to lack of light, but could hear breathing from within the cave. He called out to Ben, and could hear Ben answer back with a sound that seemed more like a sigh than a bray. Jeb tied his horse to an aspen sapling before heading inside. He lit one of the matches that he used with his pipe and slowly walked further inside. As he travelled about twenty feet inside, he could make out the shape of Ben. The ceiling of the cave was barely taller than the mule, and Jeb had to duck in sections to avoid hitting his head. Ben must have ducked in here, not knowing how to get back out. It was tight quarters, as Jeb tried to get Ben turned around and headed out in the right direction. When Jeb finally got Ben all the way out, he could see the claw marks that created deep parallel troughs in Ben's hide, and the dried blood on his coat from where the grizzly took a swipe at him.

"Don't worry, Ben," Jeb said in a calming voice. "You're gonna be okay. I'll fix you up like new as soon as we get back. Jeb tied off Ben to the horse's saddle as they rode back to the cabin. The sun was now below the trees and it would be fully dark soon. Jeb wondered if the cave he had just been in was indeed the mine they had been looking for. He had every intention of bringing Andrew back there tomorrow to find out.

Chapter XIX

"Whatta' ya' suppose could be in there?" asked Jeb the next morning, as he popped the hot biscuits out of the dutch oven that hung over the fire.
"I don't know," answered Andrew. "We don't even know if that really is the mine. Place could be filled with rattlers for all we know."
"Come on now Andy, there's got to be a reason that Ben ran in there. I'm tellin' ya', we were supposed to find that mine."
"Ben ran in there because he was trying not to get eaten, Jeb!"
"Oh shucks, you ain't no fun. Here, have a biscuit." Jeb threw the hot bread into Andrew's hand and laughed as he shifted it from hand to hand as it cooled. Andrew was just as excited as Jeb that they had actually found a cave, but he wasn't about to let Jeb know that.
"I oiled the lantern, so we can head out right after breakfast," said Jeb. "I got the pickaxe and shovels tied onto Ben, too."
"Don't you think Ben needs a rest Jeb, after all he's been through?"
"Heck, Andy, Ben's as tough as nails. He'll be just fine. Here, take a slab of bacon for that biscuit and we'll hit the trail."
Andy took his Winchester and a few extra shells as the two men left the warm cabin.

Arriving at the spot where the bear had claimed Ben's travois of elk meat, there were no scraps left to be seen. Even the bones had been carried off by coyotes or foxes during the night. When they reached the cave, Jeb took the lantern from his saddle horn and lit its wick. The walls of the cave glistened from moisture as Jeb and Andrew walked inside. The entrance seemed to be about three feet wide, but opened up to about five feet once they were a little further inside. There were many scrapes on the walls that were probably from pickaxes, and several wooden beams had been wedged in place, along with cross braces that seemed to have the purpose of keeping the ceiling from crumbling. As Jeb held the lantern at arms end, he could see that the tunnel continued and turned slightly to the west. It was narrower than the main part of the cave, and the wooden shoring stopped about six feet in.

"I'm not so sure we should go too far, Jeb. We don't know how old these braces are, and they stop just a few feet in. I don't know anything about mining, do you?"

"Not really. I done some panning a few years back, Andy, but I don't see anything here that looks like gold. Mostly gray. The rust colored streaks might mean there's some iron deposits. But this cloudy stuff looks like veins of quartz running through it." Jeb handed the lantern to Andrew and walked down the narrower part of the tunnel with pickaxe in hand.

"You just stay there and hold the lantern so I can take a few swings at this quartz. Maybe there will be some gold or silver behind it."

"Maybe this mine's been played out, Jeb. Could be there is no more color."

"Only one way to find out, Andy. Hand me that bucket."

Andrew passed the wooden bucket to Jeb and held the lantern as far into the tunnel as he could without walking in deeper. Jeb took several swings at the hard cave wall. Small pieces of rock shot from the wall and landed on the cave floor. Several more swings removed a large chunk, causing him to jump back so it didn't land on his toes. Jeb worked for five minutes swinging the pick without stopping, until he ran short of breath and wiped the sweat from his brow.

"Not too easy to breath in here," he huffed. "Let's get some fresh air and see what we have."

Jeb bent over and used his hands to scoop up several handfuls of rock into the bucket. Then the two men walked out into the daylight and tipped the bucket over on the ground. Dull gray pieces of rock, mixed with what looked to be quartz, but with a blue tinge, rolled out. Jeb ran his fingers through the mix, trying to separate most of the clear and cloudy rocks from the solid gray ones. He picked up one particular piece that stood out from the rest. It was about two inches in diameter and a small section of it looked like it was the color of a lake in the summertime.

"Look here, Andy. What do ya' make of this?"

Jeb held the stone up to the sun to give it a good look, then handed it to Andrew. "I like the dark blue part," said Andrew. "Pretty piece of quartz, but probably not worth anything."

"We should chip off some more of these blue rocks and start into Anaconda tomorrow. There's likely someone in town who'll know what this blue stuff is."

Andrew and Jeb took turns with the pickaxe, working for over an hour until they were able to separate six small rocks that contained portions of the dark blue color. Jeb carefully placed them in his pack and loaded the tools onto Ben. The two rode back to the cabin, each with a good appetite for dinner.

That evening, Andrew and Jeb talked about the blue rocks and decided it would be best to ride into town in the morning and see if they could get any advice on what they might be.

The next day, Jeb and Andrew had a discussion with Charles Evans, the manager at Anaconda Bank. He said they would need to have their samples sent out and examined by a professional gemologist.

It would take several weeks to get the samples back with a proper appraisal. Mr. Evans gave Jeb the name of a gemologist in San Francisco, who could not only tell Jeb if the samples were rich in some type of mineral, but who also worked with a jeweler who might possibly purchase any key stones. Jeb and Andrew boxed up a pound of various rocks from the mine that showed hints of the blue color and sent it off as advised.

Three weeks later, a letter addressed to Jeb Slate arrived at the Anaconda post office. Jeb couldn't read most of it, so he handed the letter over to Andrew to read.

Dear Mr. Slate,

We have examined the samples you have provided to us and have concluded that they do contain varied amounts of the gem called sapphire.

While the stone samples you sent do contain color, there were no usable stones in your deposits. We would, though, like to propose purchasing future samples from you, should they contain larger, useable stones of distinct color. We look forward to making future arrangements with you.

Sincerely,

Jacob Moreau

Gemologist

San Francisco, California

"Sapphires... Imagine us, being the owners of a sapphire mine. Why, we'll be so rich Andy, we won't have to worry about anything ever again. Why, we'll just sit back on our front porch as a bunch of workers plant our crops and chop our wood and... hey, what's the matter? Aren't you excited?"

Andrew was staring blankly into the fireplace, then looked across the table to Jeb.

"I'm happy for us Jeb, but... well, what if we don't find any other sapphires? Mr. Moreau said that we'd need better stones for them to be worth anything."

"They'll come, Andy. They'll come with lots of hard work. Yes-siree, teamwork Andy. You'll see."

"But we've got to eat in the meantime, and our money won't hold out through the winter. I guess what I'm saying is that I'm fixing to go back into town tomorrow and get me a job."

"A real job? Like what, sweeping out the livery?"

"Maybe, Jeb. But I have blacksmith experience and I can do just about any chore that you can think of. That way, I can at least get us the food we need while we're working the mine. Maybe I can work it so I'm only in town a few days and ride back here to help you the remainder of the week."

"Well, I guess so." Jeb stirred his beans as he looked down at his plate. "I can bring you a cigar every once in a while, too."

Jeb smiled and filled his mouth with a large scoop of beans.

The next day Andrew started off early and rode down into town, stopping at the blacksmith's shop, where a man was forging a large door hinge. The man stood about six feet tall. He had a stout chest and some of the hair on his forearms was scorched in places. His leather apron showed many marks from contact with red hot metal, and his shirt sleeves had a few burn holes.

Huge sparks shot forth from under his hammer, as he pounded the large piece of iron over the horn of the anvil, which created the curve of one of the two hinge pieces.

"Excuse me, sir, I'm looking for a job," shouted Andrew over the consistent, loud hammering.

The blacksmith held the piece of iron up toward his face and examined the hinge plate, scrutinizing its shape.

"Hmmmf!" he exclaimed, as if either disappointed in his work or perhaps over the fact that he was interrupted.

The smithy placed the hinge back in the coals and turned to Andrew.

"What's your name?"

"Andrew Thompson, sir."

"I'm Hardy Anderson. Ever do any smithin'?"

"Yessir, back in Altamont, New York I worked for a blacksmith. Mostly shoeing horses and forging small pieces of hardware."

"Here, look at this."

Hardy held up a brown, wrinkled piece of paper that was covered with so many different rough pencil sketches, it was hard for Andrew to tell what he was referring to.

"This here."

Hardy pointed to a sketch of a door hinge, then motioned to the hot coals. "I already started it. Let's see if you can finish it."

Andrew put on one of the leather work aprons that Hardy had hanging on the wall. Grabbing an appropriate set of tongs, he lifted the red hot metal from the fire and examined his next steps. He reworked the piece several times by burying it in the hot coals and carefully placing his blows from the hammer on target. He understood how the homemade forging would work and what part would be the hinge pin, so he hammered the hot metal around it. Andrew felt confident that his piece closely matched the drawing. With a loud hiss, the hinge was plunged into a large barrel of water where it hardened. He then placed the still steaming hinge on the workshop table and looked to Hardy for approval.

"Not bad," Hardy said. "I could show you how to save a few heat cycles and cut down your forging time."

"Yessir," replied Andrew, eager to learn as well as get paid.

"Okay, then. If you can be here Friday at eight a.m., I'll put you to work a few days a week to start."

"That suits me fine, sir. Our cabin is several hours ride north, so maybe I can work two days while I stay in town?"

"Sure. You can work Friday and Saturday. I don't pay by the hour, but will work out a price with you depending on what you're hammering and how well you do. Wasted metal gathers no pay. I keep an organized shop and I'll be looking for you to clean up, as well as prepare the following week's wood bin for charcoal before you head back north. Sound good?"

"I'll be here Friday at eight, sir."

"Call me Hardy."

"Yessir, I mean Hardy."

Andrew couldn't wait to tell Jeb about his new job. He stopped by the general store to get a cigar to surprise him with. When he walked in, he saw Willow, looking as beautiful as he remembered from his first day in the store. He was immediately drawn to her blue eyes and long dark hair.

"Hello again," he said to Willow.

"Hello, Andrew. How was your trip up into the hills?"

"Successful, thank you. Jeb and I got an elk, but more importantly, we built a cabin on a little piece of land. Just a few hours ride north from here. Turns out we're going to mine a claim."

"That's wonderful. I'm very happy for you both."

"I also got a job down the street Fridays and Saturdays helping Hardy Anderson, the blacksmith. It's only for two days a week, but I was thinking since you like to ride, maybe we could go riding together this Friday before I start work, if you'd like to?"

"Well, I think that would be nice. Sure, I'll ride with you. What time should I meet you?"

"How about seven in front of the store?"

"That will be fine," said Willow with a smile.

Andrew waved as he walked out the door. It wasn't until he was on his horse and several miles down the trail, that he realized he never got the cigar he had intended to buy for Jeb. He smiled and shook his head as he gave his horse a kick and galloped up the trail into the hills.

When Friday came, Andrew was up before the sunrise, and rode down to town to meet Willow. Arriving a few minutes late, Willow was waiting out in front of the store on her chestnut gelding. "Good morning," said Andrew. "I'm sorry I'm a little late. It's a long ride to town."

"Are you still okay to ride?" Willow asked.

"I sure am," replied Andrew. "That is, as long as we're not racing."

"Follow me then. I have a special spot I'd like to show you."

Willow led the way as they rode off into the hills. In a few minutes, they reached the spot where the stream formed a pool under the shade of a bur oak. Willow climbed down from her horse and Andrew did the same. Grabbing a blanket from behind her saddlebag, Willow spread it on the ground next to the rolling stream. She then pulled out a small bag she had carried in one of the saddlebags. "Would you like some corn bread? I baked it just last night."

"I sure would. I rode off this morning before Jeb could fix breakfast."

"Does your friend Jeb like to cook?"

"Yes, but he's partial to fixing the same things, so if I want something different, I'll usually chip in and do my share. We pretty much split up the responsibilities of running the camp."

"So tell me, did you grow up around this area?" asked Willow.

"No, I actually grew up back east; that's where my mother and father are. My real father passed away in a logging accident, but my stepfather, James, is a wonderful person. I just decided one day it was time to see the west. That way I could decide whether it was everything I hoped it was, and if I could make a life here, or head back east. I met Jeb along the way. Aside from an old woman who helped me when I was hurt, he's pretty much the only friend I have out in these parts, well, until now."

"Thank you," Willow said with a smile.

"So, you come here every morning?" asked Andrew.

"Yes, just about every morning. I've never shown anyone this spot before today. I love the running of the water and how the oak overlooks the pool. It's a place where I can come watch a sunrise or look at how the wind blows the grass or just stare at the clouds in the sky and not think about life in town."

"Well, it sure is a beautiful place. Thank you for sharing it."

"You're welcome."

"Have you always lived in this town?"

"Ever since I was a little girl. You see, I was adopted when I was young by my foster parents, John and Lucy Gaithers. My real mother was said to be Shoshone; I only have a few memories of her face. My real father was said to be a white soldier. I was told he died in the war. I guess I was brought to the adoption agency because my mother wanted a better life than she could have given me on her own. It's kind of hard not knowing who your parents were, but I am very fortunate to have a good father who loves me."

Andrew reached inside his shirt and pulled out the antler medallion, which hung around his neck. "I wasn't sure the right way to do this Willow, but I think this might belong to you."

He reached around in back of his neck and untied the leather necklace, then placed it in her hands. "Why, it's beautiful. It's a bird!"

"It's actually a meadowlark. Hiitoo' is how they say the word in Shoshone. I believe the man who gave us this might have been your grandfather."

"My grandfather? How do you know this?"

"Jeb and I came across a man called Sky With No Clouds. He was an old Shoshone brave who said he was searching for the child of his daughter, Meadowlark, whom he thought had gone to live with the Crow. Unfortunately, Sky was killed when he tried to cross a swollen stream. When we buried him we kept the necklace, hoping we could find Meadowlark and her child. While traveling north, Jeb I stopped at a camp on the Crow reservation, where we found a woman who knew Meadowlark and told of her having a child, whom she claimed to have named Willow."

"I cannot believe this was my grandfather's. I mean, I do... but for you to have found me?"

"I thought the same thing. But as my mother says back home, some things are just meant to be. Here, let me put it on for you, if you don't mind."

"Please do," said Willow, as a few tears ran down her cheek. Willow held the pendant in her hand and admired it for several minutes, saying nothing, but just smiling.

"Thank you, Andrew Thompson!" And with that, Willow leaned over and wrapped her arms around Andrew. Her warm hug felt tender and loving, and Andrew realized he had missed that feeling. His mind jumped back for a second to the train station right before he left home. He smiled at Willow, feeling warm and happy inside.

"Well, we should probably be going. I'm sure your store will be opening soon, and I need to be at Mr Anderson's by eight."

The couple rode back to town in the morning light through the blowing grass that seemed to move in unison.

"Maybe we can ride again tomorrow?" Andrew asked. "I'll be staying in town until tomorrow afternoon."

"That sounds wonderful. Seven o'clock?"

"Seven it is!"

Chapter XX

Andrew and Jeb worked hard during the late summer and unearthed many blue stones from the mountainside. They got better at figuring which stones were most likely to be valuable and which ones were likely to be worthless. Even though they had deposited many hundreds of dollars in the Anaconda Bank, Jeb still had several other bags of stones hidden in various spots of the cave. He rarely took them to town because he was afraid people might try and locate where his mine was hidden. He had heard tales of men who would jump a claim when the owners weren't working it. So he only took stones in to Anaconda once a month. With winter on their doorstep, Jeb figured he'd just let the bags of stones pile up and take them to town in one large haul in the spring.

The second week of October was upon them, and the cold chill of winter could be felt blowing its way into the cave. The men had excavated their tunnel farther into the cave, following the vein of sapphire wherever it decided to lead them. Right and left turns within the mine helped block some of the wind, as it entered the tunnel. A week later, the men could see their breath as they spoke. They had continued to cut trees and then hewed them with a broad axe to make the necessary posts to shore up the tunnel where they worked, lest they stay there forever under an avalanche of profit. Once in a while some dust would fall from the ceiling and Andrew would get quite nervous, but Jeb reassured him they were safe. They would warm their hands on the lanterns and made coffee over a small fire, so as not to put too much smoke into the tunnel.

After an end to each week's hard work, Andrew would head into town to forge at the blacksmith's shop, making time to see Willow whenever he could. They were now steady companions for morning rides in the early sunlight. Sometimes he would head over to her house in the hills above town and stay for dinner. Mr Gaithers liked Andrew and appreciated his hard work ethic, but also liked the kindness he had shown Willow. Andrew enjoyed her company very much, and found it more difficult after each Saturday evening to head back up to the cabin. It was the first week of November when Jeb called out to Andy as he finished hewing another post. "Andy, come see this thing!" he shouted. Andrew figured he's finally found a sapphire as big as his fist and they could live comfortably from here on out.

When Andrew ran in, Jeb pointed to the dull gray boulder that was taking shape in the tunnel. "Everywhere I dig, I just keep finding this type of stone. It's much harder than the other rock and seems to be almost as wide as the tunnel itself."

"Maybe the vein of sapphire has run its course," said Andrew meekly, trying not to upset Jeb too much, but almost wishing that it had.

"Hardly, Andy, hardly," Jeb trumpeted back. "This old boulder is just like a door and we're gonna have to go around or through to get to the other side. I just know there's more sapphire on the other side."

"I dunno, Jeb, looks like it might take weeks just to get around it. I'll keep helping you, partner, but I just wouldn't get your hopes up too much. Look at the bags we have in here. All totaled, they've got to be worth thousands of dollars. We won't be rich like them cattle barons, but we can fish and hunt and still live pretty comfortably with what we can put in the bank."

Jeb just crossed his arms and stood firm. "Andy, I know there's much more in here. We just have to put in the hard work to make it pay."

"Okay, Jeb, whatever you say. I'm going to head back to the cabin and fix us some dinner. Please try and be along soon."

As Andrew walked back toward the entrance of the mine, he could see nature painting a picture in front of him, framed by the dark walls of the tunnel. Leaves blew past the opening and he could hear the winds howling. As he stepped outside, rain started to fall at an angle, and a few branches from a nearby aspen fell to the ground beside him. He quickly gathered the reins of the mule and led him into the mine, out of the rain.

Running back down the torch lit tunnel, he called to Jeb to come quick. Jeb walked to the entrance and looked up at the dark gray sky, turning his head from one direction to the other and then looked back at Andrew. "Air's much colder this evening and I wouldn't be surprised to see some snow. Let's knock off for today and get Ben back to the cabin."

"Now you're making sense, Jeb."

Andrew quickly ran back and snuffed out the lanterns, and the two men headed home. On their way, the wind grew stronger and each had to tie their handkerchief around their hat and under their chin to keep it from being blown off. Halfway back, the rain turned to a thick, heavy snow and then to sleet, which stung their faces when driven by the wind. Ben locked in his hooves a few times, only to be dealt a quick slap by Jeb, to remind him who was boss. "Move it, Ben, you damn stubborn mule! We got no time to play games."

Andrew felt badly that Ben had to take some abuse, but he knew Jeb was right in using a heavy hand with him. The temperature was still dropping, and there was no telling how cold it was going to get. By the time they reached the cabin, Andrew's hands barely felt functional. He kept switching his shotgun from one hand to the other, tucking the free hand under his armpit for what little warmth there was. Neither man had planned for this drastic change of weather, and had left their wool coats in the cabin. They only had on their flannel shirts, which were now thoroughly soaked by the wet snow and sleet.

Andrew grabbed an armful of wood from the pile on the porch as Jeb led Ben around back under the roof shelter. Kindling fell from Andrew's arms as he had grabbed too many and his numb hands had lost most of their dexterity. Opening the old stove they had bought used from Hardy Anderson, he worked as fast as he could, first using birch bark and then the kindling to prep the fire. He thought of how helpful it would have been to have the fire ready to be lit, and promised himself he would prep the stove that way in the future. He reached into the tin match box and lit the tinder, just as Jeb walked into the cabin, closing the door behind him as he stamped the snow off his boots.

Jeb and Andrew both knelt beside the stove, saying nothing and only rubbing their extremities as they listened to the familiar sound of the metallic "ping," as the old stove began to warm up. The more flames grew and the fire took hold, the faster the pinging sound became. They looked at each other and laughed, knowing that they were safe from the storm and would soon be warm. The wind outside howled and a few whistles could be heard from areas of the cabin where more chinking was in need. As Andrew looked out the small window, he could see the trees swaying back and forth under the high winds. Soon it would be dark and time to turn in. The work in the mine made the days seem short, and the reduced hours of sunlight made them seem even more so. Jeb put some coffee on the stove and placed a bottle of whiskey on the table in which to sweeten it with. Andrew wiped down his Winchester as best he could and rested it against his bunk. Dinner was going to be jerky and biscuits, as neither had thought to make preparations for hunting, being so preoccupied with the mine. Andrew pulled his journal from under his bunk and wrote about the snow storm. How it was just as dangerous as it was beautiful. Old man winter had introduced himself in a bold way, and he was most likely planning on staying a while. It would be the last time either one would head to the mine without a wool coat on their back or some game aging on the front post.

With the exception of Jeb's snoring, the morning was quiet and Andrew climbed from his bunk to look out the small window. He continued his journal entry from the night before. It looked as though three feet of snow had fallen during the night, and the trees, which had most of their leaves still on them, were transformed into bent and broken forms under the weight of the snow, like men bending over to tie their boots. He could see a hawk circling above the trees in hopes of finding a hare that had not yet grown his winter white coat. Andrew stoked the fire in the stove and checked his boots to see if they were fully dry.

Jeb grumbled as he turned over, grabbing the wool blanket and covering his head with it. The nearly empty whiskey bottle bore testament to his many cups of coffee last night and now he was paying the price. His boots now dry, Andrew dressed and went outside to check on Ben and the horses, and feed them breakfast. He brought his shotgun with him in hopes of turning up some grouse during a morning walk through the pines,. After tending to the livestock, he looked off to the north. The pinkish sky glowed, and the clouds were giving way to the morning sun. His footsteps in the snow seemed to echo off the heavy laden pines as he walked between them. Looking back at the cabin, he could see the smoke curling up from the chimney with the mountains rising behind it in the distance, and he wondered how long he would live this way. Maybe for many years to come. Maybe forever. He couldn't imagine a more beautiful place to call his home. As he turned back toward the pines, he thought he saw something flutter up ahead. He walked cautiously forward, slightly bending over and trying not to make any sudden moves. He then heard the drumming of a grouse. He looked through the pines to see that the small musician had dusted off his favorite log and was drumming away for a mate. As Andrew approached, he was given away by the crunch of one of his steps. The grouse flew straight up and banked to the right, with Andrew trying to draw a bead on his breakfast. He swung and fired the Winchester as the shot missed the evasive grouse, only to fully contact the pine next to him. Cascades of snow fell from the great tree, each branch releasing more snow onto the one below it, until a heavy white shower from above was released upon him. "Uugggh!" shouted Andrew as the avalanche of snow hit him, with a generous amount finding its way down his back. He shook off what he could and wiped off his Winchester with his gloves before seeing a hawk claim the prize he had wanted. It was an hour later that Andrew's luck eventually changed, as he walked back to the cabin with a hare in hand. He then cleaned it for their breakfast.

"I like this place," said Andrew, speaking to Jeb who was only partially awake. "You should have seen the morning sky. It was beautiful!"

"Hmmph" was Jeb's only reply, pulling the blanket farther over his head. Having cleaned the rabbit, Andrew made a stew, just as his father, James, had showed him years earlier. Sitting by the warm stove, he then opened his journal and wrote more about the trip from the mine to the cabin through the surprising weather. He wrote about the grouse that escaped, and the hare that didn't. He even wrote about old Jeb, who snored too much and had again fallen back to sleep.

Chapter XXI

During the month of November it seemed to snow almost every other day. Andrew had never seen so much snow before in his life. He and Jeb had shoveled paths in the deep white powder to get to the outhouse they had built, as well as to fetch water and feed their livestock. It snowed until the cabin window was half covered, and the two drew straws to see which one had to go up on the roof and shovel that as well. It seemed as though as soon as they had finished one task, there was another waiting to be done. November ran into December, and the two men had cut their work at the mine in half. They rested every other day to conserve supplies and to rest the animals, for they both required more food just to keep themselves warm and fit. Once in a while Jeb would head down to the river and trap for beaver.

Back in town, Hardy had cut off Andrew's work at the blacksmith shop for the winter, and wouldn't have him back until spring. He desperately wanted to see Willow at the general store. When he last saw her, she had given him a guitar from the store, so he could have something to keep his mind busy during the long, slow days. Over time he taught himself a few chords, and figured one day he'd write Willow a song of her very own. When Andrew dreamed of her, it was if he was whisked away from being holed up in that cabin for so long. Just the memory of her face had a way of making him forget about the snow and the sapphire mine, and any other thing that might be worrying him. Jeb, on the other hand, made a point of going to town once a week. His visits would largely consist of stopping at the Triple Dutch for several hours of cards and whiskey, and he sometimes would not show back up at the cabin until the following day. Andrew knew that playing cards with a glass of whiskey was one sure way to ease Jeb's cabin fever, as he had admitted to having a harder time adjusting to the cold winters with each passing year.

But it wasn't just Jeb and Andrew that were having a tough time. The local wildlife also had to adjust to the early winter that was thrust upon them. Bears had gone into hibernation for the winter, while the deer were trying to dig with their hooves to find any grasses that remained. They ate all the low-lying young branches from the aspen and birch trees that they could reach. The mother fox fared better; she ate well by taking advantage of those critters who weren't so fortunate against the cold. Sometimes she would find a bird who had fallen from a tree during the freezing nights. One evening she found four mice all huddled together under the snow against a pine tree. She had seen several harsh winters, but this was the worst in several years. She would often look to outwit her old nemesis, the crow, to keep him from finding a scrap of food before she did. She would sometimes even approach the new log cabin on the edge of her territory, looking for scraps of any kind, like a discarded fish head, or a gut pile from a recent deer kill.

It was early December when she approached the cabin just after the break of day. She was on her way back to her den from an unsuccessful evening hunt. She approached slowly, keeping her body low and against the wood pile on the side of the cabin, almost perfectly blending in with the pieces of split fir, aspen and cedar. As she rounded the corner to look for the possibility of a quick meal, she froze at the sound of the voices coming from within the cabin. They slowly grew louder and more pronounced, causing her to jump back and then run off through the snow covered pines.

"Why's it you who gets to go to town, Jeb? Run outta whiskey again?"

"Listen youngin', you were the one who said you liked it here. You who likes the snowfall, all five feet of it, and who likes to tend to the fire and keep it going. You who likes the sound of the wind, the coyotes in the distance, the cracking of the ice on the lake and any other long-winded foolishness you're always spoutin' off, as you're tryin' to learn that guitar you brought back from town, or writin' in that silly book. Did you not write all these things, or was I just imaginin' them?"

"Yeah, I wrote those things; and I thought you liked when I played the guitar. Hey, wait just a minute. You were reading my journal!"

"Look, Andy, I was bored and wanted somethin' to look at. Besides, you know I don't read that good anyway. One can only be alone so long in the same surroundings, before they need somethin' else to do... and don't forget you agreed to come along on this trip of your own doing. No one forced you to come along. I said I'll be back in two days, and two days it'll be. Besides, the mule listens to me and you're the one handy with the shotgun, should we have any unwanted visitors."

"Look Jeb, you've been to town two times since November, and I've done right by you to look after the camp and our shares. Never once have I cheated you or tampered with the goods. Heck, you never even take them to the bank any more. You just let them pile up in that cave like some pirate's treasure."

"What the hell does that mean? That if I leave this time, you WILL tamper with 'em?" Jeb placed his palm squarely on top of his stag handled knife.

"No, you fool," said Andrew. "Just that you trust me to guard everything here, and now I'm askin' you to trust me to head to town and back."

"Give me one reason, why I should let you go when you're the one who's in love with these woods and damn well knows I need the comfort of a good saloon and a bottle of whiskey more than you." Andrew paused as he stirred the wood in the iron stove. Adding a few more sticks, he shut the door and stared at the glow through the five slots.

"Willow," he said quietly, almost whispering.

"Who? Speak up dammit, you know I don't hear good no more!"

"Willow Gaithers!" he shouted. "The girl from the dry goods store who helped us with our possibles."

"That skinny, dark haired gal that barely said a word? Well, if it's comfortin' you want son, I'll fix ya' up with Fat Sally at the Triple Dutch. She'll work the knots out of your line."

"I don't want Fat Sally, Jeb. I want to go see Willow. So how's about it?"

"You can see that skinny twig next month, I'm headin' out."

Jeb swung his pack over his left shoulder as he grabbed for the handle of the cabin door.

Before he could pull it fully open, Andrew kicked it shut from beside him. Jeb turned around and glared with that "I mean business" look Andrew had only seen when they fought off the train robbers back in Two Gap Pass... and the time Jeb beat that damn stubborn mule within an inch of his hide with a willow switch.

Grabbing Andrew squarely by the shirt front with one fist, Jeb swung his other bear paw at Andrew, catching the side of his face, spinning him halfway around and knocking him face down onto his own bunk. The guitar Andrew had kept tucked above his bunk came loose and landed on his head. The strings singing an unheard-of chord.

"You're stayin'!" was all Jeb said as he swung open the cabin door and walked outside to retrieve his snowshoes from the porch post.

As he slipped one foot into the binding, Jeb was tackled by Andrew and they both fell forward into the cold, waist-deep snow.

Andrew threw a fist into Jeb's face, or at least where he thought Jeb's face to be, as it was buried beneath the obscuring fluff, then followed it with another to Jeb's ribs. Standing up, he felt bad as Jeb gasped for air. It was always like that with him after an argument or fight. First the red hot anger, and then the uncomfortable pity, as if he were ashamed for his actions.

Jeb rose slowly as he caught his breath with one knee and one hand still down in the snow. Then, quicker than Andrew expected, Jeb launched his head into Andrew's midsection like a charging bull, sending them both right back through the cabin door. As their momentum carried them backwards, Andrew was able to wrap his right arm around Jeb's neck, which kept him in his bent-over position while the other hand grabbed the seat of his buckskins as he slammed Jeb's head into the back of the cabin wall. Jeb fell to the dirt floor, dazed and bleeding from his top knot.

"I'm sorry, Jeb, but I'm goin' this time, and I won't take no for an answer."

"I guess you really do like that skinny twig," Jeb said, half out of breath and dabbing a few fingers on his head where his white hair was now covered with a small spot of red. "Do me a favor, will ya'?"

"I guess... what?"

"Just bring me back a bottle of whiskey and a good cigar."

"I guess a tired ol' man needs his evening drink and smoke," said Andrew.

Once outside, Andrew placed the snowshoes on his feet, packed a few beaver pelt rolls on the mule and headed southwest into the pines.

As he reached the top of the hill onto the flat, he could hear the echo of Jeb's voice from behind. "Make that two bottles and two cigars!"

Chapter XXII

Jeb Slate was a stubborn man. When he had his mind set to something, it was unlikely anyone could change it. With Andrew off to town, he could tackle the chore of removing the large boulder, which had worn down his pickaxe and seemed insurmountable. Andrew had requested they postpone any further digging until spring, but Jeb had other ideas. Walking over to Ben, he reached into his saddlebag and pulled out a small package wrapped in brown paper no bigger than a box of cigars. He unwrapped enough of the package to confirm its contents and then saddled up his horse and trotted off, leading Ben along.

He was in a hurry to complete his chore before Andy got back from town. After all, Andy would want nothin' to do with using dynamite, he thought to himself. He didn't notice the two men, who were just inside the tree line watching him ride away.

When Jeb reached the cave, he tied up his horse and mule to a hemlock tree and took the package. Once inside the cave, he lit his lantern and fitted one of the dynamite sticks with a cap and fuse. He then tucked it in his pants pocket. The man he purchased it from in town had explained that dynamite couldn't go off by dropping it, or even burning it. You had to shove the cap inside and use the fuse to ignite the cap, which in turn would ignite the stick. He placed the remainder of the box, which contained five sticks, some caps and fuses, on the ground behind a small boulder at the entrance. He carried the lantern to light his way to the back of the tunnel, where he had left a hammer and chisel to try and create a hole big enough to hold the stick of dynamite. It was slow going. The boulder was much harder rock than what they had previously dug in. After a half an hour, he was only halfway through digging the small hole. With his arms getting tired, he put down the hammer and chisel, and pulled out his pipe and tobacco. He walked partway back toward the entrance where the cave widened, and sat down on a rock to light his pipe. The aromatic fragrance filled the tunnel as he watched the plumes of smoke rise toward the rafters and then dissipate. He thought he heard something back around the corner from the entrance, but knew Andy couldn't be back from town yet. Thinking it might just be his horse, he continued to enjoy his smoke. He jumped, nearly dropping his pipe as a familiar voice startled him.

"Place your hands up, old man."

Jeb spun around on his stone seat to look upon the man he knew to be the one from Helen's house. Directly behind him, just as familiar, was Pete Lewis. "Did you think we'd just let you run off without payin' your dues?" Luke held up the old leather map he had found at Helen's house.

"You seem to have me mixed up with someone else, friend," replied Jeb, tamping the tobacco down in his pipe with his thumb and trying to look calm, even though he was anything but.

Luke looked at the time on a silver pocket watch, which Jeb recognized as matching the one Andrew had described in his story on the train robbery that he shared at Helen's house.

He snapped the watch case shut, shoving it back in his front vest pocket. "Let's not beat around the bush, old man. Where's Andrew Thompson at?"

"I don't know any Andrew Thompson," said Jeb, as he tried to stand up, but Luke pushed down on his shoulder to make sure he stayed seated.

"I know he came west with you. He's wanted for murder back in Colorado. You try and protect him and you'll do jail time old man."

"Ha," said Jeb, as he spat out the remnants of some tobacco juice from the pipe. "You pretend to be the law. That's a joke, son. We both know you're just a two-bit bounty hunter, and a green one at that."

Luke grew impatient and took the leather thong off the hammer of his revolver. He pulled it slowly from the worn leather holster and opened the cylinder gate, removing two cartridges. "I always keep the hammer down on an empty chamber," he said. "Less two more, leaves three. You have a fifty-fifty chance old man."

"Chance of what?" asked Jeb.

"Chance of leaving this cave," answered Luke.

Pete tugged at Luke's shirt. "You never said anything about shooting, Luke. You and I can get the information another way, or just stake him out as bait."

Luke shoved a finger firmly in Pete's chest. "I told you before, we're under orders. If you can't handle the job we were given, you can ride away."

Luke turned his attention back to Jeb. "Where's your partner, old man?" Luke spun the cylinder and slapped the gate closed, drawing the hammer. He then pointed the barrel at Jeb's leg, just below his knee. "I don't have a partner," answered Jeb. Several seconds passed and then the hammer clicked down on an empty chamber. Jeb started to sweat. His nervousness made it hard for him to think. He needed to think.

"You must like gamblin'. I'll ask again, old man." A second time Luke spun the cylinder and pulled the hammer back on his Colt.

"Look, we can make a deal here," said Jeb. "This is a valuable mine. It's full of sapphires. Look!" Jeb grabbed one of the bags from the ground and opened it. As he stood up, he poured several of the bluish stones into his hand.

Pete Lewis took one of the stones and held it up to the lantern. His eyes grew wide. "These have got to be worth good money, Luke."
Luke grabbed Jeb by his shirt collar, pulled him in close and gave him a shake. "How many more of these sacks do you have here!" he shouted.
"Sev.. seven or eight," he replied, as he tucked his hands into his pockets. "But it might take me a few minutes to remember where I hid 'em."
Luke pointed his revolver at Jeb's chest. "You've got one minute."
"I'm gonna need a smoke, if you don't mind."
Jeb checked his pipe which needed to be relit, and pulled his last match from his shirt pocket. He struck the match against the cave wall and puffed hard on the bit as the embers inside once again glowed bright.
"There should be three sacks down at the end of the tunnel next to a large boulder, and another four or five smaller sacks tucked above a few of the rafters."
"Start looking," yelled Luke.
Holding the lantern in front of him, Jeb led the two men deeper into the mine until they reached the back wall where he had stopped digging.
"Here's another few sacks," Jeb said as he picked them up from the ground. He then reached up into the rafters and pulled down two more sacks, throwing them at Luke's feet. When he reached up to grab a third sack, he swung it with all his strength at Luke, catching him hard on the arm with the ten pounds of rocks. Luke's gun went off with a deafening boom and the sound of a ricocheting bullet could be heard glancing off the tunnel walls. Immediately, Jeb kicked the lantern over, breaking the glass, and quickly smothered the flame with his coat.
As the tunnel went dark, Luke fired once more, catching Jeb in the leg. He yelled as the bullet buried into his leg like a hot knife, and knocked him to the floor of the cave. Jeb knew he could use the darkness to his

advantage. The months of hard work had made him familiar with the twists and turns of the tunnel. Even with this advantage, he knew he had little time to get to the entrance before they caught up to him. Using his arms and good leg in a modified crawl, he hastened his progress toward the entrance. He stopped only to check his pipe to confirm it was still lit. When he saw the soft glow of the tobacco embers, he pushed on. Behind him he heard another gunshot, followed by Luke's voice. "I'm gonna kill you, old man!"

Pete Lewis pulled a match from his shirt pocket and lit it. He could see the busted glass from lantern on the ground and only a few feet away, the lantern itself. Ahead of him, Luke fired again blindly, using the walls of the tunnel to make his way back toward the entrance.

Jeb searched his pockets in a panic for the stick of dynamite he had tucked away. Finding it, he placed the wick in his pipe bowl and gave a big puff. Sparks shot out of the bowl as the fuse ignited. He counted as he continued to crawl toward the entrance. "One... two... three... four..." Shuffling through the dirt and debris of the tunnel floor, he could hear their footsteps getting closer, as the light from the entrance lit up the mouth of the cave just ahead and still keeping the precious count in his head. "Ten... eleven... twelve... thirteen..."

Reaching the entrance of the cave, he turned back to face the two men, just yards behind him. Luke could see part of the old man's silhouette against the entrance ahead and fired at him, grazing Jeb's shoulder. "Now this is what I call a hell of a fine exit, boys!" he shouted as he threw the piece of dynamite into the cave. He turned and pushed himself forward with his good leg, as he did his best to leap away from the cave before the fuse burnt fully down. Jeb hit the ground and rolled over several times to put as much distance as possible between him and the opening of the cave.

With a blast as loud as thunder, the ground trembled and pieces of rock shot forth from the cave followed immediately by a larger blast so powerful, Jeb could swear it loosened his back teeth. Dirt and smoke filled the air, and for several seconds Jeb could not see or hear a thing. He covered his head with his hands as pieces of rock that were shot into the sky began landing on him and all around. When the dust started to clear, Jeb's ears were still ringing, and before him was a sloping pile of rock where the entrance of the cave once was. He couldn't see his horse or mule, and only found a broken branch hanging from where their reins were tied. He figured that the remainder of the box he had left inside must have ignited given the damage to the cave. "So much for our sapphire mine," he said to himself.

Somehow, he didn't think Andy would be too disappointed with him, as he reached into his pocket and pulled out a shiny silver pocket watch with a deer head fob.

Chapter XXIII

When Andrew returned from town, his saddlebags were filled with supplies for the cabin. One saddlebag in particular contained two full bottles of Canadian whiskey. In his shirt pocket were two carefully preserved cigars. The snow made slow going for his horse, as the past few days had formed a crust on top of what had been a nice, soft powder.

The horse's hooves crunched with each step. From inside the cabin, Jeb could hear the approaching horse. He quickly put on his vest over his shirt and buttoned it up, adjusting the front over his large stomach by pulling down the bottom with both hands. He carefully placed the pocket watch in the right pocket of the vest and, wrapping the chain around a button, placed the deer head fob in the other.

"Well, it's about time you made your way back here," said Jeb, as he opened the front door of the cabin and stuck his head out.

"Not to worry," answered Andrew, not yet noticing the watch chain. "I've got your goods safe and sound."

"Hmmf. Says you. I need a taste of whiskey, son." Jeb pulled out the watch from his pocket and popped open the front, as he looked down at the time. "Three-thirty, according to my watch. Of course, I used the sun to set this thing. God knows it might be off by an hour or two."

"You should just set it by your stomach. It would be more accurate since it never misses a meal; and where did you get a watch from? You never carried one before."

"You're right, Andy. I never did. I guess I might as well give it to you."

Jeb looked down at the inscription on the lid. "After all, there is nothing so precious as family."

Andrew pulled up on his reins short of the cabin and leaped from the saddle, running toward the front door. "Is that what I think it is?"

"Yep, sure is Andy." Jeb took off the watch and placed it in Andrew's hands. Andrew hugged Jeb and thanked him several times over.

"Where did you ever find it?"

"Got her back the other day. Luke Nettle and his partner tried to rob our mine. He had this on his person, right before I blew them to kingdom come."

"Right before what?!"

"It's a long story, Andy. Come on inside and we'll talk. Oh, by the way, I tell a story better when my throat isn't parched. Grab the whiskey, will ya'?"

Jeb explained the whole story to Andy and how they probably wouldn't be able to dig out the mine until spring. Even then, it would take many weeks work to unbury the part of the cave that had come down in the blast. Andrew didn't care so much. He actually felt a relief from Jeb being so focused on it. The weeks following, Andrew and Jeb would take turns going into town. They had plenty of money deposited at the bank and between that and hunting in the hills, they lived very comfortably.

As the Christmas season grew closer, Andrew decided he would take part of his share of the money he had in the bank to buy Willow a gift. He had consulted with Jeb on the matter, but decided not to take his advice, as Jeb thought it was perfectly fine for every girl to have her own Sunday bonnet. Andrew thanked Jeb, but continued to search his thoughts, as he wanted it to be something special that would remind Willow of their time together.

Then he remembered Willow's old worn saddle. On his next trip to town, Andrew stopped at the livery on the edge of town and discussed a new saddle with the owner, Bill Meadows. While he didn't have any new saddles, he could order one that had beautiful floral carving. Ben was asking fifty dollars. That was many weeks work for Andrew, but thinking of Willow, he decided it was worth every penny.

Two weeks later, the saddle had arrived, and Andrew picked it up on his way to see Willow. Bill had placed a few coats of saddle soap on it to condition the leather, and the saddle glistened in the lantern light of the livery stable.

After he paid Bill, he rode over to the general store to see Willow, but had lost track of time. The store had closed an hour ago. He looked at the saddle, wrapped in burlap and tied on top of his saddlebags, then he looked at his watch. Eight-fifty, it read. Tucking the watch back in his pocket, he made his way over to her house. It was a little after nine o'clock when he arrived. Andrew knocked lightly on the front door and peered through the small glass panes. He could see a lantern being lit from inside and then growing brighter as it got closer to the door. The click of a lock sounded and the door opened a few inches. Andrew could see Willow's smile from behind the lantern. "Andrew, come in from the cold. What brings you out here this time in the evening?" Andrew stepped inside and Willow closed the door behind him. The house smelled of fresh cut pine and reminded Andrew of Christmas days when he was growing up back in Altamont.

"I just had to see you, Willow." She smiled even brighter.

"Jeb and me have been at odds lately, being stuck in the cabin for most of the winter. The mining has come to a standstill, and he's been pretty grumpy for the last few weeks. I would have come by earlier in the day, but I forgot how soon it gets dark and I had a stop to make."
Mr Gaithers' voice could be heard from the top of the stairs. "Willow, who is it?"
"It's Andrew, father. He rode out to see me. Everything is alright."
"Okay, well, tell Andrew he's welcome to put up his horse in the barn and stay the evening if he's willing to use the sofa in the parlor."
"Thank you, father," said Willow, as Mr Gaithers walked back to his bedroom. "Have you had dinner?" Willow asked.
"Well, not exactly. I had a few pieces of jerky on the trail."
"Jerky is not dinner. Come into the kitchen; I'll fix you some eggs and ham." Andrew watched Willow fix his meal as one would admire a beautiful sunset. She would peek over her shoulder at him every now and then, only to catch him quickly turn away at his embarrassment for staring. She laughed under her breath, and liked his boyish ways. There was something innocent and good she loved about him. "Over-easy okay with you?"
"Sure. Sounds great."
Andrew wanted to tell her so badly about the incident in Durango. He felt as if he waited too long, it would just get harder to tell her.
"Here you are. Two eggs over-easy, and a nice glass of milk."
Willow pulled up a chair beside Andrew and folded her arms in front of her, as she laid her head on them and watched him eat.
"Thank you. This sure is a fine dinner. I've always enjoyed eggs at any time of the day. Are you sure it won't be a problem for me to stay here?"
"No problem at all. Father likes you, and he wouldn't have you riding back to the cabin in the dark. Besides, not much of a moon tonight."

Willow pulled the necklace out from her nightshirt and held it in her hand.

"Remember when you gave me this?"

"I sure do. I was so troubled to bring you bad news of your grandfather. It took me a while to get my courage up."

"I'm glad you did, or we might not have become such good friends."

"Me, too."

Willow tucked the necklace back inside her shirt and smiled at Andrew. "I know it's a few days before Christmas, but I brought something for you. It's outside. I was afraid that if Jeb and I got snowed in again, I'd miss giving it to you before Christmas Day." Placing his napkin on the table, Andrew left the kitchen and went outside. He appeared moments later with the cloth-wrapped saddle in his arms and placed it on the kitchen table. "I'd like you to open it now, if that's alright?"

"I don't think father would mind," she answered. Willow untied the string that bound the burlap around the saddle and revealed the gift underneath. She gasped slightly and smiled as she looked at the beautifully carved leather saddle.

"It's for when we go riding together," said Andrew.

"Merry Christmas, Willow," said Andrew, mildly blushing, but relieved with Willow's enthusiasm. Willow hugged Andrew and kissed him on the cheek. "It's gorgeous," she said in a quiet voice, so as not to wake her father. "Thank you so much, Andrew."

Andrew sat down at the table as Willow looked over the beautifully detailed leather floral carving on the saddle.

"Willow..."

"Yes?"

"I, um, wanted to talk to you about something else that's been on my mind for a long time, only it hasn't been easy for me to share."

Willow's smile gently departed from her face. From the quietness in his voice, her first thought was that Andrew might be leaving Anaconda.

"It's okay, you can tell me anything," she said, as she took a big swig of Andrew's milk, swallowing hard.

Andrew took his time, telling Willow all about his work on the ranch in Durango, and about mean old Mr. Saunders, and how he later opened up to Andrew about his family, and how his meanness went away.

He told her about the terrible night when he found Mr. Saunders dead and how he was chased out of Durango in fear for his life. When he was done, he had eaten the last of the eggs and ham, and not a drop of milk was left in the glass.

"I just don't want to lose your friendship," he said, not sure of the response he would receive.

"You'll always have my friendship," she replied.

Willow smiled at him for his honesty and for being brave enough to share with her. She reached over and took hold of his hand. "We can work on this together," she said. "Let's get some rest, and we can talk more in the morning."

Andrew agreed and Willow walked him over to the parlor. She helped him off with his boots and covered him with two blankets so he would be plenty warm during the night. "Thank you," said Andrew.

"I thank you," said Willow as she kissed him on the forehead and went upstairs to bed.

The next morning, Andrew was up early chopping wood for Mr. Gaithers' stove. The cold air made the pieces of Green Ash pop apart with ease. When he was done, he brought an armful into the kitchen. Willow sat down at the kitchen table and poured them both a cup of coffee. "I've been thinking, Willow."

Willow looked up from her coffee, waiting a few seconds as the words had stopped.

"Yes, what were you thinking?"

"Well, I was thinking that if... well, not to presume anything, but if we were to remain good friends, I guess it would be best if come spring, I turn myself in to the law and put this behind me. I've been going back and forth in my mind about this for an awful long time. I want us to have something special, Willow, and I just can't have this bothering me for the rest of my life."

Willow got up from her chair and gave Andrew a hug. "I agree," she said. "I really think it is the right thing for you to do. I also think we should let father know. He can help. He knows the sheriff in town very well, and I'm sure getting his advice would be best."

"I'm going to write my parents and tell them, Willow. I might need your help writing them. I can't always find the right words, and I've kept this from them for far too long."

"I'll be happy to help you. We'll do it together."

Chapter XXIV

Andrew and Willow continued to ride together through the rest of the winter days. The ice that had covered the water under the large bur oak had begun to melt. As the days grew longer, the bright orange and yellow western tanagers could be seen in the hills, and water fowl that had flown south at the end of fall could be seen high in the sky, returning to the gradually opening waterways. But as spring's promise was becoming evident all around them, Andrew began to have second thoughts of his promise to himself to turn himself in. The coming of spring made him feel renewed, and his love for Willow seemed stronger than ever. The worries of being caught were pushed back in his mind, as he focused on a future with Willow, here in Montana.

The dream of settling down was becoming more real to him, that is until the day Willow reminded him of his promise.

It was a warm day in April when they rode out to their favorite spot.

"I have not noticed you writing in your journal of late, Andrew."

"Oh, I haven't had much to add to it lately. Been focusing on maybe building my own cabin in the hills."

"Did you and Jeb have another argument?"

"No. It's just that a man can't live with another man all his life. I mean, if a man is to have his own family some day, he'll need his own place. Jeb's like family, but it's not the same."

"I see. Have you thought of your family back home?"

Andrew paused, picking the petals from a wildflower and throwing them each in turn, into the water. Instead of them flowing down the creek, they just gathered together in one part of the pool.

Willow rephrased her question more directly. "Do you think it would be wise to begin writing the letter to your parents?"

"I had it in my mind to do so, but I started thinking of our life here. It's so beautiful and removed from everything back east. I was hoping you would want to be with me here – maybe build something permanent here."

"Tell me, Andrew, what would we build?"

"Why, we'd build our own place and maybe we'd raise horses. Heck, we could have a horse ranch and maybe cattle, too. I could invest the remainder of my money from the bank. We could have a cabin and we could ride together every day."

"I like the thought of being with you, but you can't ride away from your responsibilities. Would you truly feel happy, not knowing when the next man comes looking for you?"

Andrew stirred the water in front of him with a twig, pushing the petals along the bank and watching them flow one by one, down the creek.

"I guess not. I mean, I'd be happy with you, but never quite sure what would be waiting for me."

"I think we should write the letter as we planned, and ask my father for his assistance. Then when all this is behind us, we can settle down together knowing we have the rest of our lives to be happy."

Andrew stood up and walked to his horse and removed the leather journal from his saddlebag. He sat down beside Willow and started to write.

When the letter was written, Andrew tore it from the journal and sealed it in an envelope, giving it to Willow to post in the morning. He then handed her his journal.

"I want you to keep this for me Willow. It contains all of my travels. If something doesn't go right..."

"Everything is going to be fine."

"But just in case... my home address is inside. Please mail this to my folks back home."

"I will. I promise. But everything will be just fine. You are innocent, and everyone will see that."

"I have to do one more thing. I've got to head back to the cabin and tell Jeb about my decision. He'll miss me for a while, but he'll be happy I made the right choice. Better yet, let's go see him together."

Several miles away, Jeb lifted his axe above his head. The cool crisp air of the April morning acted as a catalyst as the oak log split in two. There was a small bead of sweat forming on his brow below his salt and pepper hair.
He lifted one of the halves back up on his chopping stump and quartered it. Then did the same with the other half.
He had been at it since first light, only to stop for a swig of water every now and then.

He remembered how his dog Whiskey used to watch him as he split wood when he was younger. Always nearby, knowing enough not to come too close to her master, as he swung his axe with the consistency and pace of a large time piece. Only between swings would she grab a choice piece of bark to chew on. But she'd been gone almost twelve years now, and he hadn't gotten over her enough to ever buy another dog. Several mules, yes, but never another dog. He was glad to have found a friend in Andrew, as being alone for so long had increased his love for company.

Jeb loved the spring. It was his favorite season. Not just because the weather was getting warmer, but because it was a rebirth of sorts. Everything was fresh and new. He felt as if he had taken what old man winter could throw at him, and now he had a new lease on life.

The patching of the sod roof, the splitting of the firewood, soon to be sorted and stacked in rows as high as a man's shoulders, then left to season all lay before him. He loved the preparation; the feeling of getting ahead, so the following winter would be all the more easy to bear. He loved the jumping of the trout in the stream and the call of the spring birds in the cedars. He loved the smell of the sage grass and the flowers back in the meadow.

He also loved to watch the animals as they, too, seemed to understand that hard times were over and it was time to eat and breed. Each squirrel was a theatrical act unfolding before him as one would chase off another, and then there were the bear cubs tumbling on the hillside, following their mother to where the spring grasses were sweetest. He loved it all.

He made plans to dig out the sapphire mine next month. He and Andy would shore up the timbers better than ever. Who knew what lay in store for them? "That blast probably removed that ol' stubborn boulder," he thought to himself. "Why, there could be a whole passel of blue stones just waiting to be picked up." Dreams of retiring rich entered his mind as he continued his work.

The wood splinters continued to litter the ground around him as he chopped through piece after piece. Upon hitting a knot in a particular piece of oak, he carefully removed his axe and traded it out for his wedge and sledge.

He swung the sledge lightly with his first blow, to set the wedge, then hammered continuously, driving it deeper into the heart of the knot.

He remembered the price he would pay, with his aging muscles and joints. Too much work would announce itself in the way of a stiff neck or sore back the following morning when he woke. But he wasn't going to let this piece get the best of him.

Swinging with such fury in one blow, he knocked both wedge and wood from his stump. He dropped his sledge as he lifted the heavy piece back on the stump. "Damn knot" was all he said as he turned and focused his stubborn determination back at the piece, as if it were alive, and maybe even grinning. A small wren flew down and landed on a nearby piece of wood. All of Jeb's splitting had loosened plenty of bark, which uncovered small bugs and larvae. A feast for the small wren who sang a pretty song.

"Now you stay clear, Mr. Bird," said Jeb. "This is no place to start a picnic. I've got swingin' to do."

Jeb slowly raised the large sledge above his head. With the next blow, he bottomed out the wedge, but still not even a crack or pop from the piece. "Damn!" he shouted again, scaring away the small wren. Even though there was no one around, he looked anyway, as a force of habit due to the stuck piece of wood and his slight embarrassment. It wasn't right for such a piece of wood to get the best of a seasoned mountain man.

A second wedge was driven in next. Jeb wiped the sweat from his forehead with his shirt sleeve. With blow after blow, the knotted piece absorbed the heavy, steel splinter. The heavy metal sledge head smashed down upon its adversary. Bang... bang... bang!

Then, as if someone had whispered in his ear or perhaps called him from afar, Jeb stopped and dropped the sledge. He stood there for a moment, motionless. The geese, which had come back to nest the previous week on the far bank of the pond had all taken to the air in unison. To anyone watching, it looked as though he had given up on the piece of wood and called it quits, as he stood there with a blank expression, looking up toward the sky and the flying geese.

Then his expression changed as he dropped suddenly to his knees. "Andy," he gasped, as he rolled on his back, staring at the bright green birch leaves contrasted against the clear blue sky. "What a beautiful entrance," he whispered softly, as his eyes slowly closed. His large body lay still, as the residual heat from his breath rose up into the cool, crisp April air.

That evening, Andrew and Willow arrived at the cabin just before sundown. When they didn't find Jeb inside, Andrew went out to see if Jeb was tending to the livestock. When Andrew caught sight of the mountain man lying near the pond, he ran as fast as he could to his friend's side. His first instinct was to try and sit the old man up, but his body was stiff. His face was a pale whitish-blue and his hands were cold. The split wood and tools told the story of how he had died. Andrew knelt over his friend and wept. Willow sat beside him as he let out his sorrow. Jeb had been a good friend, who had shown Andrew a different side of himself. Jeb had no family of his own, but for Andrew. There was no one to write, no one to come attend a funeral or to pass over treasured keepsakes. The things that Jeb held dearest, he had already given Andrew. The gift of adventure with riding the rails, the experience of an old man in his late years, the excitement of finding treasure within a mountain, but most of all, the gratefulness of having a family that loved him; a family to go home to.

Andrew and Willow buried Jeb under the shade of a cedar tree within view of the stream and pond. He carved a marker for his headstone, on which he placed Jeb's old worn hat. The phrase on the carved wood was simple and unpretentious. It read: Loving husband and Good friend.
After a few final prayers, Andrew packed up what belongings Jeb had. The 1860 Colt conversion revolver, he placed in his saddlebag. The remainder; his pipe and tobacco, an old worn jack knife, a harmonica and one of the blue stones Jeb had kept in his pocket, he rolled in an old Indian blanket and stored it on a shelf in the cabin. As they mounted their horses to head back to town, Andrew turned to look back at the cabin. He couldn't help but think he'd be back here some day.

When Willow and Andrew arrived back in town, the first thing they did was post the letter they had written together. Andrew felt as though he had started a series of events that could not be stopped. He worried about his parents and what they would think of his misfortune. He worried about convincing those who represented the law of his innocence. He especially worried about seeing Willow again. If the worst happened, regardless of how brave he could be, he would never see her again in this world.
They went to Willow's home and shared the story with her father, who supported the decision and credited Andrew with doing the right thing.
It was Mr. Gaithers who would accompany Andrew down to the sheriff's office to send a wire for the U. S. Marshall. Willow kissed him good bye and held his journal tight in her arms, as if she were hugging him as they rode away. It was arranged by wire that the marshall was to escort Andrew back to Durango. He was to be on the train a day after

next. Until then, the sheriff said Andrew would stay with him until released into the custody of the marshall.

Chapter XXV

Marshall Millrose arrived at the train station in Anaconda at 9:45 a.m. As he stepped off the train, he reached into his weather-worn leather vest for his pocket watch, comparing it to the time at the station. The train ride was a long one, and his back was stiff from sitting for so long. With him he carried a coat and a leather saddlebag. He paused for a minute to look up at the sky, which was full of clouds, and then decided to put on his shearling-lined coat, as his breath formed small white clouds that vanished into the crisp air.

He had been a marshall for over twenty years, which was a good run for that line of work. His job was often dangerous and the years of bringing in men who cared little for their lives, much less anyone else's, had made him as worn and callous as the vest he wore. He knew he was to meet with the town sheriff and then escort the prisoner Andrew Thompson back to Durango.

It made little difference to Marshall Millrose that Andrew had given himself up to the law. He had seen guilty men do that in the past to save themselves from a lynching, only to have some slick city lawyer get them off. What mattered to him was that he did the job he was paid to do; to get the prisoner from Anaconda to Durango, where he would stand trial. Approaching retirement, the judge in Helena had been fair to the marshall, assigning cases that were less likely to have any type of confrontation.

Inside the sheriff's office, in a chair next to the sheriff's desk, sat Andrew Thompson. He looked up at the tall man who entered the office and removed his hat and coat. The man's mustache was a reddish-brown, while his hair was mostly gray. He stood about six-foot-two and wore a gun in a holster, which was partially obscured by his vest and hung under his left arm. Instead of the gun hanging with its barrel facing down, the barrel pointed slightly upward, with the grip protruding where it could be easily accessed by the marshall's right hand. Andrew had never seen such a rig before, but it sure was a handsome one. The dark brown holster looked to be floral carved and the grip on the gun appeared to be made from stag. The sheriff had the marshall sign some paperwork and then introduced him to Andrew. "Andrew, this here is Marshall Millrose. He's going to see you safely through to Durango, where he will release you to Sheriff Belmont.

The judge back in Durango said they are working on setting your trial date. You'll be appointed a lawyer to defend your case, and remember, you'd best share all the information you have with him."

"Yes, sir," replied Andrew. His head felt light. All this was new to him and overwhelming.

"Good luck, son," said the sheriff.

Marshall Millrose walked over to Andrew and asked him to stand up. He placed a set of handcuffs on him and asked Andrew if they were too tight. "No," replied Andrew.

"Sorry, Mr Thompson. It's part of procedure."

"I understand," replied Andrew.

"You'll also need to understand, that if you should change your mind and try to flee, I am justified to stop you, any way I can."

"Yes, sir," replied Andrew.

"Good. Now that we understand each other, we'll make the best of this trip."

He then walked Andrew down to the train station.

After forty minutes waiting in the station, the two men boarded the train and were seated in the rear of the passenger car.

Marshall Millrose asked Andrew to take the window seat, so he would be away from the aisle. Andrew was embarrassed to be wearing the handcuffs. He could see people turning their heads toward the rear of the car to stare at him. "This is normal, Mr. Thompson. They'll turn back around soon enough," said the marshall.

As the train started to move, Marshall Millrose leaned over and unlocked Andrew's handcuffs. "There. That should be a little more comfortable for you."

"Thank you," replied Andrew.

The marshall asked the porter for the newspaper, and upon receiving it, handed Andrew half the paper to read.

"If nothing else, it discourages staring."

"Thanks," replied Andrew, as he opened the paper with a crinkle of noise. The reading calmed his nerves and did indeed block out prying eyes. Two days later, traveling over eight hundred miles of track, the train arrived at the Durango station. Marshall Millrose placed the handcuffs back on Andrew and walked him down the station boardwalk to where he had two horses waiting.

As the two men rode down the street together, they both noticed a building that looked to have been burnt to the ground.

Marshall Millrose rode up to a man who was loading burnt boards and broken glass onto a buckboard. "Excuse me," said the marshall. "What happened here?"

The man looked up from his job, wiping his brow. "Dry goods store burnt to the ground last week. Happened during the night and took ol' Abe Waterson with it; he lived above the store. Damn shame, too, he was a good man."

"What caused it?"

"Sheriff said it started from the wood stove Abe kept in the store. By the time the fire department arrived, it was engulfed in flames. They had all they could do just to stop it from spreading to the other buildings."

"Sorry for the town's loss," said the marshall, as he tipped his hat to the man and rode on.

"I knew that man," said Andrew. "Mr. Saunders had introduced him to me."

"Knew him well, did you?"

"No, just a one-time meeting. But he seemed to have been a good friend of Mr Saunders."

"Expect he's with his friend, then," answered the marshall.

When they reached the jail, Marshall Millrose escorted Andrew inside, where they met Sheriff Belmont.

Sheriff Belmont asked Andrew to follow him through a door to where the jail cells were.

There were several cells adjacent to one another, each with a bunk bed and a blanket. The sheriff opened one of the cells and asked Andrew to step inside. He then closed the door behind him, the metal bars reverberating with a loud clang. "The judge has the trial set in two weeks. You'll take your meals in here until then. If you need to use the bathroom, holler out and my deputy will escort you. Lights out at eight every evening."

When the sheriff left the room, all Andrew could hear was the snoring of a man several cells down.

He was now wondering if he had done the right thing by turning himself in, and if he'd ever see Willow or any of his family again.

An appointed attorney for the State of Colorado stopped by to speak with Andrew a few times. He asked for Andrew's side of the story, and then seemed to ask a lot of plain questions that weren't too focused on any of the details Andrew had given him. The attorney would only spend a few minutes at a time with him, and Andrew began to worry that something was distracting him from his job.

It was the following Monday when Sheriff Belmont brought Andrew his breakfast along with a mirror, a straight razor, a wash basin and a cup of shaving cream. "You'll be appearing in court later this morning, son. Call for me when you're ready and I'll come back to fetch the razor and such. Oh, and don't do anything funny with that razor."

"I certainly will not," replied Andrew. "I'm innocent and I expect to be set free."

At ten o'clock, the sheriff and his deputy escorted Andrew across the street to the courthouse, where the trial was set to begin.

It was Friday afternoon when Martin Perkins walked into the Diamond Belle and bellied up to the bar. The ongoing trial he had just attended at the Durango courthouse had recessed for the afternoon. Martin, a trail hand regular who had ridden for several of the local ranches over the past fifteen years, was reputed to be an honest hand. Most recently, he had worked for the Winding River Ranch, which was one of the biggest in the territory, encompassing a few thousand head of cattle that grazed over ten thousand acres. It was owned by John Nettle, who's son was recently killed in Montana while trying to bring in the man currently on trial.

He had left Winding River Ranch over a year ago, after he had been ordered by Luke Nettle to bring in any other cattle that crossed over onto his father's land. Perkins had always driven off other rancher's cattle, and considered this request immoral, if not illegal. It was because of this, that Perkins took special interest in the case.

Martin raised his hand and the bartender nodded, knowing exactly what his friend was requesting.

The heavyset bartender walked over to Martin with a mug of beer. The frothy head foamed over and ran down the sides.

"They come to a decision yet?" the bartender asked Martin.

"No. They recessed for the day. You should get a rush of folks in here any minute now."

"How's it looking for the Thompson kid?"

"They admitted his shotgun as evidence. The same model ten gauge that old man Saunders was allegedly killed with. Even had the shell casing from the scene of the crime to match it up with."

"Sounds like a rare model and gauge for around these parts."

"Yep, seems to be." answered Martin, who took a long swig of his beer and dabbed the froth that had settled on his mustache with his sleeve. "John Nettle testified that when he had asked Abe Waterson about the gun, which had been in his store for sale, Abe told him he had already sold it to Saunders, who in turn gave it to Andrew Thompson as a gift. Then Nettle said that he remembered Abe saying that there were no more in the county, as he had only stocked one model 1901 ten gauge, as it never sold as well as a twelve."

"Sure is a shame about Abe's place burning down."

"Yep, damn shame. They mentioned in court that he had probably left the door open on his wood stove downstairs before he had gone up to bed. The ledger, along with everything else, went up in flames that night."

"I find it hard to believe a young kid like that killed his own employer with the very gun that was gifted to him," said the bartender. "Did the kid have any witnesses speak up for him?"

"Funny thing was, Jake Saunders was there that night. Jake claimed he saw Andrew Thompson coming out of his father's house right before he confronted him. He also said he was so distraught about his father's death, he had threatened to kill Thompson right there on the spot. Turns out the kid got the upper hand and Jake got knocked unconscious. When he came to, he decided to ride into town for the law. He went on to say that the kid could have killed him if he really wanted to, given that Jake could identify him at the crime scene. But the kid chose to flee instead.

"And that's not all. The prosecuting lawyer said Thompson took all the money in Saunders' cash box before riding off on a gray mare he stole from the old man's corral. The next morning, several of John Nettle's ranch hands came across him on that very same horse. When the group of men approached him to turn himself in, they all testified that Thompson shot at them before hopping an outgoing train."

"Kid's guilty if you ask me," said the bartender.

"I guess it looks that way. Seems like such a nice kid, too. Speaks well and proper and all. You could almost see the innocence and hopelessness on his face as the trial wore on."

"I'd be careful with that sort of thinking," said the bartender. "Look at that there William Bonney who was shot dead down in Mexico. He was known to have been quite personable and downright friendly to people - at times. But make no mistake, he'd kill ya' dead as a doornail just the same."

"No doubt Bonney was a disturbed man, but he's one in a thousand," Martin answered. "Something just doesn't seem right to me about this case. Why didn't Thompson kill Jake Saunders too? Why would he ride toward town the next day, instead of riding down to Mexico or heading back east?"

"Dunno, maybe he got confused. I thought you said he shot at Nettle's ranch hands?"

"I did. I mean, that's what Nettle's hands say, but I'm beginning to have my doubts."

"Another beer, Martin?"

"Yeah, I'll take another... To make matters worse for this Thompson kid, the man he was traveling with by the name of Jeb Slate, ended up killing Nettle's son Luke and another hand by the name of Pete Lewis. He said under oath, that this here Slate was confronted by Nettle and Lewis when he was working a sapphire mine up in Montana. He says they tried to rob him and as Slate escaped, he brought down half the mountain on the two of them in the process."

"What was John Nettle's boy doing up in Montana?"

"He and Pete Lewis were hired by Jake Saunders as bounty hunters to bring in the killer of his father. Jake testified to it as true, as he offered each of the men two hundred dollars to bring him back to justice and stand trial."

"Seems unlikely Luke Nettle would try and rob someone, when he was going to be paid to bring back Andrew Thompson alive. And besides, why would Luke Nettle try and rob someone when his father owns one of the largest cattle ranches this side of the Rio Grande? Just doesn't add up to me."

"That's the other strange part. Thompson's friend Slate supposedly died of a heart attack up in Montana several weeks ago. Thompson said he buried him there."

"Figures. Dead men don't talk."

Martin placed the empty mug down on the bar and dabbed his mustache again. "Yep, and they certainly don't testify in court. Anyhow, we should know by tomorrow, as they are expected to ask the jury for a decision by then."

Chapter XXVI

Andrew stood in front of the small glass window. His view of the pale blue sky was partially obscured by the reinforcing iron bars. His eyes filled with tears as he thought about the likelihood of him seeing very few like it again. It was hard to believe twelve good men picked for a specific reason could find him guilty. He was innocent. Innocent men were supposed to go free. But there it was – a verdict that would mean his hanging in less than one week. He missed his family back home and wished he had written more to them. He missed Jeb, with his big laughing voice and southern drawl – he chuckled to himself – yes, even his snoring.

He saw some birds fly across his field of view, vanishing off to the east. In a way, he wished Willow was still with him, but she had stayed back in Anaconda at Andrew's request. He could hear her soft voice in his head, but it was ultimately drowned out by the men building the gallows outside in the town square. Each time the hammer fell, he tried to ignore it, but it was impossible to deny the inevitable outcome of the recurring sound. Another flock of birds flew by, but this time one small bird landed on the sill of his window. It was a wren. It pecked at the glass, perhaps curious of its own reflection. Andrew wished he could feed it some of the cornbread left over from the breakfast he had only half eaten, but there was no way he could manage it through the bars and the glass. Eventually it flew away.

As he sat back down on his bunk, he heard the click of a lock as Sheriff Belmont entered the room, which held a total of three cells. He was unarmed, as no one was allowed into the cell area with a weapon. His

deputy was just a few feet away in the other room, eating his lunch. The sheriff held a small tin tray, which contained an overdone strip of steak, some boiled potatoes and another large wedge of cornbread. To wash it down was a tin cup full of milk. Andrew couldn't believe it was lunch already. The hours seemed to flow together in the stark cell. "You best eat this lunch, son. You only ate half your breakfast this morning," said the sheriff, as he closed the large wooden door behind him with his foot. "I'm not hungry," replied Andrew, "and I'm not your son."
The sheriff unlocked the door of the cell and placed the tray on a table opposite Andrew's bunk. "Your call," said the sheriff. "If you want to see a priest, we can arrange that this week. Just let me know."
He locked the cell again and walked over to the large wooden door. Suddenly, he heard a crash from the other room. The sheriff swung open the large door, but then stopped as if frozen. He then took a step backwards and raised his hands up, level with his head. From his view on the bunk, Andrew could only see the barrel of a rifle protruding from the door. As the man holding the rifle stepped into the room, Andrew shouted in disbelief, "Pa!"
He stood up and grabbed the bars of the cell.
James Riley stepped into the room with his Winchester point blank in the chest of Sheriff Belmont. "Open the cell door, sheriff," said James with a look on his face as stern as Andrew had ever seen it.
Sheriff Belmont opened the cell without hesitation. "Step out, son," said James.
Andrew stepped out, and James pushed the sheriff back with the tip of his rifle. "You get in."
The sheriff stepped in and James closed the cell door. "Now take those handcuffs and cuff yourself to the cell door." The sheriff did as he was

told. "How far do you think you'll get after you leave here?" asked Sheriff Belmont.

"As far as necessary," replied James. "Nobody is going to hang my son for something he didn't do."

James and Andrew left the cell room and closed the door behind them. Andrew looked at the deputy, lying face down on the floor, his steak dinner strewn about him. "He'll be okay," said James. "He wasn't quite as cooperative as the sheriff."

"I'm so glad to see you, Pa! I was..."

"Not now," answered James. "I want you to wear my hat and duster, and follow me out of here, just like we were two townsfolk going about our business. I bought a bag of feed and left it just outside the door. Pick it up and throw it over your shoulder that faces the street, understood?"

"Understood, Pa."

"Good. I have two horses tied up in front of the saloon. If anyone should start shooting, you hug that horse's neck, stay low and right on my tail. You got that?"

"Yessir!"

"Alright, let's go."

James and Andrew walked down to the saloon and rode off without anyone giving them another thought. They rode up to the hills several miles outside of town where James had scouted several areas with rocks and ledge where any posse would have a hard time tracking them. He then told Andrew to stay put, as he loaded some sacks full of sand onto Andrew's horse and rode out of the camp with his horse's reins in hand. After laying down a second set of tracks, he returned to the camp an hour later.

As the sun started to set, the two men sat with a modest campfire, just big enough to warm some coffee, which complemented the cold dinner of venison jerky and corn biscuits, but small enough not to be seen from a distance.

"Do you think they'll catch up to us, Pa?"

"Not tonight, son. I laid a trail a Pawnee would have trouble tracking. Besides, I hung around town long enough yesterday to find out which horses belonged to the sheriff and his deputy. This morning I fed them so much grain, I can promise they won't be running for a while. But just the same, we'll leave our saddles on the horses tonight in case we need to ride."

James plumped up his bedroll and stretched out in front of the small fire. After Andrew was settled in, he told his father all about Jeb Slate and how he first met Jeb on a moving freight train. He told him how he met Sky With No Clouds, and how that led to him meeting Willow. He shared stories about how he and Willow would go riding together, and how if he was found innocent, they would start a small horse ranch together.

"Wonderful girl, that Willow," James said.

"I wish you could meet her, Pa. She's so kind and smart, too."

"In a way, I have met her. You see, when you sent us that letter describing how you were going to do the right thing and turn yourself in, your ma and I were proud of you, but we were scared, too. The very next day, another letter arrived. It was from Willow. She asked me to waste no time and come out right away. She was the one who told me where I could find you."

"I'm so glad you did, Pa."

"Me too, son."

James continued to share stories of home and how Andrew's ma missed him. He then asked Andrew to start at the beginning and tell him everything he could possibly remember about the trial. They sipped on coffee and talked until there was no more coffee in the pot. James stared up at the starlit sky. He started to piece together the facts in his head, but it was like a puzzle with a few pieces still missing.

With the fire dying down, they both slipped under their blankets for the night. "I'm not sorry I came out west, Pa. I'm not sorry I met Jeb or Willow, or even Mr. Saunders. He was a nice old man when you got right down to it. He just had some parts of his life go bad."

"Don't worry, Andrew. This will all work out somehow. I've been thinking about parts of that trial you described to me. I have a feeling we'll get this to all work out just fine. Even if we have to ride clear up into Canada, we'll be just fine. Now get some rest; we have some work to do tomorrow."

Chapter XXVII

The next morning, James rode back into town, stopping at the railroad station. It was a risky move, but he needed to check something with the telegraph operator there. Besides, he figured the sheriff and his posse would be out looking for him and not sitting in town. A few minutes later, he was back on the trail, making sure nobody was following him as he rode out of town.

Andrew was waiting for him back at their hiding place up in the rocks.

"Did you get the help you needed, Pa?" asked Andrew.

"Yes, if everything works out the way I've planned. We'll ride out of here this evening. It should nearly be a full moon."

"Where will we be going?"

"We'll be paying a visit to a prominent member of this town. I only hope the extra guest I invited decides to join us."

That evening, James and Andrew arrived at the ranch of John Nettle. "Stay close to me and let me do the talking. Remember, John Nettle has never seen either of us."

James tied his horse up to the hitching post in front of John Nettle's house.

It was a grand house, made from western red cedar. The porch alone looked to be forty feet long and the doors were solid oak.

Several windows ran along the front of the two-story house, for those inside to see anyone approaching from a distance. Two large stone chimneys shot out from the roof line like dark towers. James left his rifle in its scabbard and asked Andrew to follow suit. They both walked up onto the porch, but before they could knock on the door, it opened and a large man walked out in front of them holding a lever action rifle and wearing a single sixgun rig. His face featured a long dark mustache and his breath smelled of cigars. "You have business here?" he asked in a gruff voice.

"Yeah, we heard in town that Mr. Nettle might be looking for hands. My son and I had a small farm down in New Mexico, but it went under. We know our way around cattle. How much does the job pay?"

"Not so fast," said the man. "Mr. Nettle is going to want references. Wait here a minute." The man went back inside and appeared a few minutes later. "Mr. Nettle will see you in his study," said the man, who let them go in before him so he could follow behind. As they walked in, he asked them to stop so he could search them. He took the .32-20 Colt from James' holster. He searched Andrew as well, but found no gun. The great room before them had a giant fireplace with a stuffed cougar on the large mantle. Several other mounts adorned the walls of the room. "Just up here to the left," said the man. They entered the study, which was almost as big as the great room. One wall was lined with bookshelves, while another had cabinets filled with guns. A second stone fireplace was ablaze with several logs, filling the room with the smell of mesquite and alder. There was a large leather couch and two other chairs also upholstered in leather.

A tall man with thinning gray hair sat at a desk, which was in front of the bookshelves.

He was a big man, who looked like he had seen his share of time in the saddle. His hands were large and calloused, and his face had wrinkles from the sun and wind. He wore a shirt of white linen and over that, a leather vest. A pocket watch and fob spanned between his vest pockets on a gold chain.

"Michael tells me you're looking for work," he said plainly, as he puffed on a cigar.

"Yes, we are. We had a small farm north of the Zuni Mountains, but our livestock got sick and died. We could not pay back the bank, so my son and I had to leave our land."

Mr. Nettle leaned back in his chair and puffed a cloud of smoke above his head. "I'm afraid you were misinformed. We have no need for additional ranch hands right now. Michael, please show them out." Michael opened the door of the study to see them out. As James walked past him, he drove an elbow deep into Michael's gut. The big man winced in pain as he doubled over. James grabbed the rifle from his hands and smashed his face with the butt, dropping him to the floor, unconscious. Instantly, James spun around toward John Nettle, who had opened a drawer from behind his desk and had his hand clearly in it.

"I wouldn't pull that out," said James, as he pointed the lever action at his chest. Andrew walked around behind the desk and took the revolver from inside the drawer. He placed it in his belt and asked Mr. Nettle to please walk out from behind the desk and take a seat on the leather couch. Nettle walked around the desk in a slow gate, as if he really wasn't inconvenienced at all, pretending to still be master of his own den.

"What exactly do you gentlemen want? You certainly didn't come here for a job herding cattle. I would remind you that I don't keep much cash in my house, and what I do have here, you wouldn't get far with. My ranch hands are many, and they would hunt you down before you got out of the county."

"We're not here for money," answered James, as he closed the door to the study. "We are waiting for someone to meet us here."

"Who would this person be?" asked Nettle, smugly.

"You'll see soon enough," said James as he retrieved his Colt from Michael's belt and gave it to Andrew.

A few minutes later there was a knock on the study door. James motioned to Andrew to carefully answer it. Sheriff Belmont walked into the room. James pointed his rifle toward Sheriff Belmont and asked him to please raise his hands. Andrew took the revolver from the sheriff's gun belt.

"Sit down, sheriff," said James. "I thank you for replying to my invite - or should I say Mr. Nettle's invite. My name is James Riley. My son and I intend to turn ourselves over to you soon enough. But first, I have a few questions to ask Mr. Nettle before we leave here in your custody. You see, after I got into town the other day, I went over to the Diamond Belle. While I was there, it was my good fortune to overhear an interesting conversation between two friends at the bar. When they were done talking, I approached one of them. His name was Martin Perkins. Martin said he rode for your ranch for over a year, Mr. Nettle, that is before he was let go. Can you tell me why he was let go?"

"I don't remember. A lot of cowhands move from ranch to ranch. They don't like to stay put long."

"I think it was because he was an honest fella. Could it be that you were encouraging your hands to pick up strays instead of running them off, and he didn't want to go along with your orders? But then again, when you own over a thousand head, it's probably pretty easy to conceal the slaughter and sale of other's cattle you rustle, as there's no brand you can trace at that point. When they can no longer make a living, you buy them out."

"That's an outrageous accusation. You could never prove anything like that," said Nettle as his face started to grow red.

"Maybe not yet, but I will. You see, Mr. Nettle, I know for a fact that there was another model 1901 shotgun sold in this town, the same model and gauge of the gun my son was accused of using to kill Red Saunders. I think the killer made a mistake the night he killed Saunders. By habit, he ejected the spent shell, and it rolled onto the floor. It was stated at the trial, the sheriff had found it under the bed the day after the killing occurred. I think you were trying to frame Saunders' son, Jake. Everyone in town knew there was bad blood between Jake and his father. But when you found out that the sheriff knew the weapon in question was a 10 gauge that killed Saunders, you had to change plans and find out quick who else owned the other gun. Then to cover your tracks, you burnt down Waterson's shop, which contained the only information on who the two guns were sold to."

"That's ridiculous. I own no such gun."

"That's funny. I wired the Winchester plant in New Haven, Connecticut and checked their shipping records. I picked up their response this morning in town." James handed the telegraph message to Sheriff Belmont.

"They confirmed two Winchester 1901 shotguns were shipped to Abe Waterson's Mercantile. But, the defense attorney never thought to bring that issue up in court. Don't you think that's odd? Of course we'll never know who got that other shotgun, because like I said, his store had burnt down a week before the trial."

"I'm not responsible for the defense's argument," stammered Nettle. "Why don't you take that up with the judge?"

"You may not have been responsible for the defense of my son, but you were damn well responsible for the pressure you put on this town and especially the jury, whom I heard from Martin Perkins had several men on it that had worked for you at one time or another – and he'll testify to that."

"That's preposterous. Those men voted the way they saw fit. Leave my house now!"

"Not just yet, Nettle! You're a big man, Mr. Nettle. Big enough to scare quite a few people around these parts, and people will act different when they're scared. I'm also willing to bet you're not the kind of man who takes no for an answer. My son saw someone ride away from the killing that night. They rode north. Isn't your place north of the Saunders' Ranch?"

"Yes, it is, but that doesn't prove..."

"He rode in the same direction that the other men rode off to, on the afternoon when you had Luke try to buy Saunders out. Only, Andrew heard the argument that afternoon and knew Red was being pressured to sell. I'm sure that when Red Saunders caught on to your rustling, you decided one last time to try and buy him out, and when he refused, you killed him in his own bedroom."

"Lies. Lies!" shouted Nettle.

"I'm also sure that it was your son who was part of the make-shift posse who tried to kill my son before he could get to the sheriff's office. They were told to make sure he couldn't get into town, so they waited just on the outskirts, and shot at him as soon as he tried to come in."

"All I know is my son was murdered by your son's friend."

"According to my son, Andrew, your son was a thief. Evidently aside from being foreman of this ranch, he and a few of his hands robbed trains in their spare time. What Jake Saunders didn't know is that while he wanted Andrew back to stand trial, you instructed Luke not to let Andrew come back alive."

James walked over to the gun cabinet, which was filled with several makes and models of rifles and shotguns. He didn't see the shotgun he was looking for. But he did notice the initials J.N. that were burnt into each stock, as if they were branded.

"You want to lend me the key to this fancy cabinet, or do I have to find my own way in?"

Mr. Nettle said nothing as he took a small key from his vest pocket and tossed it to James.

James unlocked the glass door, and pulled one of the rifles from the cabinet. "These sure are pretty, Mr. Nettle. Not many people can afford such nice rifles. Exquisite wood."

"I'm glad you're intrigued by my sense of taste, Mr. Riley. Now if you're done, I'd like you to put it back and leave my house."

"Did you order your initials on this rifle?"

"No. I had a special brand made up in town. Many men brand the stocks of their rifles with their initials."

"Interesting piece of information, Mr Nettle."

James looked the sheriff straight in the eye and handed him the rifle. "O.K. Belmont. I'm ready to leave. But I want you to know I sent two wires this morning. The second one went to the U.S. Marshall, and I expect he'll be looking into reopening this case with this new information."

"That will be up to the judge as well, Mr. Riley. I'm going to ask for my gun back Andrew. If you and your father would be so kind, we'll be heading back to town now."

Chapter XXVIII

Sheriff Belmont escorted Andrew and James out the front door and to their horses. He placed his only set of handcuffs on Andrew, and helped him into the saddle.

"I'm sorry, son, but without more evidence, there's nothin' I can do right now. I need to say this one time. I have to get you both safely back to jail tonight, but if either one of you try something like you did with my deputy the other day, I'll be forced to stop you."

"You won't get any more interference from us, sheriff," replied Andrew.

With his hands cuffed, Andrew held onto the pommel of the saddle as he rode. He looked up at the bright near-full moon as it appeared from behind the clouds, illuminating their horses and casting a shadow of the three men as they rounded the house. Only a small, dark sliver of the bright orb was unlit.

Andrew glanced back over his shoulder at the house as the three men slowly rode past. He could see John Nettle's face peering through the curtains in one of the windows, looking anxious for them to leave. As Andrew turned away from the window, he spotted an old outhouse, set forty yards back from the house. Illuminated by the moon, he could see a carving on the top part of the door, but couldn't quite make it out. He wasn't sure why, but it piqued his curiosity. He had to see the carving.

"Sheriff Belmont, I've got to use the outhouse."

"If this is a trick, Andrew, I assure you it will be your last."

"No really, please. I'll only take a minute. Please!"

"Okay, son. Follow me. Mr Riley, please stay here out in the open where I can see you."

The sheriff held Andrew's reins as they rode over to the outhouse.

"Okay, climb down slowly," said the sheriff. He had his Winchester across his lap and pointed in Andrew's direction.

As Andrew walked up to the outhouse door, he could now clearly see the carving of a crescent moon on the door, similar to the one his father had carved in a dream. "I need you to look inside for me, sheriff."

"No, sir. That's not how it works, son. You can open that door and do what you need to, or get back on that horse now."

"You don't understand. I believe the shotgun that was used to kill Mr. Saunders is hidden in there. I just know it. Please just look for me. If we ride away now, he'll have time to get rid of it for good and we'll never find it."

Sheriff Belmont paused for a second and then slowly climbed down from his horse, looking cautiously over at James Riley.

He asked Andrew to stand aside and walk back several feet. With one hand, the sheriff grasped the latch on the door and with the other he kept his rifle trained on Andrew. The door creaked as he slowly opened it, and he could feel the tension of the rusted spring on the door. He looked down the outhouse shaft, in the corners of the small building and up toward the roof, but saw nothing.

"Sorry, son, it's empty. We really have to be going."

"Please look harder. It's got to be there," Andrew pleaded.

The sheriff paused again and then raised his voice in a serious manner. "I'm trusting you to stay still!" He then took his rifle and leaned it against the side of the outhouse.

Sheriff Belmont then opened the door again, and removed the paper catalog that hung inside the outhouse. He tore a handful of sheets off and carefully rolled them up in his hands until they took the shape of a cone. He then pulled a match from his shirt pocket and lit the papers. As he moved the make-shift torch back and forth inside the outhouse, his attention was drawn to a nail on the floor. He looked closer and found that it had come from one of the boards. Laying the dwindling torch down on the outhouse floor, he pulled his knife from its sheath and pried up the loose board.

Andrew waited nervously outside. Then he heard the sheriff from inside speak: "I'll be damned." The sheriff walked out of the outhouse holding a burlap sack, which was wrapped around a long slim object and bound with string.

Instinctively, Andrew looked back toward the house, but could no longer see John Nettle's face in the window.

Sheriff Belmont cut the string with his knife and unwound the sack from the object within. As he pulled the Winchester model 1901 from the sack, he could see the initials J.N. clearly burned into the stock. "You don't need to be a genius to know whose initials these were made for. I guess this changes everything." He held up the Winchester to show Andrew, who sighed with great relief. "Andrew, I'm going to ask you and your father to ride back to town with me. You'll have to stay in custody while I swear out a warrant for John Nettle. But given your testimony and the fact that we have this new evidence, I'm positive we'll have things set right very soon."

As the sheriff helped Andrew back on his horse, a shot rang out from the house, and the sheriff yelled and fell backwards onto the ground. Andrew knew enough to jump out of the saddle and get down onto the ground next to him. As he tried to help the sheriff, a rider took off from behind the house and rode south. "Stay with the sheriff," yelled James, as he retrieved his Colt .32-20 from the sheriff. "I'll be needing this back," he said to Belmont, and rode off after the shooter.

The shooter had a half-mile lead on James as he rode south at a gallop. Trail dust shot up from his horse's hooves, partially obscuring his silhouette from James.

Suddenly, the rider turned in the saddle and fired twice with a revolver at James. It was an old tactic when being chased by an adversary. The odds of hitting the target while at a full gallop were pretty slim. It was meant to unnerve the pursuer and make him alter his route and slow down.

But James used it to his advantage, and kicked his horse even harder as he tried to close the gap between them. The rider turned off the trail and into the grass, riding southwest. Under the moonlight, James could now confirm it was John Nettle. Another shot rang out from Nettle's Colt revolver as he pushed his horse on. The two riders rode their horses at a full gallop for several miles through the hills of grass until they came to the Saunders' ranch. Nettle's horse was exhausted and he knew it. He headed for the open barn, which had been abandoned.

Slowing his horse, he leapt from the saddle, pulling his Winchester rifle from its scabbard and diving behind the barn door.

Two shots rang out from his rifle, and James' horse fell forward onto its bent legs, with James flying from the saddle and onto the ground. Another shot kicked up dirt from the ground between him and his fallen mare. He opted to dive behind the corral for cover. All grew silent under the glowing moonlight, as James opened the gate on his revolver and confirmed the six rounds. He first thought to ask Nettle to come out, but decided it was better not to give away his exact position. Crawling on his elbows, he made his way to the side of the barn. It was too dark inside the barn to look through the spaces of the boards and see if Nettle was by the door.

Keeping still for a few minutes, James heard movement inside the barn. He knew Nettle wouldn't come out, and he was just going to have to go in. He also figured Nettle must have taken position and would be ready to shoot anything coming through that door, which would be visibly silhouetted by the moonlight.

Just then, a small bleat came from behind James. He spun on his heels with revolver at the ready. Before him stood a small goat with crooked horns, wearing a three-foot length of rope around its neck, the end of which looked to have been chewed through.

James holstered his gun for the moment and grabbed the rope that was attached to Walter. He scanned the area and found what he was looking for.

Taking a lantern from a post on the corral, he shook it close to his head and confirmed there was still kerosene inside. He tied the lantern to the length of rope and raised the globe. The goat's eyes opened wide as James struck a match and lit the lantern. Leading the excited goat to the opening of the barn, he fired one shot behind it. Walter bolted into the barn, bleating and kicking as he went, trying to stop the terrible thing from following behind. The lantern's globe burst when it struck a post, as the goat ran past one of the stalls. Pieces of hay, which were sprinkled with kerosene suddenly were in flames. The more the hay burned, the more the goat kicked and bleated, and eventually ran from the barn, dragging its blazing nemesis off into the night.

The barn was ablaze from the inside, and it wasn't long before the structure itself caught fire.

James backed off, away from the door and took position behind a water trough near the corral. "You either throw that rifle down and head on outta' there, or you can burn for all I care, Nettle! Just remember, I'm shooting the first thing I see come out of that door holding a gun!" Several seconds went by as a few options must have gone through John Nettle's head. He chose the one that would save his skin and threw the Winchester out the barn door, only to follow it seconds later with his hands held high in the air.

Chapter XXIX

It took several weeks to piece together everything that had happened at Red Saunders' ranch. But after all the information came out about John Nettle, he was eventually found guilty for the murder of Red Saunders. He was hung after the two-week trial, and not one of the townsfolk attended his funeral. His ranch was later put up for sale at auction.

Jake Saunders eventually caught up with Andrew, and made a gift of the mare, Cloud, to him. It was Jake's way of apologizing for being so mistaken about Andrew. He even offered to sell him the family ranch if he wanted it. Andrew thanked him, but declined. He wanted to put those memories behind him and create a place he could call home with Willow back in Montana.

James travelled back to Anaconda with Andrew, and met Willow and her father. He stayed with Andrew at the cabin for several days, enjoying the serenity of the woods, but realized he needed to head home to Wendy.

Two days later, Andrew saw James to the train station. He opened his pocket watch and checked the time. In the distance they could see the train coming in with its billowing puffs of smoke.
Andrew looked down at the inscription. "Your father was right, Pa. There is nothing more precious than family."
He hugged James tight. "I plan to build mine here, Pa, and I promise I won't be a stranger."

"You better not, or we'll have to come track you down."

They laughed together as the conductor called for boarding.

"Safe travels, Pa."

"We love you, son."

James waved through the open window as the train chugged away down the tracks.

It was an early summer day when Andrew and Willow rode out to their favorite spot under the bur oak tree. As they sat on a blanket in front of the running stream, Andrew asked Willow to be his wife. She said "yes" and held him tight. She couldn't remember a happier time in her life. As the two embraced, somewhere from high up in the oak, a small wren sang its most beautiful song.

Made in the USA
Columbia, SC
17 April 2018